If That Was Lunch, We've Had It

D J Colbert

Published by Rireana Press, 2023.

IF THAT WAS LUNCH, WE'VE HAD IT

First edition. June 10, 2023.

ISBN: 978-1738600311

Written by D J Colbert.

Table of Contents

Chapter 42 1

Part V 11

Appendix One.. 21

Introduction 28

Sonata in E Flat 35

The Bad Oil.. 43

Index... 53

Cornflakes on Parade 69

Chapter 48573938576748399.. 77

Chapter 42 (continued) 89

Chapter 17.2..104

Kyrie Eleison 128

Foreword 133

The Good Oil on the Bad Oil of Big Oil 163

Opus No 9 171

Glossary 186

The Short Chapter...205

Chapter -11..209

The Next Chapter..231

Requiem 235

The Rug Tying the Room Together 243

Bequest...254

It All Comes Down To This 258

This book is dedicated to Colin, Audrey, Alan, Ken, and Stuart, who have all eaten their last lunch.

With gratitude to my family, friends, and shipmates, Graham Adams for great advice, Claudia Pond Eyley for her whimsical cover, Nicholas for loyal friendship and inspiration, and finally, for tolerating a flippant idiot and being there when it matters, my wife, Lynn.

All the author's proceeds from the sale of this book will be donated to the Butterfly Trust, a New Zealand registered charity (CC38025), www.butterflytrust.org.

Chapter 42

Ten years after a man first walked on the moon, Rodney and I sat on a beach and decided to write a book. We had left school, were unemployed, and had nothing but our combined genius to sell. Unfortunately, neither of us was Oscar Wilde, but being short of cash was motivation enough. We believed that writing a book was like receiving an inheritance from a distant, unknown aunt.

"How hard can it be?" Rodney had never written anything longer than a school essay.

"Piece of piss." Neither had I.

"Pass me a pen."

"I don't have one, but hey, get a load of that alliteration."

Rodney and I had worked as little as possible. We took odd jobs when we had to and studied just enough to pass exams. At our respective homes we melted into the background when dishes were to be washed, and I was known not to change the sheets on my bed for three months at a time. You may think no mother would ever allow this, but my sweet mother had a healthy relationship with bacteria. She claimed to have avoided certain death as a young girl, when, having gobbled down a few handfuls of dirt from the garden, for dessert she ate spoonfuls of mouldy jam she found in the pantry. At a slightly older age she learnt about antibiotics and became retrospectively adamant that penicillin in the mould had saved her from some fatal parasitic infection. My mother, therefore, thought my mouldy sheets were prophylactic.

Unsurprisingly, writing a book was not our first attempt to get rich without effort. Some days earlier we had gone to Bryan's place. Bryan was a smooth but slightly geeky, punk prodigy. He was also good at making money. He owned a car with four doors and four good tyres and lived in a flat in an expensive part of town. Bryan's girlfriend was a beauty pageant contestant. She said she loved Bryan for his mind. Bryan said it was for his hair. He was very proud of his hair. It was thick, lustrous, and changed colour with the frequency of a traffic light. He attributed this love of hair-colouring products to an early exposure to chemicals. He was an only child who had been brought up on a farm in the rural hinterland where pesticides were as common as gravy.

In addition to a swag of potentially carcinogenic compounds, Bryan had acquired a dog on the farm. Scrabble was a black and tan sheepdog who now lived in a kennel outside the back door of Bryan's flat.

We were sitting around the kitchen table. Bryan was sporting an orange Mohawk cut and wearing ripped green jeans. He looked like an inverted carrot.

"What you should do is place an advertisement in the newspaper asking for money."

"Is that legal?" From an early age I'd been taught to appear respectable and law-abiding.

"I don't see why not."

"What do we say in the ad?" Rodney was more pragmatic.

"Send me a dollar. I'll take half as my commission, and you two can have a quarter each." Bryan was always magnanimous.

I thought Bryan was onto something and any objection to the legality of the plan evaporated at the thought of hard cash. "Where do they send their dollar?"

"My place." Bryan went to the telephone (back then telephones had cords and often sat on a little table, graced with a white lace doily), called up the local daily paper and dictated our advertisement. "Put it in the personal column, but not among the massage parlours." He was a stickler for detail.

Outside the kitchen window Bryan's girlfriend practised her runway walk by stepping along a rope placed on the lawn. She was wearing a purple leotard and crimson leg warmers.

"Well, I suggest you consult your legal representatives." Bryan replaced the handset as Kim fell sideways onto the grass. He returned to his chair. "Anyone got any other ideas?"

"Scrimmage!" Two Valkyries leapt through the doorway. They jumped on Bryan, threw him to the floor and sat on him. Scrabble bounded inside, barked exuberantly, and joined the melee.

"Help. Police." Bryan struggled feebly until the scrimmage sisters took pity on him and stood up. Bryan smoothed his orange locks in front of a mirror. "You've messed my hair."

"Wuss." The sisters sat down at the table, then looked at me and Rodney. "What's up?"

Scrabble took advantage of Bryan's preoccupation with his hair and hid himself between our legs. He was not allowed inside.

"We're having a business meeting." Scrabble laid his head on my feet.

The scrimmage sisters laughed. They were artistic vegetarians who designed and made their own clothes.

"There's more to life than money." The shorter dark one was on solid ground with this observation.

"Cliché." So was Rodney.

Bryan had recovered his composure. "Touché." We males bumped fists.

"Name just one thing." I believed my challenge was knowing, artistic irony.

"Literature, music, beauty." The scrimmage sisters didn't hesitate.

"Face cream." Bryan's girlfriend had come back inside. We all looked at her to see if she was serious. She was. "Can I get anyone anything?"

"Fame, wealth, unbridled power." I believed my answer was amazingly witty.

Kim now looked at me like I was intellectually challenged. "I meant a cup of tea and a biscuit." She filled the kettle.

"And make it snappy." I didn't know when to stop. I turned to the scrimmage sisters. "We're actually writing a book."

"Wow, that's cool." Trixie, the taller blonde one, patted Scrabble surreptitiously.

"What's it about?" Sarah, the shorter dark one, got up and filled the milk jug.

Rodney grabbed a couple of chocolate chip biscuits from the plate Kim had placed in the middle of the table. "We haven't got that far."

There was a lull in the conversation while Kim passed out mugs of tea.

I looked around for mine.

"What about me?"

"Make your own." Kim sat down and started painting her nails.

"Hey." Bryan had finally noticed Scrabble. "Alfresco." Scrabble gave Bryan a pained look and reluctantly dragged himself from under the table and out the door.

Another attempt by Rodney and me to enrich ourselves lazily had occurred a couple of years earlier, at the school where we wore our pants short and our hair long. That school had no qualms about using child labour to keep the grounds clean. We had no qualms about exploiting that breach of human rights. Teachers would routinely hand out detentions that required picking up discarded ice block sticks. It was a law of nature that schoolboys and litter bins were incompatible. Twenty-five sticks was an average punishment, fifty was for a serious misdemeanour, and after that you got your bum whacked with a cane. I was once awarded three strokes of the cane for copying another student's homework.

"You're just like your brother in 4C." The avenging teacher of German laid about my buttocks with gusto while confusing my relationship with a friend of mine whom he taught in another class.

"I don't have a brother in 4C."

"Another stroke for lying!" The madman choked with anger and hit me again.

"Schweinehund." I cursed under my breath in good, war-comic German. A war comic was a simplistic, militaristic, jingoistic piece of propaganda in the guise of a comic strip, that outlined in grossly unsubtle detail why the spiritually and intellectually impoverished German nation lost World War II. I relied upon war comics for my German vocabulary and an understanding of the biological, psychological, societal and institutional causes of conflict.

"Hilarious." My friend in 4C couldn't stop laughing when I told him about his violent induction into my family, or mine into his.

I do confess this teacher probably had good reason to dislike my German class. There was a German boy who sat up the back and read magazines. He had decided he knew enough of his mother tongue to pass the end-of-year exam. Compared to the rest of the class he was a linguistic genius; we would have had difficulty discussing farts with a four-year-old. Every fifteen minutes the German boy would pass one of us a note with a German phrase on it. Our role was to ask the teacher what it meant in English. For example, "Wollen Sie ein Tritt in die Eier?" I would ask the teacher. "Well," he would begin, "'Eier' means eggs...," and then he would turn red, scowl, and order me to pick up twenty-five sticks. "Wollen Sie ein Tritt in die Eier?" means "Do you want a kick in the balls?"

Anyway, Rodney and I had cleverly worked out that if we cornered the market in used ice block sticks we could sell them, in lots of twenty-five, to those objects of academic displeasure ordered to pick them up. To be truthful, we hadn't actually worked this out. If we'd known what a market survey was we still wouldn't have done one. Instead we relied on gut instinct. Gut instinct can be very valuable in business. I had read this in a women's magazine at the dentist's and Rodney could think of no reason to dispute it.

Our gut instinct told us that this plan would make us extremely wealthy, or at the very least provide us with enough razoos to buy a pie and a custard tart at the school tuck shop. Even cleverer, we would have a stash of sticks ready to go at a moment's notice when required. "Here you go," we would say to that day's academic oppressor, five minutes after we had been put on detention, and hand him his twenty-five or fifty sticks of silver. "Now that's what you call a lesson, teacher man," we would say smugly to ourselves, and waltz off into the playground, whistling coolly, with our hands in our pockets.

On the strength of this incisive strategy, we picked up as many discarded ice block sticks as we could. After days of self-imposed lunchtime labour, we had cleared the school grounds of all that popsicle litter. Have you spotted the flaw in our reasoning yet?

Our geography teacher had attempted to teach us the importance of what was known as the Inductive, Hypothetical, Deductive Spiral. This was a process of scientific, critical analysis. It was more simply described as the IHD Spiral. We thought it was something to do with birth control. We should have listened to that lesson. We didn't. Our powers of critical analysis were retarded. Years later, Rodney offered to sell me his back catalogue of ice block sticks.

"I'm not falling for that one." I wasn't completely stupid.

So, now we had decided to write a book. The book was to be titled *The Protestant Work Ethic: How to Live with It and How to Live without It*. That seemed appropriate given our history to date. We lounged in the sun. The hole in the ozone layer hadn't yet been invented. We wore no sunhats, no sunglasses and no sunblock. The only thing we did wear were budgie smugglers. We were seventeen years old. We were lazy. The sun was at its zenith. Life was marvellous.

Rodney contributed the title. Fair effort to him. He had a short attention span. We'd previously owned a boat together, a fourteen-foot racing catamaran. Rodney helped me paint it once, for five minutes. He had bigger things on his mind, namely how to entice a nurse to go out with him on a date. That was often on his mind. After I had spent weeks assembling and painting the boat, we sailed it to an island in the outer reaches of the Waitematā harbour, camping out overnight. The next day it blew a gale. Surfing down breaking waves on the sail back, we passed a ferry. We were the only two craft on the water—unless you counted that ten thousand tonne cargo ship coming down the harbour on a collision course. The ship sounded its horn, angrily, five times.

"What does he want, bro?"

"No idea." I sent our little vessel skimming under the ship's bow.

I later learnt that five short blasts on a ship's whistle means get out of the way you bloody idiot, or something similar.

Back to our novel. I liked the catchy sound of Rodney's title, its paradoxical subtext. I was convinced by its underlying philosophy. I could hear it being echoed in the three-inch high breaking waves. We used quaint words like 'inches' to describe height back then, and these waves were nano-sized, poverty-stricken, malnourished forgeries of Hawai'ian man-eaters.

Being not nearly as spontaneously creative as Rodney, I contributed nothing. So our book, and its promise of squillions of dollars, nearly ended that summer at the last 'It', snuffed out by our lethargy and the energy-sapping heat toasting us through the as yet unknown radiant hole in the ozone layer. The state of our bank balances, however, forced us on.

"What are the themes?" I was bursting the pods of a piece of seaweed one particularly lazy afternoon.

"Man's inhumanity to man." Rodney had closed his eyes to the sun and was lying on his back.

"Sounds appropriate." I thought for a moment. "War?"

"And peace. What about plot, bro?"

"Romance between a lady and a gamekeeper who leaves the estate to hunt an angry white whale."

"Is plagiarism a crime?"

"Not in my book."

"Characters?"

"Not too many. Keep it simple."

"Can I be in it?" Rodney turned on his towel and looked at me.

"Of course. You're simple."

We both studied the sand in close-up for a couple of minutes. I let some fall through my fingers. It brought to mind an hourglass.

"Do you think time is an emotionally constructed, linear flow, or just a random collection of events?"

Rodney thought hard for two seconds. "Depends how you look at it, bro. Ask Bryan."

Then we went for a swim.

Two weeks later, we still hadn't put pen to paper. In those days paper was what we wrote on. It was a very thin, flexible tablet made of wood.

"We need to get started, I'm down to my last razoos." I showed Rodney my near-empty wallet.

"How long does it take to write a book?"

"Days, weeks?" I had absolutely no idea.

"A week is a long time."

Two weeks later, we still hadn't put pen to paper.

"I think we need more life experience." I had read this advice in *Reader's Digest*.

"Can you do a course in that at the polytech?"

Apparently you couldn't, so in order to become wealthy we decided we would just have to gather up some of that life stuff ourselves. Unfortunately, in the meantime, we had budget deficits.

Catfish can taste through their bottoms.

Part V

I'd met Rodney on our first day at high school. He came from the wrong side of the tracks. He was small and weedy, with dark, greasy hair. I saw him sitting alone on a bench. Foolishly, I thought he might be in need of a friend, an ally in the lower echelons of the academic food chain. Truth be told, that's what I was looking for. I may have felt intimidated after a senior boy had thrown a half-finished ice block at me that morning. With the benefit of hindsight, I should've saved the stick.

"Hello."

"What?" Rodney glared at me.

"Just saw you sitting here, alone." I emphasised 'alone' and sat down next to him.

"Fuck off."

"Haha." I thought he was joking.

Rodney punched me in the arm.

"Hey, that hurt."

"There's more where that came from, bro."

Not much fazed Rodney, whether it was school bullies or parents. Rodney came to my place one weekend. He knocked on the back door. My father opened it. My father, unfortunately in my opinion, was a school teacher. He used to speak to us like he addressed his pupils. "You, child, whatever your name is," was a common refrain in our household.

My father's nickname was Crunch. Apparently he only ever caned one boy. Having been a successful cricketer he had a strong arm and made the one stroke he administered to that boy's rear end count. To keep discipline he never had to assault any child in his care again, except us, his biological children, and we weren't strictly speaking 'in his care'. We were more like aliens who, unasked, had dropped into his world from the nether regions of the universe.

Crunch stood on the top step and looked about him suspiciously.

"Who's there?"

"Down here." Rodney kicked at the concrete pathway at the bottom of the steps.

Crunch lowered his gaze and growled. "Who are you?"

"Rodney."

"What do you want?"

"I've come to play with Will."

"When are you leaving?"

Ever after, Rodney thought my father was a man with whom he could do business. I thought anyone who could appreciate Crunch's sense of humour must be worth having as a friend.

Some years later I pulled into a service station in a small country town north of where my father used to teach. When I went to pay, the attendant looked at the name on my credit card.

"Are you related to that history teacher, Crunch?"

"Never heard of him." Lies came easily to me in the face of potential threat. Who knows what pathological remnants of revenge may have been fomenting inside Crunch's former pupils?

"You look like him."

"Do you understand the metaphorical phrase about not judging a book by its cover?" I took back my card.

"You talk like him too."

As I drove away I saw the attendant give me the fingers.

Rodney and I spent a lot of time at the beach. We learnt to windsurf. We bought windsurfing boards from a German with bleached hair. He had a girlfriend who wasn't German but who answered every question with "Ja". It is incredible how creative the adolescent mind can be. We nicknamed her Ja.

Rodney was a good windsurfer. He had balance, something he had acquired fleeing across fences while being chased by rival gang members with cracker guns. A cracker gun is a length of pipe with a lit firecracker in one end and a projectile in the other. Lethal if used accurately. There weren't a lot of stray cats in Rodney's part of town.

I had not been chased with cracker guns, and my sense of balance had suffered accordingly. In our neighbourhood we could afford professional armaments and, to the detriment of my windsurfing ability, I had only been shot at with under-powered air rifles.

One day, soon after deciding we needed to round up some life experience in order to write our book, Rodney was lying next to his windsurfing board on the beach, in the searing sun, wearing nothing but budgie smugglers for protection. He was reading the newspaper. His back glowed like a car's brake light in a mineshaft. I was concerned for his health.

"Do you think you've had enough rays?"

"I'm Samoan."

This was true, but Rodney was also descended from Germans. The Samoans had given him the shape of his nose and his dark hair. Unfortunately, the Teutons had gifted him his skin colour.

"Have you seen this?" Rodney pointed at the paper. "It says the earth is heating up. Choice, eh?"

"Why's that?"

"Now I won't have to go back to Savai'i to see the cuzzy bros, they can all come here. It'll be hot, just like the islands."

"Yo." Bryan joined us on the sand. He was out walking with Scrabble. He looked at Rodney's back. "Wouldn't want to be you tonight."

"The earth's going to burn too." I waved a hand in the direction of Rodney's newspaper article.

"Global warming. A bloke called Svante Arrhenius warned us about it back in 1896."

"Were there people back then?" Rodney half-heartedly draped a T-shirt over his shoulders.

"And earlier than Svante, an American scientist, Eunice Foote, reckoned that variations in carbon dioxide concentrations in the atmosphere could affect the climate. No one listened to her, but when a man, an Irish physicist called John Tyndall, said the same thing, people took notice."

"If we all breathe out will it rain?" I silently predicted Bryan would ignore me as well. I was right.

Bryan scratched Scrabble's ears. "By way of female retribution, Tyndall died young. His wife gave him too many sleeping pills one night and he never woke up."

"Black widow." I dropped a handful of sand over Scrabble's tail.

"She insisted it was an accident."

"Aren't we going into another ice age?" I shielded my eyes as Scrabble flicked the sand back at me.

"Spiders don't like the cold." Rodney spoke as if he knew what he was talking about.

Things were certainly a bit frosty at my place that evening. Crunch had an exercise book in which he recorded our payments for board and lodging. Once you left school, a contribution to the household expenses was expected. Crunch was pointing out the absence of any positive entries against my name. I had meant to pay something, honestly. Crunch said nothing, just stared at me while holding up the blank page of that month's entries. I quivered a little.

"What about him?" I pointed at my brother. "He left school three years ago and has hardly paid a cent."

"I'm saving for a house." My brother slunk out of the room.

Crunch didn't take his eyes off me. "I'll come to him."

I quivered a bit more under Crunch's death stare. "I'm writing a book." This sounded feeble, even to me.

The next day, as we drank creaming soda milkshakes at the local dairy, I despondently told Rodney my plight. "Forget life experience, forget writing a book, forget squillions of dollars, we'll have to find work."

"Done that." Rodney, stirred the dregs of his milkshake with a plastic straw. He had indeed found employment, as an orderly at the hospital. "Shift work, lots of nurses." He slurped loudly.

"It's a step up from grave digging." I remembered one of Rodney's previous jobs.

"Still got to deal with the dead, bro."

This was not the first time we had succumbed to the necessity of labour. While at school we had worked as sales assistants in an upmarket menswear shop from 5pm to 9pm on late-night Thursdays.

"Can I give you a hand, sir?" Rodney would ask browsing customers.

"Thank you," they would reply, flattered by his show of courtesy. From beneath the counter Rodney would produce a lifelike wooden hand on a stand. It was used for modelling gloves. "Anything else, sir?"

"Those jeans, sir," I would say to a customer who was worried that the legs of the jeans he was trying on were scraping the floor, "will shrink 3%."

"Those jeans, sir," I would say to another customer when the legs of the same jeans finished just above his ankles, "will stretch 3%."

I deceived myself into believing I was a good salesman. I liked to think I made the customers feel at ease. I would show a personal interest in their welfare and make them comfortable in my presence.

"Shawt any tigers lately, Major?" I would drawl at the forty-something, moustached, tweed jacket-wearing, lisping, English army veteran. "Or just wabbits?" The Major, despite my weak attempts at mockery, always bought something. I think he felt sorry for me.

Prior to the menswear shop we had worked at a bakery. We had to start at 5am. Befuddled by lack of sleep, we would carry loaves of bread, cakes, pies, and tarts from the ovens, down the narrow wooden staircase to the shop on the ground floor. Employing us was a huge mistake by management, akin to corporate suicide. Teenagers, as everyone knows except teenagers, can't breathe before 11am, let alone walk in a coordinated fashion. After Rodney dropped yet another consignment of sausage rolls on the floor, I said, "Just put them back on the tray, that's our lunch." While bacteria were acceptable in my family, waste was not.

Even earlier we had gathered up empty beer bottles and returned them to the bottle shop for a two-cents-per-bottle refund. We would pile as many bottles as we could onto my homemade trolley, then drag it carefully to the bottle shop. Once, in the corner of an old shed, we found a bottle that had not been drunk. It stood before us, like a fountain of nectar in the Garden of Eden.

Beer in those days came in big twenty-six ounce bottles, meant for real men with a big thirst. We were proto real men and as dry as dusty rags. We brushed the cobwebs and dirt away from the neck. Like I said, bacteria were acceptable in my family but waste was not. We prised off the top with a pocket knife. The beer was almost flat. We thought it was meant to be like that. We were thirteen years old.

After finishing the beer we couldn't seem to keep bottles from falling off the trolley. Shards of broken glass followed us up the footpath like spiky amber breadcrumbs. We abandoned our load of empties under some hydrangea bushes, next to a garden gnome sitting on a red toadstool with a fishing rod, in a nicely manicured front garden.

"Gnome and away we go." We giggled as we pulled the now empty trolley as quickly as we could down the street. Despite that event, I like to think that Rodney and I were pioneer recyclers, even though recycling, like so many other things, had yet to be invented.

We also once worked packing Christmas food gift packages for pensioners. This made us feel noble, like we were giving something back to the society which had spawned us. My sweet mother encouraged this giving back attitude.

"It's for a good cause. Well done, you two." She was proud of us both. She didn't realise we were being paid.

"Merry Christmas." I planted my thumbprint onto the contents of a jar of Vegemite, then screwed the top back on. I placed the jar in the next gift box.

"What did you do that for?" Rodney, surprisingly, looked surprised.

"They're old. They need a laugh."

Two of our old schoolmates were also averse to hard work. What was it about our education? Their solution was to go to Australia and sell drugs. That didn't turn out well. Burdened by debt owed to underworld figures they went to where the money was – a bank. They dressed up for the occasion, in leather jackets and crash helmets.

At different times, both Tom and Jonathan had been our best friends. We played sport with them, we taught ourselves to drive in Tom's father's van, while Tom's father, unaware, sat at home and watched TV. We went on holidays together, we drank our first whiskey together (thanks again, Tom's dad), we would listen to rugby matches on the radio and barbecue sausages at three in the morning. At night we took road workers' safety lamps and street signs from where, during the day, the road workers had been digging up footpaths and laying drains. One night we stole their tent. We left it, with associated lamps and signs, on the driveway of My Friend in 4C.

"Where did those come from?" His mother was trying to back her car out the next morning.

"Public Works Department."

She swatted his ear.

Jonathan became the quintessential angry young man. He played rugby so he could assault people and not be charged by the police. He expressed an interest in going to Hong Kong, perversely to join the police.

"It's for the corruption." To him, this seemed quite logical.

He once threatened a flatmate with decapitation for running over a garden ornament. It was a plaster figurine of Little Miss Muffet. Where on earth did that level of violent revenge on behalf of a nursery rhyme character come from? He was certainly no gardener. As far as I knew he was not an arachnophobe. Was it because he felt marginalised by society? After all, his parents were librarians. Tom, on the other hand, was always a gentle, rather sweet boy, but reckless. He would steal cars then always return them after joyriding.

"I never refilled the petrol tank though." He didn't want anyone to mistake him for a softie.

When Tom and Jonathan went to the bank, by motorcycle, they carried sawn-off shotguns. The first and only time I ever fired a shotgun had been with Jonathan. We were taken to a farm by a family friend of his parents who thought we should know as much as possible about the big outdoors. That included destroying its inhabitants, in this case, cute, defenceless, just paddling about, minding their own business, no threat to humankind whatsoever, ducks. Fortunately we couldn't shoot a pool cue, let alone a shotgun, and our little feathered friends survived, but the recoil of the shotgun stock against his shoulder obviously imprinted itself on

Jonathan. I wonder if this first lesson in armed violence crossed his mind as he and Tom motorcycled their way through the morning traffic?

Much as we failed to harm any ducks, Jonathan and Tom didn't manage to get their hands on any cash. Tom was shot dead by the first police officer on the scene. Jonathan was rendered paraplegic after being wounded. Back home there was a big funeral for Tom. It was like a school reunion, except two desks were empty. For most of us this was our first encounter with the fragility of life. Knowledge of our own mortality would take a while longer.

I once went tramping with Jonathan. We were in dense bush. He was walking in front of me with a large pack on his back. I was concentrating on where to put my feet. I looked up and there was a blank space ahead of me. Jonathan had disappeared. He had slipped off the track down a steep slope, almost noiselessly, like a phantom. The weight of his pack had helped him on his way.

I was concerned at first, but when his clay-covered face popped up between the ferns, level with my boots. I mimed a kick at his nose. Two years after the failed robbery, Jonathan disappeared forever. Angry and resentful, he shot himself, with a shotgun.

Why is there something instead of nothing?

Appendix One

I suggested to Rodney that if we were going to be wealthy authors, then we should start writing notes about our experiences. I had heard that wealthy authors wrote notes. Some even kept diaries, but that sounded like work.

"Why would we do that?"

"So we don't forget anything."

"It's all up here, bro." Rodney, tapped the side of his head.

Perhaps this aversion to putting pen to paper was a result of Rodney's short attention span. Conversely, he did like to tell stories, usually based on his own experiences, and he would repeat them time and time again. When either Bryan or I recognised a repeat version we would raise a hand, signalling Rodney to stop.

"You've told us that one."

"No way, bro."

"Yes, you have." Our certainty would cause Rodney to pause and think.

"But I didn't tell you about...", and off he would go down another verbal maze.

As far as writing notes went, however, I realised Rodney was probably right. Our brains were like sponges. We were young. Recall wasn't a problem like we'd heard it was for old people over thirty. Besides, it was much less time-consuming to remember things than write them down. And further besides, at this time in our lives everything was new, and what was new was invigorating, and that meant we had little energy or inclination to record our impressions.

Like addicts we just wanted to leap to the next new and exciting thing. We had few responsibilities, we lived each day as it was gifted to us, and we couldn't imagine secluding ourselves away in order to fashion acceptable prose. We were waiting for it to materialise miraculously out of thin, inspirational air.

As a hospital orderly, Rodney embarked upon his early career of dating as many female members of the medical professions as was humanly possible. 'Dating' is a strange word. I grew up thinking it referred to a group of religious zealots hurling dried fruit at a heretic wearing sandals and sackcloth in the Negev desert. Watching American sitcoms on our fourteen-inch black and white TV cured me of that delusion.

Rodney's experiences in the dating game were equivalent to martyrdom. Girls liked Rodney, but not in the way he wanted to be liked. They saw him as an amusing interval between drinks, a hiatus on the highway of life, someone to swap pleasantries with before the real nitty gritty of pairing-up started.

Through Rodney I could date vicariously. On the upside, it saved me a lot of personal angst and what I believed at that age to be fruitless confrontation. On the downside, we weren't very successful.

"I don't know why girls aren't snapping you both up?" my sweet mother would say to us as we fidgeted uncomfortably at this intrusion into our emotional lives.

"I do," Crunch would mutter from behind his newspaper.

After each of Rodney's embarkations on the river of love, I would ask, "How did it go last night?"

"She's nice."

"Yes. But did you cross the romantic Rubicon?"

"Friends," he would confess, and redirect the conversation.

Rodney was, understandably, sensitive about his relationship failures. We all were, although we pretended not to be, and drew curtains of bravado across our youthful hearts.

The one time Rodney did hit the jackpot it ended in tears. Helen was lovely – intelligent, attractive, worked as a nurse – what more could you ask for? I can picture them now, at the beach, cheek to cheek, drinking orange and mango juice out of the same tetrapak, each with their own plastic straw. It was romantic in the extreme.

All went swimmingly until we invited Helen on a tramp in the bush. There were four of us – me, Bryan, Rodney, and Helen. To be fair, it wasn't an easy tramp. There were steep hills, it was in an isolated part of the country, there was mud, and grass that cut your skin, and a couple of rivers to wade through, thigh-deep. It was a touch cold and our boots were wet the whole day. On the upside, it didn't rain.

At the end of the first day we pitched camp and Helen, who had never been tramping before, crawled into the tent she was to share with Rodney and collapsed, exhausted. It was 5pm. Bryan, Rodney and I built a campfire and sat around it boiling tea and singing songs. Between verses, Bryan ran his fingers through his red hair, which was more dreadlock than Mohawk now. To be fair again, we didn't sing well, in fact, we were a disgrace to quavers and crotchets. But we were enthusiastic, which meant loud.

"Crazy 'bout you baby, yeah, yeah." We had learnt this song at a pub the night before. We loved it. It had originally been a blues number, but in possession of our vocal chords was rendered as a cacophony of bilious squawks.

"Crazy 'bout you baby, yeah, yeah, crazy 'bout you baby, yeah, yeah. And her name was? And her name was? Mary Jane!" Like a drunk, who thinks he becomes more witty and attractive the more he drinks, we believed that the more we sang that song, the better it sounded.

"Crazy 'bout you baby, yeah yeah..."

"Shut up!" Helen, whom I had taken for the quiet, retiring type, poked her head out of the tent and screamed at us. She was on the verge of tears. "I can't sleep." She looked pitiful.

We paused. I looked at Rodney, Bryan looked at me, Rodney looked at Bryan.

"Crazy 'bout you baby... " we chorused as loudly as we could.

The next day, by mutual consent, the tramp was aborted and we headed back the way we had come. Bryan and I strode ahead through the latticed shadows of the bush.

"We have to keep her spirits up." I was determined to atone for the previous evening.

We looked at each other, our unspoken sympathy for Helen's plight evident on our faces.

"How will we do that?"

"We could sing."

We stopped at a lake for a swim on the way back to town. It seemed like Helen had not spoken for hours. Rodney looked miserable. Again, Bryan and I looked at each other. Our telepathy was outstanding. We dropped our towels and ran as fast as we could to the water. We were in the land of hot pools and geysers, myth, magic and romantic legends.

"They need time alone." I dived beneath the surface.

"So do we." Bryan dived in after me.

We watched as Rodney and Helen, by way of mutual forgiveness, tentatively wrapped their arms around each other on the sulphur-scented beach.

"Love is a double helix." Bryan, who, in our eyes, was a love guru, should have known. He and Kim had been together since primary school. "We shared our plasticine and that was it." He had a romantic way with words.

It strains credibility, but the tramp did not end Rodney and Helen's relationship. That came when Rodney was confronted one day by Helen's mother. Helen lived at home with her mother, and when Mother was away, Rodney would sometimes, euphemistically speaking, stay over. This had not received prior approval from Mother; in fact, she had forbidden it.

On this particular day, we pulled up in Rodney's car, outside Helen's mother's house. Mother came out of the garden gate and stood on the footpath, holding a bedspread at arm's length. Rodney got out of the car. Sensing danger, I didn't.

"I need to talk to you, Rodney."

"Fire away, missus."

"This is a bedspread."

"Yes." Rodney was a little mystified.

"A bedspread from my house."

"Y...e...s." Rodney dragged out the word as if speaking to an imbecile. Mother by the way was not an imbecile. She was a psychologist.

"There are stains on this bedspread."

"Y...e...s."

"Look here." Mother brandished the bedspread at Rodney. Rodney feigned a look at the proffered cloth.

"Those, Rodney, are sexual stains."

"Y......e......s." Rodney spoke even more slowly this time.

"Well, what are you going to do about it?!" Spittle flecked Mother's lips.

Rodney looked confused, unsure what he should do or say. It crossed my mind to suggest a DNA test, but I thought that might come across as impertinent.

Finally Rodney found his tongue. "I could have it dry cleaned."

A few days later we lay on the beach. Rodney was single again, so to cheer him up I complimented him on the mature way he had handled the bedspread situation. "It's for the best. You and Helen weren't compatible."

"What do you mean?"

"No sense of humour, like her mother. Great material though. You can dine out on that story for decades, unlike most of your others. Speaking of stories, how much have you written over the last six months?"

"Heaps."

"Where is it?"

"Well, maybe not heaps, I've been busy. I was in love. My hands were full."

"You could have put that more delicately."

"How much have you written then?"

"Heaps."

Rodney didn't believe me for a second.

It takes five hours to cook a crocodile.

Introduction

The fallout from this failed relationship was cataclysmic for Rodney. He even stopped dating nurses for a couple of weeks while he recovered from the trauma. Even more cataclysmic for everyone else was the discovery of the hole in the ozone layer that occurred around the same time Helen's mother was wielding her bedspread. I am not sure which of those two events was the most frightening. But now, as if our lives weren't threatened enough by nuclear obliteration, we had to worry about getting skin cancer.

"If the hole gets big enough, will we be able to see stars in the daytime?" I was looking for silver linings. We were at Bryan's place on a gloomy, UV-free Sunday afternoon. Scrabble was curled up in his kennel keeping warm.

"Moron." Rodney picked at his toenails.

"Seriously though, can we still sniff paint from spray cans?" You can see how concerned I was about an invisible hole in the sky.

"It's chlorofluorocarbons." Bryan looked up from the table where he had dismantled a transistor radio in order to fix it. He now had a mullet with green highlights.

"Told you so." I pointed a finger triumphantly at Rodney. "Spray paint."

"Spray cans and refrigerants." Bryan waved his soldering iron in the air. "But if we change CFCs, that's chlorofluorocarbons, to HFCs, hydrofluorocarbons, we won't all die of melanoma."

"So you think everyone is going to stand around in a circle, join hands, sing the Hokey Tokey, and change CFCs to HFCs, just like a big game of Scrabble?" There was a loud bark from outside. Rodney had a point.

"The imminent threat of an ugly death can work miracles." Bryan almost burnt his finger on the soldering iron.

I always knew there had been nothing to worry about.

Apocalypse averted, I decided that, like Rodney, I too would get a job. I viewed this as only a temporary solution to being cash-deficient. I knew that very soon a flash of inspiration would strike us and our book would miraculously manifest itself in a chorus of singing angels and trumpeting bugles. This may sound overly dramatic and biblical, but so was Rodney's title. I envisaged living off the proceeds of our literary genius in Greece, lying about on a terraced villa and throwing drachmas over the whitewashed walls to the poor. In the meantime, ignoring any possible risk of heightened UV exposure, I moved even closer to the sun, having wrangled a job as a rouseabout on a sheep station in the high country. I wasn't one to be cowed by a bunch of greenies making noises about Armageddon. Besides, Bryan had correctly identified the solution. He was a greenie with brains.

The sheep station was a pristine environment. I would wake each morning to the radiant glow of colours kaleidoscoping on the steep slopes. The air was pungent with the scents of pasture, dung and new growth while lambs ricocheted about and placid ewes chewed their cud. A braided shingle river exuberantly bisected our pastoral paradise.

One morning I stood in silent reverence before this natural bounty. I was joined by the station owner.

"Beautiful land, isn't it?" I was aglow with goodwill.

"If you say so." He took his pipe from where it habitually lodged in the corner of his mouth. He was wearing gumboots, a stained beige felt hat, muddied corduroy pants and a woollen jersey. "And

I'd have absolutely no compunction in shooting any bastard who stepped foot on it without my permission."

Being a rouseabout wasn't all bucolic scenes though. It was the lowest form of labour on the station. That's how I got the job; no one else wanted it. I was given all the boring dirty jobs, like shovelling years of accumulated sheep dung out from underneath the shearing shed, mending wire fences in the biting cold, and spending days picking up stones from a paddock before ploughing it.

I also got to drive out in blizzards delivering hay to the stoic stock. One day, in whiteout conditions, the Land Rover slid down a gully and into a fence. Too frightened to tell the owner, I spent the next two hours winching it back onto a flat surface. I was swearing frequently, exhausted, frozen and tearful.

The owner studied my face hard when I eventually returned. "They say that you're no good at your job until it's made you cry." He must've come out to see what had happened, observed my tribulations, and disappeared back to the farmhouse for a cup of hot cocoa and a piece of sponge cake. Either that or he was a mind reader.

Lowly as a rouseabout ranks, I was still one step up the food chain from the stick-thin thirteen-year-old twin brothers who came to visit the station owner and his family during one school holiday. These pasty-faced lads went to a private school and spoke endlessly about 'Mummy' and 'Daddy'. The shearing gang that arrived at the same time couldn't believe its luck. As the gang roared in through a cloud of dust in their battered registration-and-WOF-free cars, Daddy was just driving off in his Range Rover. The two worlds were about to intersect.

I worked on the floor of the shearing shed gathering up fleeces, sweeping the boards, and doing whatever else unskilled labour could do. The shed was a cacophonous mix of buzzing shears, shouts and bleating sheep. It smelt of sweat, lanolin and dung. The two boys would arrive after breakfast to 'do their bit', as they put it, for a couple of hours, and the shearers soon took advantage of this desire to help.

"Can ya go and ask the boss for a long weight, mate?"

One of the boys obediently trotted off to find the gang boss and didn't return until the next morning.

"Can ya go and ask the boss for a bag of sparks for the grinder, mate?"

The other boy dutifully came back with an empty paper bag that the shearers pretended to shake over the tool they used to sharpen their combs and cutters.

The tour de force, however, occurred one lunchtime. I came back to the shearing shed early to find a bale of wool, sewn up, ready for market and suspended by a rope from the rafters. It was shapeless and it squirmed.

"Help." Two trembling soprano voices whispered from above. The bale squirmed some more. I lowered it to the floor and cut open the stitching.

"Thank you, William." The dishevelled twins tumbled out of the sacking.

"Only my mother calls me William. You can call me Will."

"Thank you, Will." The twins picked strands of wool and loose dags out of their hair.

"Lucky they didn't put you through the press first. And don't tell Mummy and Daddy, okay?"

After this event, I felt almost fatherly towards the twins and made sure the shearers came to see their positive attributes, such as being able to take a joke. I was perhaps too successful. By the end of shearing the twins and the shearers were great mates. The twins had even been invited to sit down with the gang at the end of each hard day, to smoke roll-your-owns, swear, and drink beer. I'm sure that Mummy and Daddy would have been very pleased at this rounding-out of their boys' education. I just hoped the twins held off swearing and spitting after they got home.

I had my first exposure to extreme weather events in the mountains. One morning we sat at the kitchen table, silently spooning sodden oatmeal into our mouths, while a wind roared outside. Out of the corner of one eye I saw a large, metallic object soar past the window.

"What was that?" I committed the cardinal sin of speaking during breakfast.

"Bloody oath, that was the roof." The owner also sinned.

We looked up. Through newly formed cracks in the ceiling we could see daylight. The wind roared more loudly and we heard nails popping out of what remained of the iron roof. Leaving the porridge to any passing fairytale, we decamped to the shearers' quarters. As we ran across the open yard, loose sheets of iron flew around us and trees fell across fences. Under my jacket I carried the black, house cat which had one leg in plaster following a run-in with a wild pig. The cat's name was a racial slur but this was the dark ages, and besides, I didn't understand what a slur was. Poor thing; imagine if he'd known.

We barricaded ourselves into the old wooden homestead which was used to house the shearers. Fortunately, the gang had already decamped.

"It'll probably rain now." I imagined I was being helpful, but at that age I didn't understand the value of tact. The owner's wife almost dissolved in tears. The farmhouse was new and she had furnished it with conservative rural love. The thought of its interior being turned to Weet-Bix by the wild elements was too much for her.

We spent the rest of the day being hurled around by the gale, fixing tarpaulins to the roof, under constant threat of being impaled by flying objects. I admit that on occasion, as I was clinging to the exposed trusses, I wished I'd kept my mouth shut. About an hour after we finished, unscathed, the rain started.

We later learnt that the storm was a 'one in one hundred years' event, that the wind anemometer at the nearest settlement stopped working at two hundred kilometres per hour, and that some ten thousand litre storage tanks were seen bouncing across the beach into the ocean like giant green plastic footballs. Our place was littered with fallen trees, broken fences and trashed buildings.

As we looked out on the destruction from the shelter of the shearers' quarters' doorway, the owner seemed resigned and emitted a low growl.

"It's a slippery slope, from the cradle to the grave."

For my part, I hoped he was wrong. With little understanding of the grave, I assumed I was still ascending on the escalator of life.

Is the universe conscious?

Sonata in E Flat

Almost four decades later, I'm visiting Crunch and my sweet mother. I've brought them a bottle of their favourite red wine. They now live in an apartment in a retirement village that has a rest home attached for the more frail. Crunch is eighty-nine but still manages a game of tennis on a good day. He has had a melanoma removed from the back of his left hand and holds it up to show me the scar.

"I'll die before this kills me." He inspects the wine label and seems satisfied. "Chemotherapy."

Mother is sewing at the dining room table. "Bother, blast and damnation." The cloth has become entangled in the sewing machine.

Crunch puts away the wine and sits down beside her. "I'll fix it, sugar." He gently takes the sewing machine from her and begins to unravel the bunched-up cloth.

"Sugar? I've never heard that one before."

"You don't know everything, William." Mother's smile is almost secretive.

It is hot inside the apartment. "Can I open a window before we melt?"

Crunch waves a hand idly in my direction. He is concentrating on the sewing.

"Global warming." I open the window that looks onto the driveway.

"Don't you believe it. The earth's been heating up and cooling down since Adam was a boy. Doesn't mean we caused it." Crunch stays focused on the entangled cloth.

"Have you done your own research?"

"What's that supposed to mean?" Crunch eyes me suspiciously.

A troop of residents, accompanied by caregivers in uniforms of light green, approaches down the driveway outside the apartment. They progress like a class of subdued toddlers in slow motion, uneven in their gait and direction. A dumpy woman in a smock clumps along hanging onto a walker.

"Poor old dears." Mother, who recently celebrated her eighty-sixth birthday, watches them sympathetically.

"Someone's making a fortune out of their misery." Crunch hands the now-untangled sewing back across the table.

A very old but agile resident is marching at the head of the group as if he is leading a parade. He is wearing an Oriental silk dressing gown, a British Army officer's cap, and leather slippers. He orders a left turn, but no one obeys him. After performing a snappy left turn himself, and marching five paces in that direction, he stops, barks out an about turn order, and resumes his position at the front of the procession. This pattern is repeated over and over as the residents perambulate slowly along the asphalt. At one stage the marcher orders "Halt!" and, while he stands erect in the centre of the driveway, the rest of the group just divides like a school of lazy fish and meanders on around him. Marching back to the head of the group, in time to pass the open apartment window, the marcher orders "Eyes right!" and salutes. Crunch stands to attention and salutes back.

"Happens twice a day." Mother glances over the top of her sewing machine.

The marcher looks familiar. I hesitate and look at him more closely. "You wouldn't believe it," I murmur, then call out the window, "Shawt any tigers lately, Major?" The marcher stops, looks intently at me for about ten seconds, then springs to attention again and salutes me. I stand to attention and salute him back. Whether he actually recognises me, I have no idea.

"Friend of yours?" Crunch watches as the Major strides off to re-join his regiment. He leaves behind a lingering scent of roast lamb and antiseptic.

Later, Crunch and I leave Mother to her sewing and walk across the road to Crunch's favourite cafe.

The waitress recognises Crunch. "Hello, dear, English Breakfast and a lamington?" She is in her fifties, wearing fashionable glasses with lenses the size of saucers and a tawny-coloured apron over her clothes. She has dyed, blonde hair.

"And a crust of bread and a glass of water for him." Crunch points in my direction.

"Tea, please."

"Waitresses used to say 'sir' or 'gentlemen' before I was old. Now it's 'dear'." Crunch leads me outside to a round, wrought iron and glass table where we sit down.

The waitress brings us our order. Crunch nods at her. "Thank you."

"You're welcome, dear."

A car roars past. It is occupied by four youths. A McDonald's wrapper flies out one of the windows and oscillates into the gutter like a greasy, red and yellow butterfly.

"Bloody larrikins. They should be hung from a gibbet." Crunch sees the look of mild surprise on my face. "It's pollution. I don't like it. I used to be able to swim in rivers when I was a kid, breathe fresh air, walk on clean streets. Not any more."

"Would you gibbet them alive or dead?"

"Dead." Crunch smiles. "I'm not unreasonable."

We drink our tea and watch the world passing in its rush to arrive at wherever it believes is important.

"Do you think less pollution would slow down climate change?"

"Rubbish." Crunch, flicks a fleck of desiccated coconut off his bottom lip. "What's your next trip?"

"Skippering a catamaran on an archaeological discovery voyage around Greece."

"And they pay you for that?"

"Rather well."

Crunch finishes his lamington and looks ruefully into the distance. "I wish I'd lived more like you."

"You used to tell me to get a real job... and a haircut."

"You never did do what you were told."

"Wonder where I got that from?"

Crunch smiles wryly – or perhaps it's a grimace – it's hard to tell.

The next week, Rodney, Bryan and I are in the kitchen of Bryan's swanky, downtown apartment overlooking the harbour. Bryan has turned a successful engineering career into that of a financial advisor, social commentator and speaker. He thrives on contention and his opinions leap from one side of the political divide to the other. He has discovered a latent, perverse enjoyment in offending people. He has also made squillions. After their two children moved out, he and Kim – once girlfriend and now the wife of Bryan – moved in here.

Bryan is standing by the oven. He seems to have grown thinner. His hair, on the other hand, has not. Today it has a purple haze and he is also sporting a silver ring on each finger. The kitchen is a culinary construction site. There is flour, sugar, egg and butter smeared on every surface, including Bryan. The air is fragrant with the smell of fresh baking. Kim is outside on the balcony, serenely practising Pilates.

"What's cooking, bro?" Rodney is wearing cycling pants and a Lycra jersey, having cycled to the apartment.

"Climate cookies – like fortune cookies, but with portents of doom inside."

I pick up some strips of paper from a bowl on the bench and read one out loud. "What stinks but doesn't smell? Answer: Methane."

"I give them away at global heating events." Bryan removes a tray of climate cookies from the oven.

"Global heating is a bummer, ditch the Lear Jet, ditch the Hummer," I read from another portent of doom.

"Subtle." Rodney extracts half an egg shell from the fruit bowl. "Will sunblock save us?"

Bryan hits him on his bald head with a dirty spoon.

"Does anyone want anything?" Kim has finished her Pilates and come inside. Her hair, which used to be blonde, is now platinum and drawn back, almost severely, in a ponytail. She looks at me. "Fame, wealth and a horse fart with your tea, perhaps?"

"Perfect."

She then sees the state of the kitchen. "How about we go for an ice cream?"

While Bryan cleans himself up, we wait on the balcony. "You can see my home from here." I point at the marina across the bay.

"Are you still living on that old yacht?" Kim follows the line of my hand.

"Why not?"

"And doing boat work?"

"Why not?"

"How many decades is that?"

"Only three... maybe four."

"No wonder you're not married."

"It's better than a slap in the face with a wet fish."

"Marriage?" Rodney wipes a smear of biscuit batter off his forehead.

"I meant living and working on boats."

"What about your retirement?" Kim is concerned.

Rodney laughs. "You can't retire if you don't work."

"I resemble that remark." I steal a line from an old, children's TV show.

"Don't worry, Kim, the bro is a product of socialism, a jack of all trades, a master of none, an itinerant, a wanderer, but when all else fails he can sleep in my garage." Rodney pulls out his wallet and gives me twenty cents. "Here, my good man. Go and buy yourself a cup of tea and a biscuit."

I smile at Kim. "Sorted."

"I couldn't live like that." She almost shivers at the thought of it.

"We all sail a sea of uncertainty." I return Rodney's twenty cents.

As we troop out of the apartment in search of ice cream, past a framed photo of Scrabble hanging by the door, Bryan's phone rings. He answers it, then listens for a few seconds before saying, "Well, you can tell them ninety-seven percent of climate scientists agree the earth is heating up and that we're causing the climate to change." Bryan puts his phone back in his pocket. "Trixie. The scrimmage sisters are saving the world."

"Crunch doesn't think we're to blame, and he's never heard of Facebook, Twitter, or Mastodon." I pre-empt any observation about personal research.

We walk a block to a fancy ice cream parlour.

I tap Rodney lightly on the chest. "This'll be good for your heart." He recently had a stent inserted in an artery.

"I've got a resting pulse of forty, just like the elite athlete I once was. How about you?"

"I lose count after seventy."

Bryan exaggerates licking his lips. "You can get any flavour here, from kale to kumara."

The ice cream parlour is crowded, with a queue spilling onto the street. It smells and sounds like the inside of a beehive – sweet, fermenting, and hyperactive.

Kim looks around for an alternative. "We'll have to go somewhere else."

But Bryan has other ideas. He dives into the crush of customers, pushing them aside with his arms. "Move aside, move aside, I'm a lawyer, I'm a lawyer." He repeats the phrase like a liturgical command. Miraculously, the mass of bodies opens before him like the Red Sea and Bryan places our order at the servery.

"I wish he wouldn't do that." Kim shakes her head. "It's so embarrassing."

I smile. "I agree. I can't think of anything more embarrassing than being mistaken for the wife of a lawyer."

We think we are such a clever species.

The Bad Oil

"How much have you written?" We were relaxing on the beach almost a year after first deciding to write a book. I had left the farm to recuperate after being kicked by a horse. I sent the horse a thank-you note.

"Heaps."

"Well, luckily I have." I opened up an exercise book.

"Did you steal that from school, dude?" Rodney peered at the crest on the cover.

"Excess stock."

I read out loud. "Rodney and I sat on a beach and decided to write a book. We were unemployed and had nothing else to do. Unfortunately, neither of us had passed English, but being short of cash we had nothing to lose. We believed that writing a book was like receiving an inheritance from an ancient aunt."

I looked expectantly at Rodney, waiting for effusive praise to come my way for this brilliant piece of literary craft.

"Is that it?"

"It's a start." My writer's ego rested like a naked buttock on a sharp knife edge.

"Couldn't you have given me a more heroic name?"

"Like Horatio, or Julius, or Te Rauparaha?"

"Give me a go." Rodney held out his hand for my exercise book. "How hard can it be?"

I passed it over. "It's a piece of piss really." I feigned nonchalance, as if my masterpiece of a paragraph had flowed like liquid silver from my brain, down my arm, and onto the paper.

"Pass me the pen." Rodney held out his hand again.

"I don't have one, but hey, isn't that what they call alliteration?"

Rodney had decided he wanted to do something more meaningful with his life than push trolleys and empty bedpans. He therefore spouted into a career in an oil company. This meant he got to ride around the country in oil tankers and give management advice to petrol station owners. Rodney had no idea how to manage a petrol station but was supposed to learn on the job. I met up with him at a Greenpeace fundraising concert.

"Oil is good for the environment." Rodney expressed this sacrilege between songs, with absolutely no hint of irony.

"How's that?"

"We, that's oilmen like me, look after the natural world. The company uses its profits to protect sea turtles, butterflies, bears, and lots of other animals that are furry and cuddly."

"Turtles and butterflies aren't furry, and when did you last cuddle a bear, or a butterfly, or a turtle for that matter?"

"We've even painted the petrol stations green."

"Do you really believe that crap?"

"No, but bro, have you ever got to drive an oil tanker?"

Rodney didn't last long as an oilman.

Not to be outdone by Rodney, I too changed jobs. I was still in budget deficit and inspiration was taking its time to strike. I had tried opening up the exercise book and staring at it with a pen in my hand. Nothing happened. I had tried lying naked in a dark room. Nothing happened. I had tried drinking whiskey like Ernest Hemingway. I fell out of the shower. I had tried reading Sylvia Plath. I felt suicidal. I had tried listening to Leonard Cohen. I felt strangely uplifted, but hugely unmotivated. I tried singing, "Crazy 'bout you baby...". I felt a lot better after that. Stuff writing, I said to myself, and prepared for real work.

I became a sailor and joined the merchant navy as a cadet navigator. Going to sea was like stepping back a millennium. Captains acted like feudal overlords, the officers' saloon had four-course meals and silver service, the crew's quarters were crammed into the lower decks of the ship, and words like demurrage, jackstay, derrick and dunnage were commonplace. It was a wonderful environment if you were an alcoholic, a chain smoker, a male (there were no women sailors in those days), a heroin addict, or a student of the evolution of the English language. I was only one of those, but I loved it. There is nothing like the smell of hot tar, wet rope and fuel oil, all heavily salted, to whet the appetite for casting off into horizons unknown.

My sweet mother knitted a pair of slippers for my kit. They had red, smiley lips and plastic eyes with black, joggling pupils on the top of each foot. Her theory was that if I could wear those on board ship with a bunch of drinking, carousing, swearing jack tars for company and survive, then I should be okay. She didn't seem too concerned about what would happen if I didn't survive.

This was the same mother who, some years earlier, had sent me off to my first day at school in a strange country with nothing more than verbal instructions on how to catch a bus. I was ten years old. We were in a small town outside London. We were there because Crunch had scored a scholarship to study teaching in Britain. We had been in the United Kingdom for a week. I was told to catch the bus to Monument Hill. I caught the bus to Marble Arch, about thirty miles away, in London itself. In my defence, both destinations purported to be a pile of old stones and started with a capital 'M'.

Our sweet mother had said we needed to grow up to be independent. I independently realised my mistake and told the conductor. He laughed. I squirmed, embarrassed to be the centre of attention in a strange country. "Where did you say you were from son?" The conductor laughed again. "Where did you say you wanted to go?" He laughed again. "Do you know where this bus is going, son?" Another laugh.

Once the conductor had shared my bad choice of transport with the other passengers and picked himself up off the floor, he very, very kindly directed me to wait for another bus at the next bus stop. I was late for school, by about two hours.

When I arrived home that afternoon, on the right bus, but not in the best of moods, Mother was proud that her independence theory was working. "You won't do that again now, will you, William?"

My mother also gave me a tin of home-made oatmeal biscuits to take to sea. I thought the biscuits were more of a risk to my wellbeing than the slippers.

"They're good for your bowels, dear."

"There's nothing wrong with my bowels."

Crunch gave me nothing but a baleful stare. He was up a ladder painting the weatherboards, wearing an old fawn woollen jersey with holes in it, a ripped pair of walk shorts, dirty sandshoes, and a paint-splattered green beret. His unshaven face looked like a well-worn cat's scratching post.

"Good luck." He dipped his brush in the paint pot. "You'll need it."

Painting the house was a ritual for Crunch. He would start with one wall, sanding, scraping, filling rotten boards with fibreglass filler, priming, undercoating and then overcoating. It was slow work. Once the first wall was finished he would move onto the next, until he eventually arrived where he had begun. The whole cycle would take about five years, by which time he had decided that the first wall needed touching up again.

It was Crunch's destiny, like Sisyphus, to never finish his allotted task. The work was both laborious and ultimately, in my view, futile.

In a display of filial sympathy, I once offered to help paint the house. Crunch was, after all, getting on a bit. We agreed on a fee. It was to be done in lieu of board and lodging. I knocked off the first wall in record time. I found the job went a lot quicker if you left out the undercoat. Two years later, when the paint was peeling off, Crunch eyed me suspiciously.

"Did you put undercoat on that wall?"

"What sort of moron doesn't use undercoat?"

The first ship I joined was in Dubai. It was called the *Catalina*. I walked down the wharf in forty degrees Celsius lugging a suitcase. Two men in dirty boiler suits shouted at me from the aft deck.

"Bugger off, we don't want you."

Well, they're not getting any oatmeal biscuits, I said to myself. I climbed the gangway and found the Purser's cabin. I hovered nervously at the open door. A very rotund man in a white uniform, with short-cropped blond hair, sat at a desk. He smelt of aftershave and looked like he had stepped out of a German war movie. He turned towards me.

"Oh do come in, dearie, I won't eat you." He took my passport and seaman's identity card. "I'm the grocer; you can call me Lottie."

Pursers were called grocers because they were responsible, among other things, for stocking the ship's food stores, and to be quite frank, we didn't really know what the word 'purser' meant. I imagined it could be slang for a pickpocket.

"Who else calls you Lottie?"

"Everyone, dearie. Don't think you're special."

I was happy with that response. "Okey dokey, Lottie."

"I think you'll find we say 'aye aye' on this pirate ship."

I learnt a lot at sea. For instance, in Iran I learnt that you could exchange a bottle of whiskey with the Revolutionary Guards for multiple tabs of heroin. A fourth engineer (nearly everyone had a number – it helped them remember who they were and what they were meant to do) made the mistake of taking heroin before playing a game of frisbee out on deck. When the frisbee, predictably, flew over the side of the ship into the ocean, he, not so predictably, jumped into the sea, from a height of fifteen metres, to retrieve it. We were at anchor. The current ran past us at about three knots. He was gone before you could say 'Long John Silver'.

Then it got exciting. We had a real man overboard drill. We blew the horn. We lowered a lifeboat. We chugged off in the direction of the current. About half an hour later we dragged the fourth engineer from the water. He was almost at the point of expiry, but he had a big smile on his face. He was Welsh. Did I mention this was in the Persian Gulf? That the sea was writhing with sea snakes and sharks? That it was as hot as Hades? All in all, it was a good afternoon.

Not everyone was so lucky. On a later voyage, on a different ship, we were anchored in a similar spot. A young deck boy slipped while cleaning a crane and fell ten metres, head first, to the steel deck. This was his first trip to sea. He was a cheeky, likeable lad, just sixteen years old. We kept him breathing for what seemed like hours in the sick bay. Two doctors from a Russian ship eventually arrived to help. (Only Russian merchant ships carried doctors.) They spoke no English. We spoke no Russian. They took one look at poor Davey, shook their heads, said "Nyet", and sat down. They were waiting for their bottle of whiskey.

I worried that I had killed Davey. I was trying to give him oxygen. The oxygen was contained in small, portable ventilators. We had a limited supply and I had never come across them before, so two were wasted before I managed to get one fitted over his face. It made no difference and the Russians 'nyeted' Davey soon after. Maybe, if I had not wasted those two canisters, he would've survived, I thought, a heavy, black albatross of guilt encircling my neck.

The mood was sombre when we farewelled Davey's soul on the afterdeck that evening. That was all we could farewell. The days of burying sailors at sea had gone. Davey's body remained with us for another few weeks, in the freezer with the sausages. It was not a good afternoon.

Being at sea was like that. Good days and bad days. Boring days, of which there were many, and the occasional time when you were too terrified to breathe.

Alcohol was the lubricant of the maritime world. You could achieve anything with booze. Back on the *Catalina*, the first electrician built a pyramid of beer cans. It was a metre high. He used the beer cans he'd consumed between coming off watch at 4am, or 0400 hours as we used to say, and breakfast at 8am (0800 hours). The ship was moving and he was, to employ a colloquialism, rat-arsed. How that pyramid stayed upright was a miracle known only to the Egyptians, who were just over the horizon. Apparently alcohol has been banned from merchant navy ships now and I am sure doing so has had a detrimental effect on the planet's architecture.

The *Catalina* eventually made it alongside a wharf in Bandhar Khomeini, an Iranian port some miles up the Shatt al-Arab waterway that divides Iran from Iraq. Here we were in the cradle of civilisation, just south of the confluence of the Euphrates and Tigris rivers, touching the hem of history and the glorious ascent of the human race. Two boat lengths ahead of us was a live sheep carrier. Scores of dead animals were being tossed into the river. They bloated and floated up and down on the tide. The stench of rotting flesh was enough to kill flies. A German ship was leaving as we docked. Our fifth engineer (they ran out of numbers after five) goose-stepped up and down the deck as the Germans passed. He played 'Deutschland Uber Alles', the German national anthem, on a squeezebox. The Germans ignored him. I was hoping they'd take a shot and pop his accordion.

We unloaded thousands of carcasses of frozen lamb. When I say we, I mean that all the hard, lifting work was done by Kurdish men who were as skinny and jagged as rusty nails. We watched. These men slept in cardboard box shacks on the concrete wharf. The boxes were just high and long enough that they could lie down. They had only the clothes on their backs. They cooked on charcoal fires and toileted in the desert, while we showered at the end of each day and ate four-course meals served by stewards in white jackets. Privileged Iranians in black limousines would occasionally drive past in air-conditioned leathered comfort. To my law-abiding and respectable self, this did not seem fair. Another of my eighteen-year-old selves said, "That's life."

Not much seemed fair to the second cook. For unknown reasons he tried to decapitate the first cook with a meat cleaver. The first cook's screams echoed up and down the companionways. He was a large man with a lumbering gait. The second cook was built like a greyhound. Luckily, the second cook was restrained just before he caught up with the first. We put Number Two in his cabin and locked the door. A crew member kept watch outside in the passageway.

The next morning the second cook was missing. He had squeezed through the cabin's porthole, climbed onto the dock and run off into the desert. This was not an easy or safe thing to do, but he was athletic. I secretly applauded him for his act of defiance. Luckily for him he was found before he died of thirst. It was over forty degrees Celsius and the desert was a mixture of sand, rock, more rock, and more sand. Unluckily for him he was found by the Revolutionary Guards. Luckily for him they didn't throw him in an underground cell and forget about him, or stake him out under the midday sun and cover him with honey. Instead they returned him to the ship. They wanted their bottle of whiskey.

So we locked Number Two up again, this time in a cabin without a porthole. And for good measure we put him in a straitjacket. This was maritime mental health care. You are probably appalled by this state of affairs, but before you call the health ombudsman or whatever, know that it worked. As soon as the ship left port the second cook was a changed man. It was as if nothing had happened. He went straight back to slicing and dicing, carrots that is. I have often thought that this combined use of solitary confinement and a strait jacket is how we, as a species, should deal with children who throw tantrums in malls.

The cradle of civilisation was turning out to be more cradle than civilised. Then the Iraqis decided to invade Iran. At night we could see the flares from explosions in the desert. Listening to the BBC on the ship's radio, we would hear reports of another oil refinery or pipeline attacked in the exact position we could see the flames. It was time to leave. We steamed towards the Straits of Hormuz, being buzzed by American fighter jets and shadowed by Russian warships. In our wake tens of thousands of young men would die. This too, did not seem fair, to any of my selves. Meanwhile I had received a letter from Rodney.

We are all colour blind in the dark.

Index

Rodney's words wobbled over the page like an inebriated caterpillar. "Hey dude, are you dead?"

I admit I hadn't written to him for a while.

"I got a game for the Premiers and played a blinder. Watch this space, Rodney."

Okay, 'letter' was too grandiose a term. Despite our literary aspirations, letters were not a place we thought to practise our craft. We believed we had no need of practice. Writing just happened, didn't it? Then the riches flowed.

In the last year of his teens, Rodney had gone to university to study law. He also played hockey, quite well in fact. I later heard from Bryan about Rodney's great game for the university's top team.

"Oh yes, he played an excellent game, got picked up by the press, splashed all over the papers." Bryan was no mean hockey player himself. He had been a schoolboy hockey representative. Bryan's father expected him to train twenty-four hours a day and win bucket-loads of Olympic medals. As soon as he left home, Bryan dyed his hair for the first time, had his tongue pierced, and gave his hockey stick to the local op shop.

Club hockey in those days was newsworthy. While Rodney was in the shower, his teammates were in the bar. The local sports reporter joined them. The teammates knew she was unreliable. She worked for the same publication which had refused to print our 'send me a dollar' request. In addition, she had permed and dyed blonde hair and carried a white miniature poodle. What more proof of her unreliability did anyone need?

"Who was that new player, the one who had a great game?" She downed a glass of lager.

"Oh that was Rockie, Rockie Soames." (Did I mention that Rodney's surname was Jones?) The teammates didn't miss a beat. "Have another beer." The reporter did, but let the poodle have a sip first. She and her canine drinking buddy were both gone by the time Rodney emerged from the changing rooms.

The sports pages of the evening paper that night lauded the hockey exploits of one Rockie Soames.

"You'll get heaps more chances." Rodney's teammates couldn't resist revealing how his five minutes of fame had been misappropriated by a man who never was. Unfortunately for Rodney he didn't. He only got to play one more, sadly non-newsworthy, game for the senior team.

"Story of your life," Bryan and I would later say to Rodney, in a kind and caring way of course.

I'd had a job as a journalist, briefly, before becoming a mariner. I was taken on as a cadet, also at the same publication that had refused to publish our 'send me a dollar' request. There were only two newspaper games in town, and this outfit was definitely second tier. In my third week I had to check the oil levels in the newspaper's fleet of cars. 'Fleet' is an overstatement. There were three vehicles of indeterminate age.

I came here to write, not wipe, I said to myself as I cleaned the last dipstick, failing to push it all the way back into the engine block. Later I was summoned before the chief reporter. A cloud of smoke had burst from beneath the bonnet of the car while he was on his way to a 'presser' with the Prime Minister. Seconds later the car had ground to a halt in the middle of the motorway. The oil had coated the underside of the bonnet in a thick greasy film. There was little oil left in the engine and the chief reporter missed the presser.

I chose aggressive defence. "Well, you should've hired an apprentice mechanic." He didn't ask me to check the oil levels again. He didn't have a chance. I resigned the next day. I should have known that publication was unreliable.

After paying off from the Catalina I had two months leave. Rodney, now disillusioned with hockey, had become involved in newly-invented triathlons, so I joined him. In a triathlon you had to swim fifteen hundred metres, cycle forty kilometres and then run ten kilometres. Most people would, sensibly, rather eat ice cream. Rodney and I could run and cycle well, but Rodney swam like a drunk cat. I could swim a lot better than Rodney, like a sober cat. In our first race, held around a tidal estuary, we discovered the water was so shallow we could touch the bottom and run for most of the swim section. This may or may not have been within the rules. We didn't care. It was results that mattered. I beat Rodney. I placed well, in the top twenty. I thought I had a future.

Bryan and the scrimmage sisters also competed in that triathlon, as a team. The shorter dark sister swam, the taller blonde sister cycled, and Bryan ran. Bryan's girlfriend did her nails and makeup.

Bryan's hair was now reminiscent of a coal scuttle helmet and coloured vermillion. A collection of safety pins adorned his running shorts and an envelope was hanging from one of the pins.

"What's that?" I pointed at the envelope.

"A letter from my father."

"What's he want?"

"He says I'm wasting my life, he doesn't like the way I look, and I'm a disgrace to the family."

"Why are you carrying it?"

"In case of a toilet emergency."

I also beat the combined talents of this formidable unit, although I accept my victory was slightly tarnished by the fact that Sarah, the scrimmage sister swimmer (try saying that without your false teeth), completed the swim leg without touching the sea floor. When Bryan crossed the finish line after the final run leg, the sisters shouted "scrimmage" and jumped on him.

"Help. Police. My hair."

I noticed Bryan's envelope and letter were no longer attached to his shorts.

"How's your book coming along?" The scrimmage sisters had disentangled themselves from Bryan. They often spoke in unison.

"Like a bomb." Rodney had no idea what he was talking about.

"Unfortunate choice of words. First chapter completed."

Rodney looked surprised. "You never told me."

"I've been at sea, and you don't understand Morse code."

"You could've put a message in a bottle."

"Are you going to publish?" Trixie, the taller blonde one, said this as if she thought we were rank amateurs.

"Why else would we waste our time writing?" I confirmed her suspicions.

"It'll make squillions." Rodney definitely did.

The scrimmage sisters, who knew a bit about the creative world, laughed, and laughed, and laughed some more. They often laughed in unison too.

In our second triathlon, the race marshals had set the first leg of the triangular swim course at an enticing angle to the beach. They had also forgotten to rope off the swim start area. When the hooter to begin sounded, Rodney and I, with an eye for the main chance, and to compensate for our lack of training, sprinted up the beach. Mathematicians will understand we intended to enter the water at ninety degrees to the first mark, thereby cutting about two hundred and fifty metres off the fifteen hundred metre swim. We had both failed maths at school, but this was applied maths, we convinced ourselves afterwards. Had he been a triathlete, we were certain Isaac Newton would've done the same.

The race marshals shouted at us, and at the others who had taken our lead, in what can only be described as a very restrained fashion.

"Swim you fucking... fucking... wankers!" A short man, with the incendiary words 'Race Controller' displayed across his T-shirt, shouted the loudest. I paused momentarily, weighing up our moral options (my law-abiding and respectable self was conflicted for a nano second) then surged ahead.

"I owed it to Rodney, and the other competitors who followed me. Their faith in leaders would have been severely undermined if I had changed course. Think how bad that would have been for the future of our country." My post-race explanation convinced no one.

I beat Rodney by hectares of space. I placed well, in the top twenty. I still thought I had a future.

In our third race, the swim leg was cancelled just before the start. The large brown puddle masquerading as a lake was declared unfit for human activity due to pollution. That pollution was caused by runoff from nearby dairy farms – nitrates, phosphates, sulphates, caliphates, e.coli, b.coli, c.coli, g.coli. Are you paying attention? I wrote 'caliphates'. If you spotted that, you definitely know your shit from your sheikh. Okay, I also confess, G. Coli (better known as Giovanni) was an Italian painter who lived in the 17th century. He has nothing to do with this book. Nothing whatsoever. I promise.

Back to the race. Instead of conducting the swim and being sued for losing half the field to waterborne diseases, a second run was substituted. I finished third. The guy who finished fourth ran a fantastic race, brilliant in all respects. He did come in a long way behind me though. It was Rodney.

The race had been sponsored by the local business community which contributed the prizes. They obviously had some old stock to clear. I won a pair of running shorts that were sized for a twelve-year-old, and a glass sherry decanter that was cracked and leaked as soon as it was filled. I showed off my spoils to Rodney.

"Smart move by those sponsors, bro. Twelve-year-olds shouldn't drink, not sherry anyway."

After these initial problems, however, the organisers upped their game. They set swim courses that actually required immersing your whole body in water for the full fifteen hundred metres. Rodney and I found it increasingly difficult to compete to the level our egos required. To compensate, Rodney turned to multisport, where he could kayak instead of swim. I, fortunately, was ordered back to sea. It had turned out I didn't have a future after all, at least in triathlon.

Before embarking on my next voyage, Rodney and I decided to send *The Protestant Work Ethic: How to Live with It and How to Live without It*, or *TPWE:HTLWIAHTLWI* for short, to a publisher. Rodney found the name of one – Stables & Stately – in the yellow pages of the phone book. We had both yellow pages and white pages in those days, and incredibly, they were made of paper.

"Send them a teaser. In business you have to keep some powder dry." Bryan was wearing black leather pants and a torn white T-shirt. His hair was parted on one side, slicked down, and coloured indigo.

"Just the title then?" Rodney was holding onto his one small contribution for all he was worth.

"What's the title?"

Rodney told him.

"You're restricting your market. How are you going to sell it to the Catholics, Muslims, Buddhists and Hindus? They have a lot of purchasing power." Bryan had a point.

"Do they have work ethics?" Rodney was suspicious of anyone who did.

"Not sure about the Catholics." Bryan thoughtfully extended one of the rips in his T-shirt. "They spend a lot of time dressing up, inhaling incense, and drinking wine with crackers."

"And the Buddhists just sit on their bums and hum." If what I said was actually true, I thought I could fancy being a Buddhist.

We drafted a suitable covering letter and sent it off, with the title, to Stables & Stately. Surprisingly, we received a reply. It was a pro forma letter but we found that encouraging. It was addressed to 'Messrs Rockwell & Herringbones'. After his hockey experience, Rodney was quite comfortable using pseudonyms and one name was as good as another to me.

"They wouldn't have wasted their ink if they didn't like it." Bryan had cleverly intuited the publisher's business practice.

Apparently our covering letter had not been at all suitable and we were asked to submit more information than Bryan was comfortable with, but we had no choice.

First, we were asked what the title was.

"Are they morons? We've already sent them that." I couldn't believe their stupidity. Nonetheless we repeated the title. At Rodney's suggestion, we also included the acronym, *TPWE:HTLWIAHTLWI*, to make it easier for them to understand. Then we were asked who the author was. We stuck with Messrs Rockwell and Herringbones. They also wanted some background information about Messrs Rockwell and Herringbones. I thought hard.

"How about Rockwell learnt to read at the age of two months, was made a member of Mensa at three months, and is a budding winner of the Nobel Prize for Literature. Herringbones is a graduate of the French Foreign Legion, a collector of Regency chamber pots, and truffle farmer. He once gave birth to five kittens?" At the mention of kittens, Scrabble barked loudly in the background.

"You can't say that." Bryan was shocked. "Take out the bit about the kittens." Scrabble barked some more. We took out the bit about the kittens and wrote down the rest of it. Next we were asked for the category of the book. They gave examples, such as history, current affairs, and health.

Bryan was decisive. "Say bestseller."

We did as instructed. Then we were asked for any books that were similar to ours.

I looked at the ceiling for inspiration. "How about *The History of the Decline and Fall of the Roman Empire*? And by the way, you've got mould."

Bryan also looked at the ceiling. "I wonder how long that's been there. Never heard of the book, but it sounds good, and first impressions count. Write it down." We wrote it down. Next Stables & Stately wanted to know why we were the right people to write this book.

Rodney sighed with exasperation. "Are they morons? It's about us for God's sake. Who else could write it?"

We wrote, "It's about us." Then we were asked if we had any expertise in the area we were writing about.

I shook my head in disbelief. "They really are morons. It's about us!" I added the exclamation mark to make sure the imbecile receiving our letter got the message that Messrs Rockwell and Herringbones were not to be truffled with. We were beginning to worry we were being scammed.

Rodney was the first to sense this. "Maybe they just want to steal our title?"

"And the first chapter." I had to look after my own interests.

Next we were asked about the intended market.

Bryan didn't hesitate. "Readers."

We wrote it down. Finally we were asked to list our previous publishing history, awards and writers in residencies. We wrote down "Heaps". We were also asked to send in the first chapter.

Bryan was not happy at all about this. "Never give up your intellectual property without a fight. Tell them it's in the mail. Incidentally, what is the first chapter?" Bryan looked from me to Rodney and back again.

I reluctantly handed Bryan my exercise book, open at the first page. He read silently, while Rodney and I assumed poses of relaxed disinterest that were at odds with our internal fears of being exposed as literary sawdust. This is what Bryan read.

Chapter 42

Rodney and I sat on a beach and decided to write a book. We were unemployed and had nothing else to do. Unfortunately, neither of us had passed English, but being short of cash, we had nothing to lose. We believed that writing a book was like receiving an inheritance from an ancient aunt.

Rodney and I had been NASA astronauts. You may find this surprising, especially given the fact we had failed English, but because Americans don't speak real English that was not a problem. You may also think that being unemployed and short of cash does not fit with people who have recently been astronauts. That too is easily explained, by the further fact that we had been fired, not out of a Saturn V rocket, but out of the lunar lander we took for a spin over Houston one night. We had set down outside our favourite bar.

"Cool wheels!" A group of joint-smoking, hippie chicks who were wearing flowers in their hair, psychedelic miniskirts, gold round-rimmed sunglasses and crocheted sandals gathered round us. "What does this button do?" asked one, reaching inside and pushing the ejector ignition.

Houston at night looks great from a parachute, but not so good from the inside of a military police van. The President cut up our Green Cards and with our aerial revenue avenue now closed, we were considering other options.

So, bro," said Rodney, "have you written a book before?"

"No, bro. Have you?"

"No, bro."

"So, bro. Who's going to write it?"

"You, bro."

"No, you, bro."

"Too slow, bro. I said 'you, bro' first."

"No, bro."

"Yes, bro. Go back four lines."

"Well, what do you know, bro?" I said, reading what I had written four lines earlier.

"Told you so, bro."

"It's going to be a great book, bro."

Just then, from out of nowhere, four, beautiful girls, wearing nothing but bikinis, came and sat down beside us.

"What are you two hunks doing?"

"Writing a book."

"Wow, that's really amazing. You must be really smart. Mind if we hang out with you guys?"

"We're kind of busy," said Rodney.

"But has anyone got a pen and paper on them?" I asked.

Rodney came up with the title, "The Protestant Work Ethic: How to Live with It and How to Live without It". I said I thought it was a bit churchy but Rodney said so was the Bible and that sold a lot of copies. I couldn't dispute that so I got stuck in and wrote all these words you're reading now. I hope you like them and please tell all your friends so they buy copies of the book and make us squillions.

Writing a book is not easy. By the time you get to here, I've written four hundred and sixty-nine words, make that four hundred and seventy-six, okay, four hundred and eighty-two. It all adds up in the end but it's already taken two years to write this much, so I hope you appreciate all the effort that has been put into launching you on the path to enlightenment.

There are lots more chapters after this one, and if you want to add anything yourself, please feel free to chime in. See you on the next page. Ciao.

Bryan was captivated. "Wow, that's really good. It's almost like a real book."

"Genius, bro."

I smiled modestly. "Let me know when we have to sign the contract."

"This could be a turning point." Bryan caressed his hair.

Two days later, I flew out to join the jolly ship *Rangitoto*.

In my absence, Rodney focused on multisport. His subsequent recounting of this part of his athletic career became one of his staple stories. Bryan and I delayed for years in raising our hands to indicate we had heard it all before. We had always enjoyed a spot of schadenfreude.

In Rodney's telling, his experience of multisport was short-lived, but spectacular. He trained hard, learnt how to kayak in white water, and declared himself ready to race from one side of the South Island of Aotearoa to the other. This was a gruelling event over mountains and down fast-flowing rivers. There was no swimming involved. Rodney, however, discovered he had missed the date of entry. He was distraught. He was outside in the garden at Bryan's flat, oiling his bike.

"Time is but relative, bro." Rodney looked skywards and shook his fists. No one, except Scrabble, was paying much attention. "I could enter after I finish and the world wouldn't suffer." Scrabble howled in sympathy.

"Muffle!" Bryan was inside, rearranging his collection of fridge magnets.

"Me or the dog?" Rodney poked his head through the door.

"Neither of you is bloody Hamlet."

Scrabble retreated to his kennel with a whimper.

"He's good with words, bro."

"When he was a puppy he ate half a dictionary. I had to sit up with him all night. He had chronic verbal diarrhoea."

Luckily for Rodney his multisport career was not yet fated for destruction. In his time of need, up stepped The Energiser. The Energiser was three axe handles high and two axe handles wide. He could kayak like an Olympian, cycle blindfolded up mountains of shingle scree, and run for weeks without sleeping. He had no hair and no front teeth. He grew tomatoes.

The Energiser had a cousin who suffered from a compulsion which caused him to enter every multisport race known to humankind. Then, at the last minute, before the race started, the cousin would pull out. There was always something that prevented him from competing, such as washing his hair (baldness didn't run in the family) or eating ice cream. The cousin's name was Rodney.

On the day of the big event our Rodney lined up at the start. He was competing as Rodney MacFarlane while the real Rodney MacFarlane, The Energiser's cousin, cut his toenails.

Our Rodney outshone his wildest predictions. At the end of the first day, halfway across the mountains, he was the race leader. The Rodney part of his name appeared on the leaders' board. The other competitors were not impressed. "Who is this MacFarlane guy? Where did he come from?"

Rodney skulked around the back of the camp, keeping to the shadows. This was embarrassing. What if he actually won the event? He could be prosecuted for fraud and thrown in the slammer for the rest of his natural life. At the very least he would be disqualified and his mates would take the piss out of him.

Rodney slept on his conundrum. It was uncomfortable, like the night he slept in the tent on the tramp with Helen. Waking around 3am he decided there was only one way out of his dilemma; he would race slowly and lose. In the loneliness of the dark hours before dawn he reflected on his sporting life, recalling the unfulfilled promise of his hockey career. Now, here he was being usurped by a pseudonym for the second time. He hoped his third encounter with pseudonyms, namely Messrs Rockwell and Herringbones, would prove more successful.

The second multisport day began with a long kayak leg down a raging river. It hadn't rained for months and the water level was low, meaning there were a lot more rocks to hit. Rodney made sure he didn't paddle too hard. It was his undoing. In the most inaccessible part of the river, deep in a rock-walled gorge, Rodney half-heartedly steered his kayak into what seemed to be the biggest, sharpest, ugliest rock in the river. He was thrown into the water and bounced off the rock-strewn river bed. Perfect, thought Rodney as he struggled for breath and careered off the walls of the gorge, no way I'll win now.

But it wasn't perfect because after he washed up on a gravel beach below the gorge, Rodney discovered he couldn't scratch his nose. He couldn't take off his lifejacket, he couldn't eat the banana tucked into his purple Lycra race jersey. In fact he couldn't move his right arm without a grinding sound and excruciating pain. He had broken his collarbone.

Luckily for Rodney he was spotted by a race marshal. Unluckily, the only way to get him out of the river was by helicopter. Rodney's arrival at the finish was therefore not the low-key anonymous event he had planned. After landing to the curious looks of hundreds of spectators and having a TV camera thrust in his face, he was rushed off to hospital in an ambulance.

The Energiser picked up Rodney when he was discharged. "Well, it could've been worse. If you'd died, my cousin would've been in the shit."

The Energiser himself was not immune to embarrassment. In another multi-day race, with Rodney acting as his support crew, The Energiser lost his way. It was in the mountains. The sun had long set and he had still not arrived at that day's finish line. All other competitors were accounted for. The organisers were very concerned.

"Where is he?" They stood, almost threateningly, around Rodney.

Rodney waved his hand vaguely in the direction of the bush. "He's a slow runner." He sounded apologetic. "And he doesn't have a good sense of direction."

The organisers immediately called in Search and Rescue. The mountains echoed to the staccato pounding of helicopters, their airborne observers armed with night vision goggles. Dogs and their handlers combed the bush. Searchlights played in sweeping patterns across the night sky.

It was about 11pm when The Energiser stumbled, unnoticed except by Rodney, across the outskirts of the camp at the finish. On Rodney's advice he merged with the shadows then slipped inside a Port-a-Loo to gather his thoughts. After ten minutes of somewhat nauseating spiritual contemplation, he decided he would have to front up.

"Where the bloody hell have you been?" The very relieved chief organiser couldn't help shouting.

The Energiser clasped his hands together and bowed his large frame. "I cannot tell a lie." He paused for a moment, soaking up the fresh mountain air. He looked the organiser directly in the eye. "Meditating."

Rodney led him back to his tent. "Like your work, bro."

The Energiser was also a conservationist, long before that term became fashionable. His speciality was ridding the bush of possums which preyed on native bird life and chomped down truckloads of tree foliage every night. He would set traps for the possums and, when caught, dispatch them to their maker with a whack on the head from a hammer.

"This job is not a good way to pick up chicks." He meant girls. "How do you explain that you bash out the brains of furry cuddly little animals?"

The Energiser was a clever man. He could recite from memory the names of the capital cities of all the nations on earth. In his heart, he confessed to Rodney, he knew the possums were innocent and that it was humans who had caused the problem by introducing them to this environment.

"Perhaps we should just let nature sort it out." This was The Energiser's response when asked about his occupation by an enlightened chick one night when he and Rodney were in a bar. Not long after, the chick and The Energiser got married and, in the appropriate fullness of time, produced two large toothless and bald babies.

How strange we must look to other animals.

Cornflakes on Parade

Eating our ice creams, Bryan, Kim, Rodney and I are walking along the seawall on the waterfront. Away from the apartment and inner-city traffic we can smell traces of brine and seaweed, mixed with the aromas of coconut-scented sunblock and hot tarseal.

We enter a park by the water's edge where a crowd of people is gathered. They are looking at a collection of temporary sculptures made from papier-mâché and corrugated cardboard. Among the vividly coloured sculptures are emaciated polar bear cubs with severe mange, planes disgorging filthy pollutants, gorillas crammed into cages no bigger than the animals are, an electric car being mown down by a diesel-guzzling semi-trailer, tropical islands drowning in environmental agony, and smug-looking male politicians of various nationalities juggling gold bars and barrels of oil. Each sculpture has script written on it.

"Scrimmage!" Trixie and Sarah execute a synchronised geriatric bounce from behind an apocalyptic conflagration of the Amazon rainforest.

"Don't you dare." Kim stands protectively in front of Bryan.

"What d'ya think?" Sarah waves her arm around the art installation. "We popped it up this morning."

"Hey." Rodney, while taking a lick of his neon cherry cone, has just read the script on a sculpture of a burping and defecating cow, its tail raised like a trumpet to the heavens. "It says ice cream has tested positive for glyphosates and glyphosates can cause cancer." He looks worryingly at his remaining scoop of emulsified fat droplets and sugar.

A twelve-year-old carrying a skateboard has also stopped at the exhibit. He is drinking soft drink from a can.

"Here, bro, have a treat." Rodney holds out the remnants of his ice cream to the twelve-year-old.

We all look more closely at the exhibit. The script also tells us that slurry, which is just another word for liquid cow shit, finds its way into the rivers we used to swim in, into our drinking water, and into the food we eat. I read the next part out loud.

"And methane from cow burps traps about thirty times more heat in the atmosphere than carbon dioxide."

Skater Kid refuses Rodney's offer, takes a gulp from his can and lets out a reverberating belch of his own. "I coulda told you that." His jeans are baggy and, fashionably, deliberately patched. He is wearing a loose black and grey hoodie.

Trixie looks at him in a motherly fashion. She and Sarah have recently retired from teaching adolescent artists at an urban commune. "What else can you tell us?"

Skater Kid points to a sculpture of the blue planet vomiting plastic and pesticides out of a gaping mouth which protrudes fleshily out of the Pacific Ocean. He reads the script aloud. "Planetary health. If we don't look after the earth, it won't look after us."

"I did that one." Sarah attempts to sound modest.

Skater Kid looks at her admiringly. "That's sick."

"What's your favourite?" Trixie continues in mother mode.

Skater Kid leads us to a sculpture of Greta Thunberg. "She's awesomesauce. We get Fridays off school because of her."

Trixie looks impressed. "That's really cool. So you use that time to protest against the destruction of the earth and all its species?"

"Nah. I go to the skatepark."

We wander around some other sculptures. Skater Kid looks closely at a caricature of George W. Bush who is playing a violin while standing on top of the Statue of Liberty's head. The Statue of Liberty is drowning in sea water.

"Who's this Bush dude?"

"He was a politician who thought saying 'global warming', or 'global heating', would scare the public so he came up with 'climate change' instead." Sarah can't keep the disdain out of her voice.

Skater Kid reads aloud from the script. "The Kyoto Protocol of 1997 was designed to reduce the emission of gases that contribute to global heating. George W. Bush thought it would harm the American economy so he withdrew the USA from the Protocol. The USA is one of the world's top two carbon emitters. This wasn't George's only miscalculation while in office. Remember the Iraq war? George didn't have a good strike rate on the big calls."

Skater Kid looks at Sarah. "Did you do this one too?"

"Can't say no."

"You're a beast, for a coffin dodger."

"You're off the hook." Sarah and Skater Kid exchange high-fives.

"Hey, look at this one." I have moved onto a sculpture of what looks like a nuclear bomb survivor. Her skin is peeling off in flesh-coloured strips, clumps of hair have gone from her scalp, and she is emaciated to the point of starvation. I read the script. "Don't you think that's a bit over the top for sunburn?"

"Skin cancer has increased a lot since the 1970s." Trixie is a little defensive.

"Possibly caused by ozone depletion and air pollution." Skater Kid causes us all to stop and look at him, surprised at his erudition.

"Read the small print, or do you need your glasses?" He laughs and hands Rodney his empty soft drink can. "Here oldie locks, have a treat."

Rodney self-consciously rubs his bare pate. "I had hair once."

Skater Kid jumps onto his board and pushes himself away. "Ride hard or ride home. I'm off for a sesh of nose picks." He skates away into the crowd.

I look after him, wonderingly. "Were we the same?"

Rodney is searching for a litter bin for the soft-drink can. The scrimmage sisters look at him sternly. "You'd better recycle that."

We admire some more sculptures then walk back towards the road.

Trixie waves at us as we leave. "See you tomorrow, Bryan."

"He's giving a talk." Kim doesn't sound enthusiastic.

"To the Anarchists of Aotearoa. I've called it 'Cool Cash on a Hot Planet'. Come along."

We walk on in silence for a few minutes, dodging fruit boots (that's in-line skaters to most of us), runners, power-walkers and exercising parents pushing prams. Rodney is right at home in his cycling Lycra. Eventually, Bryan suggests turning round.

On the way back I notice that the wife of Bryan is subdued. "What's up Kim?" I put my arm around her shoulders. Bryan and Rodney have pulled ahead of us.

"It's all this talk about the world in trouble... and cancer."

"History goes in cycles. We'll come out the other side before we grill our guts into charcoal. Trust me, I'm not a lawyer."

Kim laughs a little. Encouraged, I start to croak, "Crazy 'bout you baby..."

Bryan and Rodney turn around. They pick up the beat. "Yeah, yeah."

"Crazy 'bout you baby, yeah, yeah." We all croak together, looping our arms around each other's shoulders and moving in ragged time with the music, one staggered step to the left, then one staggered step to the right.

A jogger takes evasive action as we stumble like a quadruply-envisioned drunk in front of his path. "Bloody wrinkletons."

We shout after him. "And her name was? Mary Jane!"

The jogger turns and gives us the fingers.

"He should wear gloves, or he'll end up like Crunch." I don't think he heard me.

The next evening, Rodney and I catch the train to a ramshackle hall in an outer suburb. The hall is owned by the local Bahá'i faithful and the anarchists have hired it. There are approximately thirty people in the hall. "Protection By Protest" reads a banner hung on one wall. "Resist Capitalism" reads another hung as a backdrop to the stage. We find Kim and the scrimmage sisters and sit down in time to hear Bryan take the microphone.

Bryan's hair is canary yellow. He is wearing shorts, jandals and a ripped T-shirt with the slogan "Words are Turds" on it. He introduces his lecture by discussing war.

"Just think of all those emissions caused by the world's militaries in producing weapons of destruction and then blowing them up, along with all that collateral damage, by which they mean people like you and me. It has been estimated that the US military, which is by far the biggest producer and consumer of instruments of war in the world, emitted about 1.2 billion metric tonnes of carbon between 2001 and 2017. Can you believe that?"

"We don't usually believe anything," mutters a voice in the audience. "But yes, we can believe *that*."

"What does 1.2 billion tonnes of carbon actually look like?" asks one of them.

"One tonne is five hundred CO_2 fire extinguishers, so think six hundred billion of them. That's almost one hundred fire extinguishers of CO_2 for each person on the planet. It's a hell of a lot and the world would be a much better place if it hadn't been produced at all. Just think of an earth without armies, guns, gold braid and epaulettes, where we resolved all issues at a hangi in the park on Sundays. What a blast that would be."

The audience applauds vigorously.

"The US Department of Defence, by itself, has a bigger carbon footprint than most countries on earth. And before I forget, Vladimir Putin recently budgeted US$79 million for global heating research. At the same time he was blowing close on US$500 million a day in razing Ukraine. What a tosser."

The audience whistles, applauds, and stamps its feet. Bryan then proceeds to explain why he believes the world still needs capitalism and a cash economy to counter the threat of global heating. He either hasn't read the banner behind his head or, most likely, doesn't care.

The response from the audience is as sage as it is subtle. "Hiss! Boo!"

This does not deter Bryan. "Properly incentivised capitalism can help solve the technological problems of the heating planet."

A woman in her late twenties, with a multitude of visible piercings and vibrant green hair, rattles angrily to her feet.

"Who do you think you are lecturing us about our welfare, you superficial, selfish, ego-driven, dishonest, lazy, old, pompous hypocrite? Where were you when it all started? Roasting on a beach in your undies probably and drinking through plastic straws. You could've stopped it then."

"Go, sister." The audience roars its approval.

"Pompous is a bit of a stretch." Rodney's comment is drowned out by the noise.

Bryan is not to be outdone. He shouts over the hubbub. "If it's all the same to you, I would like to live a long, comfortable life, and not be barbecued to death. In this instance, being selfish is a virtue. If we all, selfishly, wanted to live out our natural lives without having to walk over hot coals to get to the finish line, then we would be motivated to do something about the state of the planet. We have to bring the capitalists on board. They are the gold standard of 'selfish'. So I'm lecturing you, because unfortunately, we can only achieve this, much as I hate to say it, if we all work together, and that includes working with the capitalists. So let's all be selfish and unite. It's our only hope. And consume less. That will..."

"Blasphemy!" The green-haired woman jumps onto her chair and turns to the audience. "No, no no." She thrusts her fist into the air. "No to capitalism, no to climate change, no to everything." The rest of the audience leaps to its feet.

"No to capitalism, no to climate change, no to everything." The volume of their chant increases with each phrase. "No to everything. No to everything." Their fists are pumping away like Texas oil wells.

Bryan attempts to explain that climate change is not the correct terminology and they should be chanting "no to global heating", but his words shimmy away in the turmoil. Recognising a lost cause, he picks up a basket at his feet and heaves its contents at the audience who are now stamping their feet in time with their chant. Small, butterfly-shaped biscuits shower down around them.

"Have a climate cookie. Doom be upon ye all!"

Back at the apartment later that night, Bryan is aglow with energy. "Wasn't it great? I love it when they start shouting."

"Have you spoken to the anarchists before?" I sense the answer is obvious.

"Oh yes, many times."

"It always ends like that. I don't know why he goes back. Life's too short to play games with." Unlike Bryan, Kim is not euphoric.

"Carpe diem." Bryan gives her a big grin.

Octopuses have nine brains, three hearts, and blue blood.

Chapter 48573938576748399

While Rodney continued to flex his multi-sporting muscles, I was confined to shipboard life on the *Rangitoto*. My opportunities for sporting activity were few. In Jeddah, the second electrician and I would go for a run at 0200 hours. We did this to avoid the daytime heat. We were not permitted to leave the port. This was a common restriction in the Middle East. So we ran round and round a warehouse on the wharf. Each lap took about three minutes. The Bangladeshi stevedores, working nights, would cheer us on. We thought they were considerately boosting our morale against the energy-sapping, nighttime heat.

"No, mon, they are takin' bets, mon, on which one o' you two fol down first." Our Barbadian greaser found the Bangladeshis' gambling instincts amusing. This should have come as no surprise. No one was doing social work out there in the maritime world.

A greaser was a crew member who worked primarily in the ship's engine room and was responsible for keeping the machinery lubricated. He was not of the same status as a ginger beer. A ginger beer was an engineer, one of those officer people numbered one to five who also worked primarily in the engine room. This was Cockney rhyming slang. In that slang, a ginger beer also had another meaning, but in the nautical context, a ginger beer was not a homosexual. Although one chief engineer may have qualified as both. Sorely interrupted, he once attended an emergency alarm in the engine room, in the middle of the night, dressed in lace negligee, fishnet stockings and suspender belt.

The second cook, no relation to the slicer and dicer on the *Catalina*, also decided to take a trip around the warehouse on the wharf at Jeddah. He, however, walked, carrying a case of beer, on his way to visit another ship. This was not a smart thing to do. From nowhere, a squad of machine gun-toting soldiers appeared. They took his beer. They took his arms. They handcuffed his wrists. They took him to the slammer. Even the ship's cat knew that alcohol was banned in the Kingdom of Saudi Arabia.

That cat had sneaked aboard at Basra, in Iraq. Seamen are a creative bunch. We named him Basra Cat. He lived under a crane on deck and would approach no one but the second cook, who fed him. Basra was as mean and lean as a species-inappropriate junkyard dog. At sea one day in the Persian Gulf, in a dust storm, visibility was nil and the wind howled at forty knots. An exhausted bird, blown off course from the land, landed on the heaving deck, seeking shelter, near Basra Cat's crane. The bird's plumage was wet and ragged, it shivered with fatigue. You can imagine how relieved it was to discover this magical, floating oasis in the middle of the ocean. The poor bird had all of a nanosecond to appreciate its good fortune. After that, not a feather remained. It was a dangerous life for other animals as well as humans.

The arrest of the second cook created an international incident. The British Embassy was involved (this was the British Merchant Navy after all). The shipping line's owner was involved. The second cook's parents appeared in their local Liverpool paper, lamenting their incarcerated son.

"'E's like a sandwich short of a picnic, d'ye no warra mean?" his father was quoted as saying.

Five days later, someone paid a large fine, bottles of whiskey changed hands, and the second cook was returned to us. A sojourn in the slammer hadn't dampened his enthusiasm or his Scouse accent.

"It were great. De Saudi prisoners luked out for me someding special like. We had te sleep on de concrete floor and dey swept me space clean, every night! 'Ow good is tha'? Der was no beer though. D'ye no warra mean?"

Sad to say, but I think his da was right.

In addition to running on the wharf in port, while at sea we also got to follow sporting pursuits on board ship. This could be life threatening. Frisbee throwing, as we have already seen, could have negative consequences. Dangerous too was the football we played in an empty hold. Steel bulkheads (sailor-speak for walls), combined with a rolling sea, made for a game more like a salty version of rollerball.

Before the *Rangitoto* docked at Jeddah, we had navigated up the Red Sea and been astounded by the variety of marine life. Giant manta rays glided across our wake, dolphins tumbled around the bow, and huge globes of phosphorescence, pulsating like mirror balls in an underwater disco, lit our way. So, on a day when we were drifting, awaiting orders from head office, what did we do among this splendid display of nature's imaginative genius? We decided to kill some of it and went fishing. I say 'we' but I was not a huge supporter of this activity. I believed the creatures we observed were as much entitled to live their lives as naturally as we were. The collective 'we', however, settled on fishing for sharks. Big ones.

The ginger beers made a steel hook, about thirty centimetres long, in the engine room workshop. It was attached to the cable of a crane, as if the intended target was the shark equivalent of Moby Dick. The first cook was cajoled to hand over a slab of steak. The hook was baited with the steak and swung out over the ocean. The baited hook was lowered into the sea and everyone waited. And waited. And waited. We could see the black fins of sharks circling the temptress hook. We waited some more.

"Haul it in," someone eventually said. The steak was gone. The process was repeated again. And again. And again.

"Bugger off." The first cook was not impressed when asked for yet another steak. "And you can forget about a BBQ this weekend."

It was perhaps fortunate for the second cook on the *Rangitoto* that, after his incarceration, there was a crew change at Jeddah. He got to fly home before he did something else to get himself executed, along with the rest of his crew mates. The old crew was replaced by a Chinese crew. When I refer to 'crew' here, it means all the sailors who were not officers. In other contexts the word 'crew' can include officers. It is a duplicitous word of which there are many in the English language. If this worries you, you can always speak Esperanto.

We received further orders to sail up the Gulf of Aqaba and discharge our cargo of newsprint in Jordan at the eponymous town of Aqaba. Aqaba was separated from the next-door Israeli town of Eilat by a shaky barbed wire fence running down the middle of the beach. Where I come from, a sheep would have seen this fence as an invitation to greener pastures, if in fact there had been greenery of any sort in the surrounding desiccated wastelands.

The Israelis were very pleased to see us. They sent a gunboat with an eye-piercing searchlight to light our way the night before we anchored. Over the radio, they also, very kindly, wanted to know who we were and what we were doing. They were such good conversationalists. Not once did they talk about themselves, just asked lots of questions about us. They also pointed out, quite helpfully, that the Gulf was actually called the Gulf of Eilat, not the Gulf of Aqaba. We thanked them for correcting our imperfect knowledge of geography and improving our knowledge of Zionism.

Seagoing was a spiritual experience. From the cradle of civilisation, here we were now, anchored at Aqaba, in the midst of ancient Biblical peoples, surrounded by deserts of forty-day and forty-night proportions, breathing in the vapours of the world's great religions.

On the Jordanian side of the barbed wire fence, five times a day, we would hear the muezzin calling out the adhan, the call to prayer, from the many mosques' minarets. From the Israeli side, on a still night, we would hear dance music booming from nightclubs, the bass lines throbbing through the dust-encrusted gloom. After such a night we had to disagree with that well-known line from the pre-dawn adhan – "As-salatu Khayrun Minan-nawm" or "prayer is better than sleep".

Everyone in this part of the world, except perhaps the Israelis with hangovers, seemed imbued with religious spirit. Wandering ashore, I shared in this spirit as I bought a music cassette tape at an inflated price from a pious roadside vendor. I knew he was pious because he was a Hajji, a Muslim who has made the pilgrimage, or hajj, to Mecca. I knew he had been to Mecca because he told me. He said it had cost him a lot of money and that was why he was now having to make ends meet as a roadside vendor. I felt a little sorry for him, so didn't haggle. The tape's outer cover stated that this was music by those well-known, God-fearing men, the Sex Pistols.

I opened the tape's outer cover back in my cabin. The cassette player stood open, ready to compete with the Eilat nightclubs. The inner writing on the cassette tape read, "The Best of Joan Baez". Well, I thought, still vibing with the religious spirit, Joan is a few steps closer to God than Johnny Rotten, so I was not totally displeased with my purchase. I placed the tape in the cassette player, closed the little plastic window, and pressed play. Hallelujah! From the speakers came, not the crystal bell, clear notes of Joan Baez, but the warm, embryonic fluid tones of the Hare Krishna mantra. How thoughtful for that street vendor to have been thinking of my soul when he ripped me off and gave me what was, in most parts of the world, a free giveaway.

Like my street vendor, the Jordanian stevedores also professed to be pious. We were discharging our cargo at anchor as the wharf wasn't big enough to accommodate the ship and each day the stevedores would be transported out to the ship in lighters. Whenever the adhan sounded they would roll out their prayer mats on deck, face towards the Kaba, the central shrine in Mecca's Great Mosque, and bow down to Allah. One noon, as the stevedores genuflected on their mats, the ship turned with the tide. The stevedores were now facing in the opposite direction from the Kaba. Did this invalidate their prayers? I suspect not. The prayers could just travel the long way around the globe to the Kaba instead of merely hop-skip-and-jumping over the nearby desert. Their prayers, however, would be at the back of the queue when they arrived at Mecca. Any miracles requested would therefore take a little longer to implement. It is the same in any bureaucracy.

Unfortunately, all the prayers in the world were not enough for one stevedore. A roll of newsprint did exactly that and rolled on top of him. These were not rolls you would buy at the local stationery shop – these were industrial-sized rolls. They must have weighed at least half a tonne each. He was badly crushed. We don't know whether he lived or died. He was evacuated in a lighter and the discharge of cargo continued. It was a bad morning, but just another day at sea.

After all the rolls of newsprint had been unloaded from the forward hold, I helped the ship's carpenter affix dunnage to the lower bulkheads to protect our next cargo. 'Affixing dunnage to the bulkheads.' What a terrific sentence, I thought, I should make a note of that.

I had not forgotten that Rodney and I were writing a book. If I'd pilfered a roll of the newsprint I could've written down two thousand years' worth of notes. It would've been like amalgamating the *Bible* and the *Koran* into one consolidated volume of spiritual guidance. Interestingly, as a side benefit to Rodney's and my early retirement plan, that would also have provided the perfect solution for Middle East peace. Muslims and Christians would have all been preaching from the same prayer book and there would've been no need for division, war and other calamitous global upheavals. Unfortunately, I didn't pilfer half a tonne of newsprint, so someone else will have to solve the problem.

Dunnage is packing material, usually cast-off pieces of poor-quality wood, used to protect a ship's cargo from damage. In this case we were breaking down old wooden pallets and using the planks of wood to frame and line the bulkheads. The ship's carpenter was an elderly Chinese man. He spoke no English. I spoke no Chinese. He wore khaki shorts, sandals and an off-white singlet. He looked as fragile as a starving sparrow. What teeth he had were yellow. He possessed a handful of wisps of white hair. He came from the southeast of China and spoke Cantonese, and probably another dialect or two as well.

One of us would hold the nail and piece of wood, and the other would hammer the nail into place. He hammered. I held. Until he offered me the hammer.

"Are you sure you want to do this?" I intimated in sign language. I hadn't hammered anything of substance since school woodwork classes as a twelve-year-old.

"Yes, yes, yes," he said in Cantonese, or whatever dialect he favoured. At least that is what I thought he said. The carpenter held the next nail and piece of dunnage, and I nailed the wood to the frame. I offered the hammer back to him.

"No, no, no." At least that is what I thought he said. I nailed on the next piece of dunnage. He smiled at me. I smiled at him. He nodded enthusiastically and smiled again. We were having such a merry time nailing dunnage at the bottom of the forward hold. My memory of what happened next is hazy. But I can remember a slight roll of the ship and the oath the carpenter screamed as the hammer hit his thumb. Well I can't actually remember the oath – it was Chinese, I assume – but it was very loud and sounded like a very bad word.

Can I just say what a trooper that old carpenter was. I took him to the sick bay. The top of his thumb was a pulpy mess. You may remember that only Russian merchant ships carried doctors. The person usually responsible for medical matters on our ships was the chief mate. He was also known as the first mate under the numbers system outlined previously, and sometimes he was just called 'Chief'. A captain would sometimes call him 'Mr Mate'. Other times, and this is my favourite, he was simply called 'the mate'.

The mate's main knowledge of medicine derived from a large illustrated book called *The Ship Captain's Medical Guide*. This door-stopping tome contained 'cut along the dotted line' diagrams of how to perform appendectomies and other life-threatening operations at sea. If you're not already feeling nervous, let it be known that this mate was an alcoholic. The primary doctoring function of mates on most ships was to inject penicillin into the buttocks of errant sailors. They were the lads who had committed 'indiscretions' ashore, and a few days later developed symptoms consistent with STDs. They would line up outside the sick bay after breakfast, drop their strides, and the mate would proceed along the line, jabbing them in their buttocks. You can understand why the mates did this after breakfast.

Returning to the current medical emergency, our mate bent his florid cheeks over the carpenter's thumb. He wiggled his own thumb, indicating that the carpenter should do the same. (The mate, not surprisingly, didn't speak Chinese either. He was from Birmingham.) The carpenter gingerly bent his thumb.

"Not broken then." The mate washed the thumb with his alcoholic breath and iodine, bandaged it and gave the carpenter some aspirin. "Time for a drink." The mate walked out the door. It was an hour after breakfast. For the hundredth time I apologised to the carpenter. I did really feel guilty about this. Besides, the roles could've been reversed and it may have been my thumb which was smashed up. It made me wince at the thought of it. The carpenter raised his thumb into the air and held it in front of my face.

"Ouch." He spoke in English and smiled in Esperanto. Great, I thought, no lasting damage there, either to his finger or my reputation. I smiled in return, tapped him on his bony shoulder blades, gently, so as not to knock him overboard, and whistled as we went back to work, still friends.

The ship's bosun showed me a map of China one day and explained that he and the crew came from Guangdong Province in southeast China. The bosun was required to speak English because he had to implement the orders of the mate. The mate was responsible for running the deckside of the ship. The mate and the other officers were mostly English. The bosun was like the foreman of the deck crew. He organised the able seamen, ordinary seamen and deck boys to do their work. The chief ginger beer on the other hand was responsible for running the engine room and other mechanical bits on board. The captain oversaw the whole shebang.

Now all that is clear, why were there Chinese crew on a British ship? It was all to do with money. If British crews were employed, they had to be paid British wages. Chinese crews, however, could be paid at a rate commensurate with what they would earn in China. This was a lot less than British crews expected. It was a simple equation for the ship owners. Not only were their rates of pay substantially less, the Chinese crews' conditions of work were also harsher. The Chinese on our ship could expect to be away from their homes for over a year at a time. Some would be absent for two or more years. And remember that, while on board, everyone was expected to work seven days a week. Weekends and days off were illegal in the merchant navy. British crews, on the other hand, expected to be repatriated every four to six months.

Even I could see this was unfair. And it was not just Chinese crews who suffered. Crews from the West Indies, Bangladesh, India and the Philippines were also commonly found on ships. The practice of paying them rates determined by their home countries' standard of living continues to this day, even though they do exactly the same work as crews from wealthier nations. Some may call this racism, and I can't really think of an argument against that charge. Back then, we just got on with sailing the globe, polluting the air with the ships' exhaust fumes, and delivering a lot of often useless stuff from one country to another. It was simply the way things were.

Notwithstanding the unfairness in the system, at Chinese New Year the Chinese crew invited everyone to a ten-course meal in the crew's mess. They cooked for us, waited on us and poured alcohol into our mouths at every opportunity.

At each boozy gulp we shouted the only Chinese words we knew – "Yam seng!", meaning drink to victory – and then drank some more. Drinking made it easier to eat the eyes bulging out of the fish heads. It was a wonderful gesture from men isolated from their families on a tin box for years at a time and being paid a pittance. Why would you put up with it? I asked myself, admiring their resilience and self-sufficiency, and popping another piscean pupil down my throat.

It was implied earlier that the Muslim religion was a bureaucracy. Please do not take offence. In my admittedly limited experience, most religions operate like bureaucracies, albeit with a little bit of theatre and razzmatazz thrown in. I mean, have you seen the clothes they get out of the fancy dress box on holy days?

The shipping company was also a bureaucracy, although not on the scale of Islam. Disappointingly, it was also very short on razzmatazz. But it did hold sway over our lives. The company now decided I had been on this voyage long enough. It ordered me to take some leave.

Life is significant and it's not. That's the big paradox.

Chapter 42 (continued)

When we were given leave from shipboard life, the company was legally obliged to fly us back home, or to an equivalent place of our choosing. Young men, wanting to explore the world further, would often ask to be flown to a country they hadn't visited before.

"I'm not a bloody travel agent," roared the captain of the *Rangitoto* down the companionway at one of my shipmates. He had only asked to be flown to Vladivostok so he could ride the Trans-Siberian Railway. Where was the harm in that? We were paying off in Singapore. This time, I was heading home.

"So where have you been, dude?" Rodney and I were sitting at Bryan's kitchen table drinking tea. Bryan was outside doing jazzercise with Kim. It was part of her fitness regime for her next pageant. Scrabble was crunching a bone he had been given by the local butcher.

"Fabled and promised lands." This was surprisingly accurate. "Speaking of promised lands, where's our contract, Rockwell?" I expected Rodney to have heard something in my absence.

"Nothing doing."

"They must've lost our letter."

"It's been four months."

"That proves they've lost it. Any reasonable person would've replied by now."

"Perhaps publishers are bastards?" We sipped our tea and pondered Rodney's hypothesis. Eventually I broke the silence.

"How much have you written?"

"Volumes."

"Neither have I, but I did make some notes."

"What for?"

"Inspiration."

"Such as?"

I opened up my exercise book. "We affixed dunnage to the bulkheads."

"What the hell does that mean?"

"It's a Chinese thing."

We sipped our tea some more. Rodney looked around the kitchen.

"Do you know where Bryan keeps his biscuits?"

"He doesn't." Kim returned inside. "Because he's become very health conscious." Bryan coughed very unhealthily in the background. "We have celery sticks." She glared at Bryan and went to the fridge.

"I've been thinking, bro, maybe we should join a writers' group." Rodney, surprisingly, sounded serious.

"What for? I've been to a writers' group. It was called school."

"We need a catalyst."

"I'd rather chew barbed wire."

"I've heard a lot of women go to writers' groups." Kim bit into a celery stick wrapped in a lettuce leaf.

"Sign me up." I wasn't stupid.

It was university holiday time and Rodney was working at a centre for at-risk youth in the city. I say 'working', but most of his day was spent playing basketball, or squash, or space invaders, or the jukebox, or swimming in the pool, with the clients of that charitable establishment. This was exactly the sort of employment we had been looking for. I volunteered to help out at the youth centre while I was on leave. I had a record in working with youth.

I had once helped out at a Scout camp. One day the boys were put through an obstacle course. At the end of the course they were covered in mud. They were told to strip off and clean up in the river. They obeyed orders and jumped naked into the water. They were Scouts after all. We threw them a box of laundry powder to use as soap.

"Why don't we steal their clothes?" someone suggested. "That will test their initiative." It was five hundred metres back to camp along a country road.

"Excellent idea." The other, responsible, caring, mature camp leaders couldn't agree fast enough. In a flash we had scooped up all the discarded clothes, stuffed them in a sack, and walked off down the road.

Let's pause a moment to illustrate the calibre of leaders at this camp. One of them, a few years previously, had forced me to pimp my sister. He was a senior pupil at the school where Rodney and I were still getting acquainted. He approached me one day outside the gymnasium. "Bring your sister to the pool at the weekend." He was referring to the community swimming pool where idle youth gathered to show off, get sunburnt and inhale excessive amounts of chlorine gas.

"She doesn't like the pool."

"So?"

"She can't even swim." This was a lie.

He moved closer and cracked his knuckles in front of my face. "Bring her to the pool." He enunciated his words very slowly this time.

This was the person who was renowned for throwing an axe at his next-door neighbour in a fit of anger. By way of excuse, he had red hair and was volatile. I should clarify that. It was the axe thrower who had red hair and was volatile, not the next-door neighbour. I didn't mean to imply that it is perfectly acceptable to throw axes at gingers who exist on a short fuse. If you disagree, shame on you. Luckily the axe missed, ricocheted off a wheelbarrow and impaled itself in the neighbour's letterbox. This perplexed the postman when he arrived, but otherwise no damage was done. I therefore have to confess that, out of fear mind you, I did pimp our sister.

Fortunately, the redhead, who was romantically known as Grubby, and our sister got on well. Crunch, however, was not impressed. He would hang out at the end of our driveway at nights with a powerful torch, waiting for Grubby to deliver our sister home after a date. "Good night," Crunch would growl at Grubby by way of greeting.

Since my acquiescence at the swimming pool, Grubby and I had been on good terms. Leading a Scout camp was a no brainer. I had learnt how to deal with young boys from an expert.

Back to enforcing nudity on vulnerable minors. It was a Saturday morning and the usually quiet country lane was busy with traffic heading to the beach. Once the boys discovered their betrayal, they set about fashioning skirts from the surrounding foliage to hide their modesty. One boy decided he would just hold a rock in front of his groin. Ready to run the gauntlet, they grouped at the farm gate leading to the road. They were twenty near-naked adolescent boys. They waited for a decent break in the traffic, then, as one, they ran. Poorly-secured grass and ferns flew in all directions. The rock was soon discarded. It was an impediment to sprinting, like the weights added to horses in a horse race, not to mention the chafing effect. Twenty pairs of unadorned youthful buttocks bounced above the tarseal. Cars stopped and the occupants leant out the windows, sounding their horns and cheering the boys on.

"It was character-building for them." Grubby felt the need to justify our actions after the event.

In another age we could've taken photos and sold them on OnlyFans. No, we couldn't, don't even think about that.

Due to his excellent people skills and caring nature, Grubby later qualified as a doctor, and later still, due to his proficiency with sharp-edged chopping instruments, became a surgeon.

I had another ploy to build the boys' character. My plan was to tell them there was a psychopath, recently escaped from a psychiatric institution, on the loose in the vicinity of the camp. I gave instructions that if anyone spotted the psychopath, they should not approach him, as he was dangerous, but notify the camp leaders.

"It will be a test of their powers of observation and ability to function under stress." I felt the need to justify my actions before the event.

That night, after the boys were in their sleeping bags, I put on a balaclava, a heavy woollen jersey and gumboots, and ran madly around the camp. I shook the guy ropes of tents, knocked down tent poles, and shouted in my best German. Some of these boys were only eleven years old and away from their mothers for the first time. They were terrified; some started screaming. I, on the other hand, was enjoying myself. I tipped over tables and cooking utensils.

"Sieg heil. Sieg heil! Wollen Sie ein Tritt in die Eier? Schweinehund. Schweinehund!"

There were more screams. Unfortunately it was very dark, and I had not thought to take a torch with me. Rushing to terrorise the next tent, I fell through a privacy curtain of sacking and into a pit latrine.

One of the senior boys, who did have a torch, came and stood over me. "Do you want me to tell the other camp leaders, Will?"

Despite this history, Rodney's youth centre for troubled young people agreed to let me volunteer. I wondered what sort of intellectually challenged person was running the show. Given my experiences in the outdoors, whoever it was even sent me away on a camp with a van load of at-risk youth. A couple had intellectual disabilities, and one seventeen-year-old had a history of bipolar disorder and suicide. He was only three years younger than me, for goodness' sake. I was totally unqualified to be doing this. What sort of intellectually challenged person would appoint the intellectually challenged person who was running the show?

Our van towed a trailer. The trailer was overloaded with camping gear. Going up one steep hill on a gravel road I found I could spin the steering wheel from one side to the other but the van wouldn't alter course. This is not how it's supposed to be, I thought. The weight in the trailer was causing the front wheels of the van to lift off the road.

"Righto kids, who had pies for lunch?"

I chose the three heaviest to sit on the bonnet. They sang rude songs as the stones and dust flew around them. This is good for morale, I decided. I couldn't see out the windscreen, but they indicated with their arms which way I should steer. We made it to the top in no time.

At the camp one afternoon, my bipolar man lay down in the tent. I responsibly went to check on him. He had collapsed on top of his sleeping bag.

"I'm not feeling good."

"Something you ate?" I was more hopeful than realistic.

"More like something inside my head."

"Would some aspirin help?" Again, I was leaning towards hopeful.

"It hasn't before."

"Before what?"

He was a lovely lad. Very bright and obliging.

"Just before." He began to cry.

I sat with him for what seemed like the whole summer but was more like half an hour. Suddenly, he sat up.

"I'm fine now. Thanks."

"No problem."

We walked out into the sunshine laughing like old mates. Perhaps I was growing up? What a terrible thought.

It was at the youth centre I met Stan and Ajit. Stan was fair, tall, angular, and geeky. Ajit was dark, short, and could work a room with as much ease as Father Christmas giving out presents. Together they ran a hostel on the top floor of the youth centre. The hostel was for backpackers and any profit it made went towards the running costs of the youth centre.

Stan, Ajit and I got along well. We went flatting together in a house owned by Stan's parents. I needed a base following my departure from the *Rangitoto*. I had finally been dislodged from home after Crunch threatened to rent out my room. In lieu of any board and lodging arrears, I left behind my collection of road signs and a parking meter.

Both Stan and Ajit were also volunteers. They had day jobs so their volunteering was done at night. They were allergic to sleep. Stan, however, was known to nod off at inappropriate times, like when his mother came to our flat for dinner. Stan's head would gradually sink to his chest, his knife and fork drop gently from his hands, and he would begin to snuffle out a gentle snore. Stan's mother was not offended.

"He once fell asleep at a function for the Prime Minister. I don't take it personally."

Shunning sleep, Stan and Ajit would drive out to the airport at all hours of the night to meet backpackers on incoming flights. They would entice them to the hostel with promises of a swimming pool, squash courts, a gymnasium and a central city location. They didn't mention that they would be sharing those facilities with a wide range of juvenile delinquents, many of whom were serial glue sniffers, petty – and not-so-petty – thieves and crooks.

"It's local colour." Ajit was never short of an answer when the backpackers later questioned him about their security.

Stan had a predilection for lighting fires. He was a suburban pyromaniac. He would burn household rubbish, gardening debris, old clothes, old toys, old magazines, old people, in fact, anything combustible. It was his way of dealing with waste. As we know, recycling hadn't been invented then and lighting bonfires in your backyard was seen as a socially acceptable activity for a Sunday afternoon. One such afternoon, soon after my leave had begun, Stan was tending his backyard fire. It was a large blaze and he was enjoying the heat and sooty grittiness of it. A strong wind merely added to the drama. The inside of the house smelt like an incinerator.

"Stan?" Ajit poked his head out the lounge window. He and I were playing a board game of world domination. "Is that smoke I can see in the garage?"

"No, it's just the dirty windows make it look like smoke."

Ajit resumed conquering Asia.

"Boom!" The garage windows blew out.

"Oh dear." Stan ran for the garden hose. "My car's in there."

"Boom!" The lawn mower exploded. Flames were leaping up the outside walls of the garage. Stan's efforts with the hose were as good as spitting into a blast furnace. Ajit stuck his head out the window again.

"Fire brigade? Or have you got this under control?"

The fire brigade duly arrived and extinguished the blaze. The garage and Stan's car were write-offs.

"It was time for a new motor." Stan always looked on the bright side.

Just three weeks later, shortly after we had disposed of the wreckage of the garage, Stan was burning old paint from under the eaves of the house above the front door, prior to painting. He spent a lot of energy on painting the house, much like Crunch. The wood under the eaves was old and dry and it was a hot, windy day. Stan stopped for lunch. Ajit looked up from our current board game of world domination.

"Can I smell burning?" He cursorily sniffed the air then threw the dice to acquire more artillery.

Ajit was addicted to board games of world domination. He could spend twenty-four hours on the trot following in the horse steps of Genghis Khan.

"War is relaxing," he explained. He once flew nonstop from the other side of the world, began a game as soon as he walked through the door of the flat that afternoon, and finished it at breakfast time. He hadn't slept for three days.

"We know that address." The emergency phone operator I spoke to sounded pleased to have a repeat customer. The fire brigade duly arrived and extinguished the blaze.

"See you next time, Stan." The firemen shook hands with him as they left. The damage was not too substantial.

I looked at the water dripping out of the ceiling in the hallway. "We could've put the fire out with the hose."

Stan mopped up the water on the floor. "The fire brigade has really made a mess this time."

"I'm going to put them on speed dial." Ajit dropped what remained of the incinerated heat gun into the rubbish bin.

Ajit should have done what he promised. A month later, he took the floor mats from his own car, washed them, and left them to dry in front of a heater. He was the only person at home. Stan was helping the next-door neighbour paint his house. Inexplicably, Ajit fell asleep.

"Can I smell burning?" Ajit woke up to billows of smoke. The mats had caught fire and dropped onto the carpet.

"Oh dear." Stan jumped back over the fence.

This time, after the fire brigade had left, promising eternal friendship on their way out the door, an insurance investigator appeared.

"That's the third fire in two months, Stanley. What are you going to do about it?"

Ajit answered on Stan's behalf. "Buy a fire engine?"

The idea of purchasing a fire engine was not as preposterous as it sounded. We found one – advertised, perhaps unsurprisingly, in that same newspaper which had refused to print our 'send me a dollar' advertisement. It was a rural fire engine, now deemed surplus to requirements. If we all pitched in we could afford to give it to Stan as a present on his next birthday.

In keeping with his love of a good blaze, you won't be surprised to learn that Stan was also an aficionado of fireworks. If he'd had any say in the matter, he would've been born on the fifth of November. At the merest whiff of a celebration, he would delve into his wardrobe and appear with a bag full of Tom Thumbs, double happies, thunder sticks, Catherine wheels, Mt Vesuvii, and any number of star-laden skyrockets. He would then proceed to terrorise the neighbourhood pets by putting a match to as many wicks as possible.

For someone so empathetic, it was a surprise Stan didn't like domestic pets, especially cats. One morning a neighbourhood stray gave birth on top of Stan's best pair of work shoes, in the same wardrobe where he kept his fireworks as it happens. Stan was not prone to swearing but this time he made an exception.

"Jeepers creepers. I've got to go to work. I need those shoes." Okay, this was not actual swearing, but it was as close as Stan could get. You could tell he was really, really riled up.

"So do I, got to go to work, that is." Ajit, having looked at the mess in the wardrobe, quickly raced out the door.

Mother cat looked at Stan disdainfully and went back to suckling her kittens. Her choice of birthing suites was not a coincidence. This was her revenge for the many times Stan had set off his artillery barrages or chased her with the hose on full pressure.

The shoes didn't clean up well. I took a cursory glance after Stan had extracted them from beneath the cat and kittens and was trying to wipe off the mess with a tea towel. "You won't get much support from an inner sole of feline placenta." Following Ajit's example, I walked quickly out the door.

Crunch didn't like cats much either. This was another thing he and Stan had in common. My father would keep small piles of rocks around the section which he would reach for whenever a cat entered his territory. He may have been a good cricketer but I never saw him scone a cat. Unlike schoolboys, they didn't stand still to be punished.

Crunch was big on protecting his territory. Early one morning the local Hare Krishna were snipping flowers from an area of our garden that fronted the footpath.

"What do you think you're doing?" Crunch's voice reverberated around the neighbourhood. He had emerged from the house wearing a blue pair of our sweet mother's knitted slippers, pink-striped pyjamas and a green checked woollen dressing gown.

"What do you think *you're* doing?" One of the Hare Krishna stood on the footpath holding an open pair of secateurs. "Auditioning for fashion week?"

I thought this was a bit rich coming from someone with a shaved head, beige yogi pants and an orange chadar, but we children, staring out of the lounge window, admired his courage.

"I'm calling the bloody police, that's what I'm doing."

Another of the Hare Krishna walked up to Crunch and offered him a stem of Crunch's red fuchsia he had just plucked. "Peace and love, old man."

From the lounge we cheered and applauded loudly, then scattered as Crunch, his face verging on purple, lurched around to see where all the noise was coming from. The Hare Krishna took advantage of the distraction to flee. They didn't forget the flowers.

"Hare Krishna, Hare Krishna. Krishna Krishna, Hare Hare." They speed-walked down the road banging a drum and a tambourine.

Putting aside his lack of animal welfare credentials, Stan was still ahead of his time in that he recycled our empty beer bottles. He would line up half a dozen bottles, place a sky rocket in each, and attempt to light them all from the same match. Salvo after salvo would cascade onto the roofs of the houses around us. Stan called them mass weapons of marginal destruction.

Now you probably think you know where all this talk of fires and fireworks is going, but you don't, because Stan was not the only one with a fetish for spending large amounts of money on domestic ordnance. My brother began his childhood as a suburban sapper. Like Stan, he would collect as many fireworks as possible, at any time of the year, for any purpose whatsoever. I once joined him in blowing up our letterbox. We also made lemon bombs. We would cram double happies into lemons, light the crackers, and then throw the citrus grenades at each other. After one Guy Fawkes Night we collected up all the unexploded fireworks, emptied the gunpowder onto the verandah, and put a match to it. The resulting flare-up left a very satisfying, charred circle in the paintwork. But that was okay. We knew that sometime in the next five years Crunch would repaint it.

One day, my brother conducted an inventory of all his armaments. He laid them out on his bed, scientifically grouped by type. Big bangers in one pile, small bangers in another, big rockets in another, small rockets in another, big pretties in another, and so on. For some reason he thought he would test fire a few. Usually this is something that, like nuclear bomb testing, would best take place on a tropical island stolen from its indigenous owners, or at the very least, outdoors. My brother, who was quite the pioneer, decided he would carry out this experiment indoors.

Unfortunately for him, there came into being a chain reaction. The spark from his initial lighting jumped species, spectacularly, from one group of ordnance to the next. Our sweet mother rushed down the stairs as soon as she smelt the tart scent of sulphur and heard the introductory explosions. She bravely gathered up all the fireworks, exploding, exploded and unexploded, in the bedspread, and threw the whole bundle out the window. It fell onto the lawn and leapt about like a sack of scalded cats. I know that is an unfortunate analogy given our recent nod to animal rights, but it was sadly accurate.

"You're a fool, you're a fool." Our now not-so-sweet mother randomly hit upon this very succinct description of my brother who was cowering in a corner of the room.

"I know, I know." He dissolved into tears. He wasn't crying because he was berated for being an idiot. He was crying for the loss of his stash. His Guy Fawkes Night was ruined.

Stan was a gentleman, honest and fair. Everyone liked him. He soon married. His wife evidently liked him too. This was a blow to me and Ajit who had to move out of the house. I bought a small yacht and moved onto that. Ajit went and stayed with his grandparents in their retirement village.

"It's only temporary." Ajit meant what he said. Two years later he still meant it.

Stan managed to stay awake for the duration of his wedding, but soon after was diagnosed with sclerosing cholangitis. This is a disease of the liver, not caused by excessive drinking. Stan took the news with his usual aplomb.

"I should've drunk more then."

Sclerosing cholangitis is life threatening. Instead of a fire engine we all chipped in and raised enough money to send Stan to Australia for a liver transplant. The transplant failed. We sent him back for a second liver. This operation was more successful. We learnt a lot about sclerosing cholangitis. One of the early symptoms is fatigue that can cause someone to fall asleep at inappropriate times.

Seriously, does transhumanism have a future?

Chapter 17.2

Later that year, Rodney's summer university holidays were spent hitchhiking around Australia. A friend of his, a nurse, had suggested that he and she throw caution to the wind and point their combined thumbs up the kangaroo highway, platonically of course. Rodney needed little convincing, it was better than working, and after all, she was a nurse, and platonic may not necessarily have meant platonic. I wasn't invited. Three into two doesn't go. But I didn't have to get on the plane, I could live the experience vicariously, just as, through Rodney, I had dated vicariously. I knew that when he returned, Rodney would regale me and Bryan with the story of his journey as many times as he could before we raised our hands to prevent further damage to our sanity.

Before Rodney left, however, as he had suggested, we joined a writers' group. The group had advertised for new members in the same newspaper that had refused to print our 'send me a dollar' request. We should have known they would be unreliable.

"Like to write?" read the advertisement, "So do we. Elite writers' group seeks new members for literary intercourse and inspiring times. Come and see if together we gel."

"Jeez." Bryan read the ad while twisting his recently formed, blonde forelock around his index finger. "Was it in with the massage parlours?"

We went to our probationary Saturday afternoon 'grouping', as the writers' group liked to call their gatherings, a week before

Rodney was due to fly across the Tasman. It was held in a run-down old villa in a fashionably seedy part of town.

"I'm Maggie." The woman who answered the door emerged from a cloud of incense. "You must be the new..." she paused and looked us over rather too keenly, "... men." She stretched out the last word like it was bubble gum. Maggie was dressed in a yellow kaftan and her hair was pulled back under a cerise tie-dyed head band. She was ancient, at least forty. "Welcome," she purred, and oozed her way down the hall, leading us into the lounge.

There were another five versions of Maggie sitting round the room, like a family of vividly-coloured budgerigars.

"We're just waiting for Ralph, our moderator. He's looking after his sick mother." Maggie sighed. "He is so good to her."

At that moment, a man wearing faded jeans, a white polo shirt and a creased blue suit jacket sidled into the room. This, apparently, was Ralph. His slightly protruding stomach held his jacket apart and his dark hair was plastered back, like plastic, over his skull. He sat down and placed a scruffy leather satchel at his feet. He needed a shave. "Sorry I'm late everyone, but Mum was feeling unwell. The doctor thinks it could be pancreatitis."

Maggie and the budgerigars made soft sympathetic chirping noises.

Although only in his late twenties, Ralph was the moderator of the grouping because, as we found out later, he was the only member who had actually published anything. He called the gathering to order and turned his attention to us.

"Welcome to the grouping." His welcome was not like Maggie's. It was more of a grimace. "If all goes well today, and we think you're both a good fit for the grouping, then we will be delighted to have you join. Perhaps you'd like to begin by introducing yourselves and telling us why you are here." He had a pompous English-sounding voice.

Rodney, quite seriously, said he and I were writing a book and thought it would be good for our collective abilities to be exposed to writers of the calibre of the grouping. Ralph nodded in sage approval and Maggie and the budgerigars twittered and preened.

"And you, good sir?"

I had decided I didn't like Ralph. I know that may seem harsh given I had just met him, but sometimes I just reacted to people like that. I had once experienced it sitting next to a complete stranger in a movie theatre. The poor man hadn't even looked at me. Perhaps it was something to do with pheromones. Anyway, Ralph had marked all the wrong lampposts as far as I was concerned.

"I came for the crumpet."

There was an awkward silence. Maggie and the budgerigars appeared confused, then subtly preened a little more. Ralph looked like he was suffering from severe indigestion. Rodney turned his gaze out the window. Suddenly, one of the budgerigars stood up.

"Rat Boy!" We all stared at her. I thought she seemed familiar. She had grey hair tied up in a bun, similar to our sweet mother.

"Rat Lady?" I studied her face to make sure.

"Who else?" She gave me a hug.

"Where are my mice?"

I'd last seen Rat Lady when I was nine years old, before our family went to England. She was a neighbour and had offered to look after my pet mice while we were away. Before we left, I had christened her Rat Lady, and she had reciprocated in kind. When we returned, she had moved, and so had my mice.

"Sorry. Rodents aren't known for their longevity." Rat Lady looked me up and down. "I could hardly recognise you, but when you opened your gob, I knew it couldn't be anyone else." Perhaps I hadn't grown up after all. That was a relief. "How's Crunch? And your dear mother?"

Rodney and I kept our mouths shut for the remainder of the grouping.

"Tell your parents I'll drop in for a visit." Rat Lady waved theatrically as we left.

"Well, that could've gone better." Rodney smiled wryly as we made our way back to Bryan's place for a cup of tea.

"Do you think we should apologise?"

"What do you mean, 'we'? Besides, I won't be here, dude, I'm off to Oz."

The next day Rodney received a phone call from his travelling companion. She seemed excited, and this is how Rodney's Australia story began. I will recount it as accurately as I can remember from his endless retellings. (If at any stage you feel the need to raise a hand to prevent unwanted repetition, you can just turn a page or two.)

"Guess what? Something wonderful has happened." Travelling Companion's words tumbled over themselves like froth in a waterfall.

She's won the lottery, thought Rodney. *Now we can fly first class.* He pictured them staying in expensive hotels and lying on beaches drinking cocktails from coconut shells with little pink paper umbrellas in them.

"First prize?"

"Absolutely. I've met a man."

I'm a man, thought Rodney. *What's that got to do with the price of fish?* "That's nice." He couldn't think of anything else to say.

"His family have a beach place, a private beach, with a boat, and water skiing, and windsurfing, just like you do, and guess what?"

Oh, I don't know. They hunt down poachers with a bailiff and a pack of hounds? "I can't guess."

"He's invited me for Christmas!" She announced this fact as if she'd just been voted Miss Universe.

Later that week Rodney flew to Australia, by himself, in economy.

My Friend in 4C, who, as you've probably worked out, had long left 4C and his school shorts behind, now lived in Sydney with his parents. I had mentioned this to Rodney.

"You can go and stay with them."

I omitted to tell My Friend in 4C, or his parents. In the rich orange-tinged citrus-smelling heat of a Sydney summer's morning, Rodney knocked on their door. My Friend in 4C's mother opened it.

"Who are you?" She was a pianist. She sang her sentences.

"Rodney."

"And what do you want, Rodney?" She glanced at his backpack.

"I've come to stay."

"How long for?"

Slight sense of déjà vu there, thought Rodney, as he followed her inside.

My Friend in 4C dropped Rodney on the highway north when the time came to test out his thumbs. After two minutes on the side of the road a tropical tempest set in. Luckily Rodney was prepared for this. He dug in his pack and pulled out his bright yellow poncho. It didn't do much to keep the rain off but it made him feel as if he had met his first test on the road and passed.

"What the fuck is that?" The man in the jeep, who had picked Rodney up, gestured at his outer garment.

"It's a poncho."

"Are you gay?" Well, Jeep Man didn't exactly say that. Remember we are still in the dark ages here and what he actually said I cannot write. You will have to guess. Think poncho and alliteration.

Rodney denied this kindly meant observation and steered the conversation to more impersonal things, such as the weather.

"Heavy rain." The windscreen wipers flopped from side to side in front of their faces.

"Not as bad as 'Nam."

"You mean Vietnam?" Rodney was not sure he had heard correctly.

"Course I fucking mean fucking Vietnam. Are you gay?" (See above.)

"What were you doing in Vietnam?" Rodney was the model of politeness.

"Intelligence. Behind the lines, interrogations, that sorta shit."

Rodney was not sure where to steer the conversation next. How did you make small talk with someone who spent their time strapping people to chairs in dimly lit rooms, blindfolding them, and administering electric shocks to their genitalia?

"Satisfying work, bro?"

Jeep Man looked at Rodney strangely. Rodney was beginning to feel uncomfortable. They drove along in silence for some minutes before Jeep Man jabbed a finger in Rodney's direction.

"Where are you going?"

Rodney tried to keep his answer as non-committal as possible. "Nowhere special."

"Same."

That's a shame, thought Rodney. They lapsed into silence once more.

"I don't go anywhere without protection." Jeep Man nodded his head sideways as the jeep lurched to overtake a semi-trailer. "Arsehole." He gave the truck driver the fingers as they bolted past.

Jeep Man nodded his head sideways again, three times in rapid succession, in Rodney's direction. Rodney wondered if Jeep Man was having a seizure and looked blankly back at him. "Beside you, for jeez sake."

Rodney glanced down at the inside of the passenger door. There was a machete strapped to it. "The bang stick's in the back." Jeep Man tilted his head towards the jumble of dirty clothing and canned food behind them.

Rodney thought he had a reasonable idea of what a bang stick was. Not wanting to pursue this angle of conversation further he nodded sagely, as if it was quite normal for every vehicle on the public highway to carry a machete and a bang stick. How do I get out of here? he wondered.

By now Rodney was not feeling quite as pleased with himself as he had when he first pulled his bright yellow poncho over his head. He had heard about hitchhikers going missing, their dismembered bodies later dug from shallow graves in the sun-shrivelled stony ground of the outback. He had not planned on being a newspaper headline, at least not this early in his hitchhiking career. Besides, he was going to be a wealthy author. He briefly imagined himself dressed in a silver-bordered tuxedo, on a red carpet, waving to adoring chanting fans at the premiere of the film adaptation. "Rodney. Rodney!"

"How about we get a motel room for the night?"

Rodney grasped for the red carpet but it had been pulled from under his fantasy feet. He uttered the first plausible excuse that entered his mind. "I'm actually going to the youth hostel, bro." Sensibly, he had no desire to spend the night with a homicidal maniac.

"What youth hostel? There's no youth hostel around here." And, indeed, Jeep Man was right. Through the early-darkening, afternoon gloom, there was not a building in sight. Rodney thought hard. He remembered YHA marked on his map in this vicinity. And before you ask, there was no Google Maps back then, just pieces of paper with coloured lines and little churches marked on them. You folded them up and carried them in your pocket.

"It's in the town at the next intersection. I can walk from the turnoff." Rodney tried to hide his eagerness.

"I could drop you off. We could get a room at the youth hostel." Jeep Man stared fiercely at Rodney.

"No rooms, only dorms, you have to share with, oh, I don't know, hundreds of people."

Jeep Man dropped Rodney at the next intersection. As he drove off into the rain, still heading nowhere special, Rodney heard another homophobic slur thrown his way.

Rodney looked at the signpost at the turnoff. It indicated that the small town where he thought he had seen the YHA symbol was ten miles away. It was wet, he was cold, it was late afternoon, his yellow poncho didn't keep the rain out. I'll get a lift no problem, said Rodney to himself, and started walking.

Two and a half hours later he was still walking when he blinked and almost missed a rough collection of half a dozen rundown houses and a cemetery. It was getting dark and Rodney was hallucinating hopefully. He told himself it looked like the perfect place for a youth hostel. Across the road from the cemetery he stood in front of a large, corrugated iron shed. The sign above the door read "Youngs Helicopter Academy".

"Bugger." Rodney succinctly addressed the wet slimy nostril-clotting air. The building was a hangar. "Led up the rural flight path by a three-letter acronym."

Rodney looked around. Not a single human neuron synapsed, other than his own, and they were bordering on dysfunction. "I thought every town in Australia had a pub." The silence was foreboding. Not a single human vocal tract vibrated in reply. The only neurons and vocal tracts in this place were composting, mutely, across the road. "This dump must be the exception that proves the rule."

Rodney walked across the road and pitched his tent in the cemetery. He collected fallen branches from underneath some gum trees and piled them around the edges of the tent. In those days tents didn't have built-in ground sheets, and sleeping mats were still a twinkle in some mountaineer's eye. We'd just dig a hole for our hip in the hard ground, lie down and go to sleep. The next morning, we'd be up at first light, all bleary-eyed and limp-tailed, thinking that was a terrible night, there's got to be a better way. The branches were a symbolic attempt by Rodney to keep snakes out. No self-respecting snake would think 'roadworks', and look for the detour signs when coming upon a piece of kindling in its path, but it made Rodney feel better.

Rodney ate baked beans, cold from the can, then levered his wet body into his wet sleeping bag. He felt like a worm in a bottle of mezcal, without any of the many advantages conferred by being cocooned in alcohol. He said good night to himself.

"Night night, Rodney, sleep tight, hope the reptiles, and spiders, and leeches, and centipedes, don't bite, causing severe anaphylactic shock, toxic organ failure and certain death." On that cheery note he went to sleep.

"Flash! Bam! Bam! Bam!" Rodney's first thought, as he lurched awake at midnight, was that Jeep Man had tracked him down. He searched around for his can opener, wishing instead that he too had a machete and a bang stick. "Flash! Bam! Bam! Bam!" Percussion waves of energy stampeded through the cemetery. Through the thin walls of his tent, Rodney could see the tombstones illuminated by lightning. It was only a thunderstorm.

"No problem." He laughed at his fear. And that's when the screaming started.

Rodney had never heard screaming like it. Raw cackling screams, like a swarm of angry turbo-charged razor blades, swooped upon him from all directions. Unlike many in his family, Rodney was not a religious man, but now he began to have second thoughts about the wisdom of pitching a tent inside a storage facility for the dead.

"Flash! Bam! Bam! Bam!" Lightning and thunder curdled the air. Rain fell in cascades and the wind howled. The screaming intensified. Rodney imagined himself fried to a crisp in the bowels of hell. All I need now is the riders of the Apocalypse, he thought wryly. That's when he heard the staccato rush of horse hooves in full flight. Rodney didn't sleep after that.

By daybreak the thunderstorm had passed, and as soon as it was light Rodney ventured outside the tent, all bleary-eyed and limp-tailed. It was a beautiful sunrise. The light glowed beatifically upon the gum trees, and in the paddock next door half a dozen tired-looking horses ambled about.

That could explain a few things, he said to himself. A flock of creamy brown birds busied themselves in the branches of the gum trees. As Rodney admired them they broke into a chorus of raucous croaks and caws. So that's what kookaburras sound like, thought Rodney, curiously, much like the screaming banshees of my night.

"Bastards." Rodney shook his fist at the birds. The kookaburras just laughed, and laughed, and laughed, and laughed.

Rodney trudged back to the main highway. He hitchhiked north. He eventually came to a small town where he had heard there was work for itinerant travellers. He was running short of pineapples. A pineapple was a bright yellow, fifty dollar note. He got a job picking pineapples, the fruit, not the note. Our parents taught us at an early age that money doesn't grow on trees, or other leafy plants, and to this point in time, unfortunately, they had been proved right.

Rodney got a bed at the local youth hostel. This youth hostel was not an aircraft hangar and there was not a tombstone in sight. Even better, the town had a pub. The next morning Rodney was picked up at 5am by a group of men in a truck. The mood was quiet and sombre. Rodney thought someone may have been in need of a tombstone after all.

One of his new workmates saw Rodney's concern. "Too many tinnies, mate." Rodney understood him to mean they were merely hungover, not dead.

They drove to a property in the countryside, which was peppered with pineapple plants, and pulled up beside a rusty corrugated iron shed.

"Your job, mate, is to pick the bastards off the plants and put them on the conveyor." The foreman burped a vapour of deceased alcoholic yeast in Rodney's face.

Rodney pointed to a number of elongated criss-cross tracks pressed into the dusty ground. They led into the pineapple plants.

"What made them?"

"Snakes."

At 5:30am, Rodney and three others began wading through the rows of pineapple plants in pursuit of a conveyor fixed to the back of a tractor. The conveyor dropped the fruit into a trailer hauled by the tractor. It was summer. It was hot work. Hard yakka, as they say in those parts. By 8am it was twenty-eight degrees Celsius in the shade. The plants were shoulder high and, like a hothouse, trapped the heat underneath their wide stiff leaves.

As he had been instructed, and like the others, Rodney was dressed for the heat. He was wearing a long-sleeved shirt, jeans, thick socks, boots, thermal underwear, ear muffs, and a heavy woollen balaclava. Okay, I lied about everything after 'boots', but I think you get the point. This outfit was not a rouseabout's answer to Yves Saint Laurent, nor did it, by any stretch of the nasal passages, reduce body odour. It was simply for protection from the leaves and snakes. The snakes liked to coil up and hide at the base of the plants. Apparently it made it easier for them to ambush their prey, or some pineapple picker's ankle.

At 8:30am the gang stopped to drink water. At 9am the first man fell.

"Strewth." The foreman, who was driving the tractor, scowled. "Are you pulling a sickie, Bruce?"

"Don't be a drongo, mate, I'm crook." The person, Rodney quite validly believed to be called 'Bruce', crawled to his knees. The foreman took this opportunity to prove he was not completely devoid of compassion.

"Then go chunder in the dunny, take an early smoko and have a durry before I crack the shits." 'Bruce' wandered off in the direction of the shed. Rodney wondered what language they were speaking.

At midday they stopped for half an hour for lunch. Rodney had brought some sandwiches in a paper bag. The others all had small eskys from which they produced cold dog's eyes, snags and tinnies.

"I could sink a slab." 'Bruce' was obviously feeling a lot better. He peered at Rodney's food. "You won't get far on them sambos."

They finished work at 3:30pm. The truck drove them to the pub.

Rodney picked pineapples for five days and left with two of the other pineapples in his pocket. It was enough to keep going. On Christmas Day he found himself sitting underneath a bridge by a muddy river in the provincial town of Rockhampton. The river was swollen by recent rains and, as well as mud, carried with it truckloads of rural and urban detritus. Pieces of wood, rags, branches of trees, dead chickens, decapitated dolls, sodden cardboard, a thong of the flip-flop, not underwear, variety – all washed past in a seemingly endless procession to the nearby Pacific Ocean and the previously pristine Great Barrier Reef. In addition, the river carried with it a scent of overly nutritious compost. What couldn't be seen of course, were all those nitrates, phosphates, sulphates, e.coli, b.coli, and c.coli mentioned earlier. As promised, I have not mentioned that other coli whose first name means John in English.

Rodney was not alone under the bridge watching this infectious liquid poultice of pollutants flow out to the Great Barrier Reef. Mr Bojangles sat next to him. Mr Bojangles had spent Christmas Eve in the slammer. He had been detained for being drunk and disorderly. Sobered up, he had been freed. But he was very thirsty. To his credit, Mr Bojangles was not drinking more alcohol. Instead he was drinking river water. He was in possession of an empty stubby. Periodically, he would fill the stubby bottle from the river and drink the nicotine-brown water. Mr Bojangles was the first Aboriginal Rodney had encountered on his journey.

"We're the oldest civilisation on earth, mate, but these bastards wouldn't let us vote till 1962." Mr Bojangles waved his hand generally in the direction of Rockhampton when he referred to 'these bastards'. "Who's your mob, mate?"

"I'm from New Zealand, dude, but I'm part Samoan." Rodney was keen to assert his indigenous credentials. The week on the pineapple plantation had not been kind to Rodney's complexion. His face was pink and peeling.

"You gammin with me?" Mr Bojangles paused, took a sip from the stubby, then gestured at the river. "You know where all this shit's going, mate?"

"To the sea?"

"To the GBR." Rodney looked confused. "It's a three-letter, bloody acronym, mate. CNN, the American TV station, they like three-letter acronyms, they called it the GBR. They said it's one of the seven bloody wonders of the world, and Yanks are always fuckin' right, right?" Mr Bojangles took another gulp from his stubby. "My mob knew about the reef for tens of thousands of years before any of youse fellas arrived."

Rodney was tempted to raise his Samoan heritage again but decided he didn't want to suffer more ridicule.

"During the last ice age, when sea levels were much lower, my mob lived right next to the reef. Today it's all under water, our hunting grounds, our art..."

"I never knew that."

"No-one wants to know, except us." Mr Bojangles looked sadly at the putrid water.

Rodney didn't know how to reply to this. He gazed at the endless stream of rubbish in the flooded river. It reminded him of a mouldy beef stroganoff.

"The bloody reef's over two thousand three hundred kilometres long and is the world's largest reef system. It covers the same surface area as Germany and is about five hundred thousand years old. It's living coral growing on top of dead coral, mate."

"So the dead are propping up the living, bro? That's like being forced to pay taxes after you've popped your clogs."

"The first of your mob to come here, he bumped his bloody bilges on the reef. It was eleven o'clock at night on a Sunday, mate."

"Who was that?"

"Captain fuckin' Cook, mate." Mr Bojangles said this with a sewage pond full of contempt. "He almost sank his bloody boat. Shame he didn't." Mr Bojangles stood up and threw his stubby into the water. "Plenty more where that's going." He watched as the bottle bobbed away into the distance.

"How come you know so much about the reef, bro?"

"I used to be a guide out there, mate. Until the bastards fired me." Mr Bojangles turned and wandered away, haltingly.

On Boxing Day, Rodney was on the outskirts of Rockhampton, thumbing for a ride.

"Climb aboard." Big Tony was driving a battered blue panel van. Rodney hopped in the back with his pack.

"Gidday." Another voice emanated from the dark recesses of the floor of the front seat.

"That's Grant." Big Tony turned onto the highway, steering with his bare feet, his knees against his chest.

Rodney was beginning to seriously consider the sanity of Australian drivers.

Big Tony saw Rodney's worried look. "It's all right. Grant works the pedals."

Well ahead of their time, Grant and Big Tony had invented the concept of driverless cars. A family car on holiday overtook the panel van. Two young faces, squeezed together, looked out of the back passenger window. They giggled and pointed as Big Tony waved at them with both hands.

"Works every time." Big Tony lowered his legs. He was sitting on a cushion so he could see out the windscreen.

Grant, who was almost twice the size of Big Tony, removed his hands from the pedals and sat up. "Where yer going?"

"Nowhere special."

"So are we." Big Tony took his hands off the wheel again and thrust a battered black antique top hat onto his head. "Yeeha!" He accelerated until the old van shook like a maraca at a Mexican fiesta.

This time it was Grant who observed Rodney's worried expression. "It's all right mate, we're not crazy." Rodney was relieved. Grant and Big Tony looked sideways at each other, sniggered a little, and then exploded in ruptures of hysterical laughter.

FNQ, stands for Far North Queensland. It is best to say FNQ quickly, with a blocked nose, if you want an Australian to understand which area of their country you are referring to. And for the sake of completeness, Australia is actually a place called Straya. Australia is just an illusion invented by Strayians to stop the Chinese from buying up the real Straya. Most of Australia, especially the rocky bits underground, has been sold to the Chinese, but Straya itself remains an impregnable fortress. Just ask any boat person fleeing across the Timor Sea to escape persecution. Australia on the other hand is now just a crisp pie crust, with all the filling having been spooned out and sent to Shanghai.

Rodney spent two weeks tripping around FNQ with Big Tony, Grant and their mate Pong who joined them in Cairns. Pong had a shaved head and was immaculately dressed. In case you're wondering why Pong was called Pong, it's because he was previously called Ping.

"And before Ping?" Rodney asked Pong.

"Peter," said Pong, whose surname was King.

"P. King?" asked Rodney.

"Spot on," said Pong.

Somewhat ironically, Pong was fastidious about his personal hygiene. For instance, he carried a toothbrush in his pocket, in a custom-made toothbrush container embossed with his initials, and brushed his teeth after food of any description had crossed his tongue.

One day, Rodney came across Pong sitting outside his tent in the campground where they were to spend the night. Pong was perched on a camp stool with the legs of his designer jeans rolled up to his knees. He was concentrating on his index finger which was performing small, circular motions on his left calf.

"What's up Pong?"

"Gotcha." Pong brought his thumb and index finger together and plucked something from his leg. "Hair." He flicked what he had plucked onto the grass. "Body hair makes you smell."

Rodney noticed that Pong's calves were completely hairless and smooth, like a baby's bottom. "All right, bro." He paused, thinking, then nodded downwards, towards his groin. "So I guess…"

"You guess right."

"Ouch. Doesn't that hurt, bro?"

Pong stood up and looked Rodney in the eye. "Pain is transitory, Grasshopper. Cleanliness is godly."

With that they went and bought pizzas for dinner.

Rodney's time in FNQ came to a premature end after Big Tony surfed a waterfall in the Tablelands. His surfboard was a piece of plywood he had found on the side of the road.

"Yeeha!" Wearing nothing but his top hat and scarlet budgie smugglers, Big Tony hurtled over the slippery lip of the cascading stream. The waterfall was a mere minnow, less than two metres high, but rocks in the sub-tropical highlands of FNQ are as hard as those at Niagara. Big Tony missed the pool at the bottom of the fall, concussed himself and broke three ribs. Pong and Rodney supported Big Tony in the back of the van while Grant drove to the hospital. Big Tony, still wet from the stream, moaned at every bump in the road.

Pong sniffed at the hospital air as Big Tony was wheeled out of A&E and off to a ward. "At least he's had a good wash."

The next day, Grant and Pong dropped Rodney at the side of the highway.

"Big Tony's the crazy one, not us." Grant leant out the driver's window, then looked sideways at Pong in the front passenger seat. They dissolved into giggles as they drove off, leaving Rodney standing by his pack, looking for his next ride.

Rodney had discovered Australia was too big to circumnavigate, so he headed inland, to the outback. It was in the outback that Rodney met Onion Man.

Rodney was in a remote part, heading towards Adelaide. One afternoon, on the outskirts of a very dry and very wizened hamlet, which had a pub as a redeeming feature, Rodney was picked up by a very dry, and very wizened, old gentleman. He wore walk shorts and a pork pie hat. In between those two items, hung on craggy bones, dwelt a buttoned-up-to-the-neck, short-sleeved, red and white checked shirt. This gentleman had clearly dressed up to make an impression on someone. He smelt of beer and pungent aftershave.

He drove a dusty and dinged-up Holden. Rodney climbed into the front passenger seat.

"Where yer headin'?"

"Nowhere special."

"Aha." The gentleman changed from first gear into second. Manual gears in a car were common back then. Today they are only found in race cars and wreckers' yards. Rodney looked at the odometer. They were cruising along the very straight empty asphalted road, at thirty kilometres per hour.

"No traffic." Rodney hoped this hint would spur the gentleman to take a risk and depress his accelerator foot. Rodney had a long way to go to the next town before nightfall. Ten minutes passed. Rodney was growing a little impatient. "What's the speed limit around here?"

"Oh, yeah," and, like a rocket, they reached fifty kilometres per hour. Another ten minutes passed. A road speed sign dawdled past. Inside its little red circle there was a one, followed by two zeroes. A car overtook them and disappeared from sight in a jiffy. Wish I'd caught that one, thought Rodney.

Rodney was about to say "Problem with the fuel pump?" when the gentleman said, "There's an onion in the back."

"Sorry?" Perhaps this old Holden ran on biofuel and they were going to grate an onion into the fuel tank?

"Under the back seat, there's an onion." The gentleman paused and looked hard at Rodney. "For yer tea."

"Oh." Rodney was now quite confused.

"Yer can reach over and get it."

Rodney thought he should humour the old bloke, so he twisted in his seat and leant over the back. There was indeed an onion, swaying around on the floor. It is worth noting here that Rodney was wearing a T-shirt and running shorts. The running shorts lived up to their name in that they were, indeed, short. Stretched out over the back of the front seat, Rodney retrieved the onion, his nylon-covered buttocks pointing to the incessant sun.

Another ten minutes passed. Onion Man was about to lose his gentleman moniker. He took his left hand off the wheel. It hovered in no-man's land for a few seconds and then, after a slight flourish, landed on Rodney's bare knee.

"Bugger off." Rodney chose a phrase to show his displeasure which was either appropriate or unfortunate, depending on how you look at it.

"Oh." Onion Man spoke in a flat, almost aggrieved manner, before putting his errant hand back on the wheel. Rodney backed himself up against the passenger door. Ten more minutes passed as the speed dropped to thirty kilometres per hour before Onion Man pulled over to the side of the road. "This is as far as I go."

Rodney was pleased to disembark but not pleased to be dumped in the middle of nowhere. He watched as Onion Man turned and drove back the exact way they had come, back to his dry and wizened collection of shacks. Rodney looked at the onion in his hand then threw it in the direction of the departing vehicle. It bounced on the hot seal, shedding skin, before rolling into the dust on the side of the road. There was nothing but desert and scrub in all directions. It was as hot as Hades. The flies couldn't believe their luck and came in their thousands to suck every ounce of sweat off Rodney's body.

Rodney spent the night camped in a dry creek bed under a bridge. Early the next morning he was picked up by a truck. The truck driver kept his hands on the wheel. That's an improvement, thought Rodney, as they purred down the highway at one hundred kilometres per hour. At the first town he stopped and ate bacon and eggs, followed by a schooner or two. A schooner is a glass of beer. Do not expect to see a two-masted sailing vessel in the outback. It was 10am. Life is good, dude, Rodney said to himself.

Rodney eventually arrived in South Australia.

"Want a ride to Melbourne?" Rodney looked up from fixing his jandals, in the direction of an English-sounding voice. He was seated on his bunk in the youth hostel in Adelaide.

"It's a long way."

"We'll make stops." Andy was rotund, fair, and wore milk-bottle-thick glasses.

"What sort of car have you got?"

"A Kawasaki."

The next day found Rodney and his pack perched on the back of Andy's motorbike. There was a law against wearing helmets in those days and shorts and jandals were de rigueur safety gear.

"Lean with the bike." Andy's words merged with the wind as they wobbled around the first couple of corners on the Great Ocean Highway. At the next left-handed bend Rodney still leant against the turn. Andy was a genial bloke. He slowed down. "It's like this. Lean in the direction I lean, or walk." He said it quietly, with a smile.

"Sorry, bro. I thought you said lean *to the right*." Rodney soon cottoned on and they made it to Port Fairy by mid-afternoon, unscathed.

"Fancy a game of bowls?" Andy was eating coleslaw at the local takeaway. He was a vegetarian.

Rodney had not expected to be asked this question for another fifty years. "Why not? Everyone should practise being old."

They walked to the local bowling club.

"What do youse fellas want?" A florid-faced pensioner wearing a green cardigan had answered their knock at the gate.

"We want to play bowls." Andy's tone implied he was stating the obvious.

"Youse are too young."

"We're old at heart."

The pensioner looked them over for a few seconds. "All right then." He took them inside and gave them each four bowls. "They're biased."

Rodney inspected his bowls for signs of prejudice. "That's unfair."

"Nah, not like that. They lean one way or the other when youse bowl 'em." The pensioner gestured left and right with his hands.

"Like a Kawasaki?" Rodney had learnt his motorcycling lesson well.

"Wouldn't know, son. I only drink Aussie grog."

Andy and Rodney were guilty of mild incompetence on the bowling green. Game over, they went to the pub. Andy ordered two schooners of beer.

"Pom?" A local man, who was using his elbows to prevent the bar from levitating, looked sideways at Andy.

"Too right, cobber." Andy did a passable Australian accent.

"Are you takin' the piss, mate?" The man burped and wiped his lips.

"Not at all, my good man." Andy now adopted a faux upper class English accent. Rodney did not think this was sensible.

"Bloody oath, y'are. D'ya wanna go, mate?" The local put his drunken face up against Andy's and sneered. Rodney looked around for the nearest exit.

"It wouldn't end well." Andy was as calm as you like.

"Why's that?"

"I was on the British Olympic team. Judo."

"How do I know that?" The man backed away slightly.

"You don't."

"Orright then, just remember, orright?"

"Orright." Andy returned and sat down next to Rodney with the two schooners. "Cheers."

"Were you really on the Olympic judo team?"

Andy took off his glasses and cleaned them on his shirt. "Baggage handler." He squinted hard into the distance.

After three months on the road Rodney arrived back in Sydney. He had lost weight but gained what almost passed for a tan. His face was a melange of fawn and pink splashes, like a piece of modern art. He knocked on the door of My Friend in 4C. My Friend in 4C's mother opened it. She didn't recognise him.

"Who are you?"

"Rodney."

"Do you have ID?"

"I know who put the roadworkers' tent on your driveway."

"Pass, friend."

"Haha," laughed My Friend in 4C. "Have you looked in a mirror lately? And thanks for all the postcards." Rodney hadn't sent any.

After three days of fattening up and facial care, Rodney flew home. My Friend in 4C and his mother drove him to the airport in Mother's Mini Cooper. She was driving. My Friend in 4C was in the passenger seat and Rodney nursed his pack in the back. Mother was a motor socialist and driving for her was a communal activity, something to be shared by all occupants of the vehicle.

"Tell me when that light turns green," she would sing-song, for example, and, "Do you think there's room to squeeze between those two, incredibly huge trucks?" At one intersection she turned to My Friend in 4C. "Are there any cars coming?"

My friend, who, extremely unlikely as it may seem, later worked in public relations for American President Bill Clinton, looked to his left.

"No."

Mother pulled out to join the traffic. There was a screech of brakes, a violent blast of horn, and the fleeting image of an angry driver's face as a blue and white Mercedes Benz bus ricocheted past in front of them. Mother glared at her son.

He shrugged. "You only asked about cars."

Does time even exist?

Kyrie Eleison

Three months after the Anarchists of Aotearoa meeting, I am helping the scrimmage sisters set up another pop-up art installation at an inner-city park. The grass has been mown recently and the juicy scent of clippings is fermented and rich.

"What's this one?" I am unloading from the truck a large, corrugated cardboard bed with a wire and papier-mâché skeleton languishing on it, in a pose suggestive of an agonised death. The cardboard sheets are decorated with pools of blood, lumps of what look like decaying flesh, and clumps of discarded white hair with bits of scalp still attached.

"Read the headboard." Trixie helps me position the bed next to a man in a suit who is vomiting an outsized quantity of oil from his mouth.

Before I can read the script I hear a voice behind me.

"'Sup."

I turn around. "What are you doing here?"

Skater Kid is wearing the same baggy patched jeans and a loose red T-shirt. He has black and white sneakers on his feet and a bandage around the middle of his left arm. He swings his board by its wheels.

"What are *you* doing here?" Skater Kid points across the way to a large concrete bowl with multi-coloured graffiti painted on it. "This is a skatepark."

"What happened to your arm?"

"Swellbow. I had a slam trying a burly."

"Yo." Sarah greets Skater Kid by slapping hands and bumping fists.

"Where's the child molester? The oldster who tried to give me an ice cream?"

"Oh, him. Out cycling." I'm not sure Rodney would like to hear himself described as an oldster.

"Rad!" Skater Kid has noticed the skeleton. He reads aloud from the headboard. "Hotter nights as a result of global heating mean less sleep. Our bodies need to cool each night as we fall asleep and if we can't cool down our sleep quality will suffer. The impact of hotter nights is especially clear anywhere nighttime temperatures rise above ten degrees Celsius."

"You don't think a leprous skeleton is a bit dramatic to demonstrate the consequences of a poor night's sleep?" I confess to adding a dash of sarcasm to this well-meant observation.

"Global heating is the stuff of nightmares." Sarah stalks off haughtily to help Trixie with another sculpture.

"I wish she was my gran." Skater Kid looks after Sarah and starts walking towards the skatepark. "Peace, love and skate, boomer." He makes some sort of complicated farewell gesture with his fingers and fist.

"Have you got a name?"

Skater Kid turns briefly, grins, makes another complicated finger gyration, then continues on his way to the bowl.

That afternoon I call in at Bryan and Kim's apartment. I have been away skippering a boat on a film shoot, so haven't seen them for a while. Kim answers the door. She looks washed out.

"Are you all right, wife of Bryan?"

"Bryan's asleep."

"No, he's not." Bryan emerges from the bedroom. He is wearing crimson tracksuit pants, a fluorescent green T-shirt and, unusually for him, a beanie. He looks as thin as ever.

"Nice outfit." My voice betrays a hint of concern.

"It took hours to get right." Bryan sits in an armchair.

"It's not like you to be asleep in the afternoon." Bryan doesn't answer, so I tell him about the skeleton on the bed.

"That research also showed that women's bodies drop in temperature earlier in the evening than men's. So no more headaches, just, 'Sorry, darling, I've cooled down early tonight.'"

"Stan was always falling asleep."

"And if the 'Rona hadn't delayed his next liver transplant, he'd still be alive."

"Fickle thing, life. He was a good bloke, Stan." I look out over the harbour.

Bryan seems distracted but eventually breaks the silence. "Whatever happened to Ajit?

"Spent a couple of years in hospitality, then joined the army."

The conversation halts again. Kim seems tense. "Can I get anything for anyone? Will?"

"Cup of tea and a biscuit, please." A trace of a smile crosses her face.

"Bryan?"

"Just tea, thanks."

"Feeling all right?" I am alluding to the fact Bryan hasn't asked for a biscuit.

"Never better."

In the kitchen, where she is boiling the water, Kim breaks into tears. Bryan gets up, goes to her and gives her a hug. "It's okay. Carpe diem." He looks at me, pausing uncertainly for a moment. "I lied. I've got bowel cancer."

"You're joking." Shocked, I get up to join them.

"No, but it's under control. It seems I have a natural affinity for drugs. Wish I'd known that when we were young."

"You never said anything. When did you find out?"

"Six months ago."

I put my arm around Bryan's shoulders. I can feel the bones beneath his clothes. He feels like a wire coat hanger. "Why didn't you tell us?"

"It wouldn't have made any difference."

"We could've been nicer to you."

Kim laughs a little.

"Have you told Rodney?"

"I need a doctor, not a lawyer."

"He could make you a will." Kim pours milk into the tea.

"Do you want me to tell him?" I take a mug from the bench and give it to Bryan.

"No, I'll do it. He'd think you were joking."

The ocean is not a silent world.

Foreword

After his four months' hitchhiking around Australia, Rodney arrived back in town a few days before the next grouping. We were sitting at Bryan's kitchen table, drinking tea and eating celery sticks wrapped in lettuce leaves. Scrabble was lying on the doorstep. Rodney had just finished treating us to the first recital of his Australian adventure. It had only taken two hours. Bryan and I were ready to fraudulently raise our hands just to get some respite. Rodney, sensibly, read the mood of the room.

"So where's our contract? And where are the biscuits?" He looked around the kitchen. At the mention of biscuits, Scrabble let out a sharp bark.

"Publishers are bastards." Relieved by the change of subject, I took a bite of crackly green fibre.

"How much have you written, bro?"

"Volumes."

"Neither have I."

"Any notes?" Bryan passed Rodney a packet of biscuits he had hidden behind the fridge.

"Nada." I took a biscuit too.

Our lack of progress was becoming depressing and repetitive.

"Should we try another publisher?" Rodney picked up the yellow pages from beside the telephone.

"Who publishes the phone book?" I took a gulp of tea. "They've got a big readership."

Bryan thought it was too early to stoop that low and we should send a follow-up letter to Stately & Stables, our original publisher of choice. "Take this down."

I opened my exercise book with the school crest on it and waited for Bryan to dictate.

"Dear Sirs or Madams. We are Messrs Rockwell and Herringbones. Some months ago we sent you a submission for the publication of our book, *The Protestant Work Ethic: How to Live with It and How to Live without It*. It is a winner. We have not yet received the courtesy of a reply. The time for nominations for the Nobel Prize for Literature is fast running out. If you don't act now, you will miss the deal of the century and forever be known as losers. Yours faithfully etc. etc."

I wrote it all down.

"One more thing." Bryan inspected his yellow hair for split ends. "PS. We enclose the first chapter. There is more where that came from."

I wrote that down too.

"It pays to end on a positive note." Bryan tossed a biscuit outside for Scrabble and put the remainder back behind the fridge.

I took the scissors from the kitchen drawer and carefully excised the letter from my exercise book. Rodney and I signed it and we put it in an envelope along with a typewritten copy of the first chapter.

"That'll stir them up." I put the rest of my lettuce and celery experience in the bin.

"They're back." Maggie led us into the lounge. She was wearing a dark blue kaftan and a cucumber-coloured tie-dyed headband. Everyone went quiet and looked at us.

Rat Lady broke the silence. "Well, we need some males, I mean men."

Maggie and the budgerigars nodded their assent. Ralph frowned and looked as if he wasn't getting the respect he felt he deserved.

Rat Lady waved her cigarillo at me. "And at my age, I'm happy to be described as 'crumpet' by anybody."

I looked at Maggie, Rat Lady and the budgerigars. "Sorry, I can't resist a cheap laugh. It was probably just my artistic nature." Rodney coughed and looked out the window. I ignored him. "I think you're all lovely."

The budgerigars twittered and preened and made space for Rodney and me to sit down. We took this as confirmation that we had indeed gelled, as the grouping's advertisement required.

"How's your mother, Ralph?" Rodney looked genuinely concerned.

Ralph looked at Rodney suspiciously. "She's got a bad back."

Maggie and the budgerigars cheeped sympathetically.

"It wasn't pancreatitis then?" Rodney didn't look quite so concerned.

"No, fortunately." Ralph quickly turned to his notes and began pontificating. "The secret to getting one's work published is simply the quality of one's work." He paused to let that sink in. The budgerigars wrote it down in their notebooks. "Publishable quality is not subjective. It is immediately apparent to all discerning editors, purveyors of literature, and readers of the highest calibre. It is..."

"Excuse me." Rodney half-raised his hand.

"Yes." Ralph impatiently tapped his fingers together.

"How much money did you get for your books?" Rodney, quite appropriately I thought, was getting to the essence of why we all attended the grouping.

Ralph didn't agree. He rolled his eyes and ignored Rodney's question. "There can be a fine line between acceptance and rejection, so it is vitally important that when you send your submission to a publisher, you have been through it with a fine-tooth comb, ironed out any imperfections, and made it as appealing as possible."

"Excuse me." I, too, half-raised my hand. I couldn't leave my mate to fight alone.

"Yes." Ralph uttered the curtest affirmative reply in the history of spoken language.

"Shouldn't you just send them a teaser first?"

Ralph regarded me mockingly. "Well, I suppose any submission of *yours* could be described as a... teaser."

Rodney half-raised his other hand. "Our mate Bryan says you have to maximise the market potential."

Ralph cocked an eyebrow condescendingly. "That is true, but the quality of the writing must still be preeminent."

Rodney was unfazed. "You didn't earn squillions, did you?"

There was a fiscal crack in Ralph's composure. "I made enough to... to pay tax."

The budgerigars glanced knowingly at each other. It was common knowledge that Ralph struggled to make money off his writing.

Rat Lady went sotto voce. "This is the most fun we've had since reading aloud from *Wuthering Heights*."

I was beginning to feel a bit sorry for Ralph, but before he could resume, Rodney changed tack. "Is it okay to tell little porkies in a submission?"

The following week I sailed out towards Australia on my next voyage. Our sweet mother gave me another large tin of oatmeal biscuits.

"They're good for your bowels, William." How could I forget?

I left the slippers behind this time. In forty-degree heat they made me feel overdressed.

I had joined a vessel called the *Madrigal Star* whose best days were long lost in her wake. Worse, she was commanded by a direct descendant of Blackbeard. It was a legal requirement that commercial ships of that size had two working radars. The *Madrigal Star* had zero working radars.

"We're sailing anyway. Just like it was in the war." Captain Blackbeard, I mean Stretton, had gone to sea when he was fourteen years old in World War II. He emphasised the word 'war' in a loud, guttural and threatening way. I soon realised he always spoke like this.

It was a rough trip across the Tasman with cloud cover the whole way. This fact is important because we were in the days before GPS and, as previously mentioned, Google Maps. Instead, we found our way around the oceans using a sextant. A sextant is a roughly triangular collection of brass and mirrors, about the size of a baseball or softball glove. It enables you to measure the angle of a celestial body above the horizon. A celestial body is not a reference to your main squeeze. It's just a fancy way of referring to the sun, moon, planets and stars. From this measurement, with a bit of massaging and coaxing, you can work out your position on the surface of the earth. Neat, eh? Not so neat when you can't see the celestial bodies for days on end. Then you have to rely on what sailors call 'dead reckoning', which is a nautical term for guessing. So we guessed our way across the stormy Tasman Sea.

After three and a half days we guessed that Wilsons Promontory, the big rocky bit at the south-eastern tip of the Australian mainland, should be just off to starboard. Unfortunately it was the middle of the night, raining in sheets, and blowing a gale. The light on Wilsons Promontory could not be seen. Now, if we had had an operational radar, just one, we could have turned it on, seen the outline of the Australian coast on the screen, and steered around it safely, stress-free, without running aground and gasping our last water-soaked breaths. Off down Bass Strait we would have scooted on our merry way. Not having an operational radar, we could not do this. Instead, six of us hung over the starboard bridge wing, soaked to the skin, binoculars clamped to our eyeballs, seeking a glimpse of the Wilsons Promontory light.

We could almost hear the sound of the surf when someone shouted, "There it is!"

"Where?" Our eyes were riveted ahead.

"There." He pointed. We swivelled as one to the left. It was like line dancing in the shower. The light flashed far too brightly. It flashed to port. It was very close and in the wrong place. Or we were in the wrong place. Whatever.

"Hard-a-starboard!" Stretton, who was standing directly behind the helmsman, blared his order into the helmsman's ear and the helmsman threw the wheel over. The old ship heaved and groaned in an emergency turn away from the beckoning rocks.

"Perfect." The second mate marked our position on the chart. "Twelve hundred miles dead reckoning across the Tasman and only two miles off course. Steady as she goes, helmsman."

"Did someone say something?" The helmsman cupped his ear and looked around the bridge.

The chief mate on the *Madrigal Star* was named 'Mike'. I called him 'Chief'. Captain Stretton called him 'Mr Mate!', always with an exclamation mark. The mate was my immediate boss. One of the first tasks he assigned me was to scrub the deck of the bridge. It looked clean enough to me, but who was I to argue? Being an old ship, the deck was teak. I got on my hands and knees with a bucket of water and a holystone. A holystone was a lump of sandstone, traditionally used on ships to clean wooden decks. Why was it called a holystone? Probably because scrubbing a deck on your hands and knees is like praying. Large holystones were known as 'bibles', and smaller ones were called 'prayer books'. I was wielding something about the size of Genesis.

I thought I did a good job of holystoning the deck of the bridge. It only took two hours. The mate inspected my work.

"Fing is, it ain't good enuf, do it again." The mate was born within earshot of Bow Bells. He was a Cockney.

"Fing is, sorry, I mean the thing is, it's lunchtime." I was feeling peckish.

"Do me a favour." The mate turned on his heel and went below, down the apples and pears, for silver service and a gin and philharmonic. He meant tonic.

I disregarded the pedigree of the holystone and said something I can't repeat. Well, actually I can. I said, "You are a simple-minded, bone-headed, imbecilic runt of a sailor who couldn't navigate his way around a bathtub without water wings and a rubber duck." Or words that may have rhymed with a couple of those I've just written. Two can play at that rhyming slang game.

It is fair to say that the mate and I didn't get off to the best of starts. I'm not sure why he disliked me. Perhaps I reminded him of his children.

"Me cuwant bun puts bloody dead woss on 'is cornflakes." He made this complaint to me one afternoon.

"Beg your pardon, Chief."

"On 'is bloody cornflakes." I looked blankly back at him. "Tomato sauce on 'is ceweal." He looked at me like I was stupid.

"Really?" I was unsure what relevance his current bun's (son's) weird culinary preferences had to navigating a ship through the Indian Ocean. Usually, I thought, when you get a nutter for a captain, you get a gentleman for a mate, or vice versa – it's the way the universe balances things out, yin and yang, and all that woo woo stuff. On the *Madrigal Star* I appeared to be stuck with two superiors who were competing for the title of tit of the year.

The mate decided he was going to make my life as difficult as possible. He gave me the ugliest, dirtiest jobs. I didn't like that, but I wasn't going to let him know I didn't like it. He also decided I had to learn the International Regulations for Preventing Collisions at Sea. These regulations were more simply known as the Rules of the Road, or even more simply, which suited the intellect of those of us actually at sea, as 'the Rules'. The mate decided he would teach me. His method of teaching was as ambitious as it was revolutionary.

"Wule 1. Learn it and wepeat it to me tomowow."

Our classroom was the bridge. The mate used to keep what was called the four to eight watch. That meant he was the officer in charge of navigating the ship between four o'clock and eight o'clock every morning and evening. Usually, we dropped the 'watch' word and just called it 'the four to eight'. The second mate kept the twelve to four, and the third mate kept the eight to twelve. You could say our days were numbered. Anyway, the mate decided that every afternoon, at 1600 hours, I would join him on the bridge while he taught me the Rules.

I dutifully, defiantly, or both, learnt Rule 1. The next day, at 1610 hours, soon after his watch commenced, the mate asked me, "Wule 1, wot is it?"

"It says that the Rules apply to ships on the ocean and rivers..."

"Nah. I don't wanna know wot it says, all genewal like, I want to know wot it acshully says, wot are the wowds. Compwendez?"

"You mean you want me to repeat it word-perfect?"

"If that's wot yer call it."

"I can't do that."

"Then go an' learn it be'er." The mate made a habit of misplacing his 'd's' and 't's'.

I didn't like having to do this, but I still wasn't going to let the stupid rubber duck know.

Now I don't know how many of you have read Rule 1 of the International Regulations for Preventing Collisions at Sea, probably the vast majority of you, but for the sake of completeness, I will point out that it has five parts, (a) to (e), inclusive. Those five parts are written in a foreign language understood only by lawyers and other obfuscators of the truth.

As a child I had never heard of 'obfuscation', and this reminds me of something I have carried for a long time, a psychological scar that needs healing. Whenever we children asked Crunch, or our sweet mother, what the meaning of a word was, or to enlighten us on some fact of the world, they would always reply, often in unison, "Look it up in the dictionary," or "Look it up in the encyclopaedia." This, as I keep reminding you, was in the days before the internet, so instead of dubdubdubs and urls we had a dictionary and an encyclopaedia. An encyclopaedia was a pile of paper with words in it, about the same size as a laptop but much fatter, and without the lights. A dictionary was similar, but more like a fat tablet without the lights. Needless to say we learnt nothing, because it was too much effort to look up either of those things.

Rule 1 of the International Regulations for Preventing Collisions at Sea was incomprehensible. Just so you understand how unjust was the mate's order, and why my mood was touching on annoyed, here, by way of example, is Rule 1(e).

"1(e) Whenever the Government concerned shall have determined that a vessel of special construction or purpose cannot comply fully with the provisions of any of these Rules with respect to number, position, range or arc of visibility of lights or shapes, as well as to the disposition and characteristics of sound-signalling appliances, such vessel shall comply with such other provisions in regard to number, position, range or arc of visibility of lights or shapes, as well as to the disposition and characteristics of sound-signalling appliances, as her Government shall

have determined to be the closest possible compliance with these Rules in respect to that vessel."

Well if you're so smart, learn that off by heart, and then tell me what it means, without going to a dictionary, or an encyclopaedia, or one of those dubdubdubby, urly things.

I again, dutifully, defiantly, or both, learnt all of Rule 1 by heart. The next day I applied for the Chair of International Legal Studies at Oxford University. No, I didn't, I recited Rule 1 to the mate on the bridge. He seemed slightly taken aback, as was I, when I got it right.

"Wule 2 tomowow then."

I accepted this as praise.

There are thirty-eight rules in the Rules. Many of them are as convoluted as Rule 1(e). Then there are all the annexes and appendices. This was going to be a long trip. Worse, the mate did not stop at the Rules.

"Splicing, lashings and whippings," he announced one afternoon.

Now don't get excited, splices, lashings and whippings are just fancy bits of ropework. To further test me, the mate had decided I would also have to learn a new splice, lashing, whipping or knot every day. So I learnt how to do eye splices, back splices, long splices, short splices, common whippings, West Country whippings, palm and needle whippings, square lashings, diagonal lashings, round lashings, tripod lashings, shear lashings, bowlines, reef knots, figure of eight knots, sheet bends, double sheet bends, carrick bends, clove hitches, half hitches, rolling hitches, monkey's fists, sheepshanks, and a host of other arcanely named twists and turns of rope.

"Wot's that?" The mate peered at my latest attempt one afternoon.

"It's a Turks Head." I proudly held out the circular tangle of strands like an offering.

"Turks Head my arse."

I got better with practice.

I had dutifully, defiantly, or both, as usual, learnt all the Rules by rote, and the next day had promptly forgotten the wording of the rule I had recited the afternoon before, but I became quite good with the ropes. I could feel a new career beckoning, in a circus, as an escapologist.

At 1600 hours every afternoon, at the commencement of his watch, the mate was invariably tipsy. This was not good practice, especially as at that point in time he was responsible for thirty lives and a few million dollars' worth of vessel and cargo. Another thing I learnt at sea is that it is unwise to ask alcoholics to police themselves. In this regard, a ship was the antithesis of an AA meeting. Instead of the participants supporting each other to stay off the grog, at sea they were encouraging each other to drink the bar dry and build pyramids of empty beer cans.

In his defence, however, the mate had a cast iron excuse. He had caught malaria years previously, up the Amazon River, and, according to him, it would routinely resurface and strike him down with fever, chills and shakes. Unless, of course, he drank a lot of gin and philharmonic. This was because the philharmonic allegedly contained quinine, and quinine is a treatment for malaria. The mate, as the medical officer on board, had therefore prescribed himself large daily doses of quinine, mixed with a splash of gin. Or was that large daily doses of gin, mixed with a splash of quinine? He couldn't remember.

During our lessons on the bridge, the mate and I would sometimes veer onto subjects other than the role of the give-way vessel, or whether it was a fox or a bunny that went through the hole when tying a bowline. One afternoon, we even discussed the existence or otherwise of an omniscient, omnipresent god.

The mate was a supporter. "'Ow else do you explain all this?" He brandished his arm around the horizon.

"Evolution?"

"Do me a favour." The mate dipped his words in more than a soupçon of sarcasm.

Another afternoon he said to me "Y'know wot?" I shook my head. "When I go on leave, it's like I don't belong at our 'ouse."

"Why's that?"

"They got their woutines. They go on doing wot they always do, and I just sit in a lion's and watch 'em." He paused and looked at the horizon. "This ain't a good life for a mawied man. They don't need me."

Once I established that a 'lion's' was a chair (lion's lair), I felt a bit sorry for him. Something weird was happening here. The mate was opening up. He and I were actually beginning to like each other.

As well as spending time with the mate, I also saw a lot of the Barbadian deck boy. Benjamin was fifteen years old and this was his first trip to sea. He couldn't read.

"'Ow about you teach 'im then? Fing is, dustbins gotta know 'ow t'wead." The mate meant dustbin lids, or kids in English.

Three times a week I gave the deckboy reading lessons in my cabin, on the company's time. I thought this was very generous of the company. Not that it had been consulted. Remedial reading lessons weren't part of its growth strategy. The mate told Stretton I was teaching the deckboy how to tie knots. "'E's got a fewcha." He meant Benjamin, not me.

Benjamin hardly said a word. In fact, he barely spoke more than he could read. The ship, fortunately, had a library. Unfortunately, it was a dingy cupboard containing an out-of-date selection of musty paperbacks, some antique classics, a handful of dog-eared, joke books and the occasional bodice ripper. The rats on board paid more attention to those books than the crew did. They had taken a particular liking to *Catcher in the Rye*, excising numerous portions of the pages with their teeth. There were a lot of depressed, adolescent, angst-ridden rats on that ship.

Rats weren't the only stowaways on the *Madrigal Star*. We also carried a full complement of cockroaches. I once came off watch in the middle of the night, and feeling a little peckish, stopped by the galley. The benches and deck were bustling like a crowded train station. It was a cockroach carnival. I can handle bacteria like a pro, but even I decided my grumbling stomach should wait until breakfast. I was hoping the cockroaches would have wrapped things up by then. Perhaps they would go off to the library and read Kafka, or have a chuckle over a book of Gary Larson cartoons.

Surprisingly, given the calibre of our crew, there were no children's books on board, so I decided to write my own, about a couple of boys, a year or two older than Benjamin. He'll be able to relate to that, I thought. I wrote about two teenagers writing a book. That's clever, I thought, writing a book about writing a book, who would ever think of that? It was five pages long with ten words to a page. Good practice for the real thing, I told myself. Stick that up your quill and sharpen it, Ralph.

Benjamin was not inspired by my handwritten masterpiece. In fact he didn't show much interest in learning to read at all, until we tried the dinner menu. Benjamin was fond of food, and although there were some difficult words, like 'roasted' and 'pudding', he knew what they tasted like. I had stumbled upon a new pedagogy. By the end of the voyage Benjamin had decided his fewcha was to become a steward.

"Ya cahn eat a Turks Head."

I was almost knocked down by this torrent of eloquence, but was tempted to point out that you could, although it was probably not something that would go down well with the good people of Istanbul. On reflection, I held my tongue. I didn't want Benjamin to argue with me and use up his quota of words for that month in one hit.

Soon we found ourselves back at anchor off the entrance to the Shatt-al-Arab waterway. We were at anchor for two weeks. If you went out on deck in the sun, after two minutes you were standing in a puddle of sweat. The air-conditioning broke down. If you stayed inside in the shade, after two minutes you were standing in a puddle of sweat. At last, to our great relief, the pilot arrived to guide us up the waterway. He started climbing up the pilot ladder hanging over the side of the ship.

"Two bloody weeks!" Captain Stretton fired a broadside of syllables at the pilot, the pilot boat, and the whole of Iran and Iraq. "Who's going to pay my demurrage?! My demurrage! Who's going to pay it?!"

Demurrage is the extra cost to the consignee for delayed cargo and was of little concern to the pilot. He looked up the side of the ship at the demented figure in a white uniform ranting at him in a foreign tongue from the bridge wing. He paused. He looked down at the comforting, peaceful, familiar deck of the pilot boat. He chose the pilot boat.

"I woulda offered a' Awistotle of gay and fwisky before I bollocksed 'im." The mate looked on gloomily as the pilot boat disappeared over the dusty horizon. That's a bottle of whiskey to you.

We waited another week at anchor. When the pilot next arrived, Captain Stretton held his tongue. Even then we didn't get to go alongside. We anchored off the wharf, rafted up to another of the company's ships. One afternoon, the second mate, the fourth engineer and I lowered a lifeboat for testing. The engine puttered into life and, like the adolescents we had recently been, we pretended to be David Attenborough and chased sea snakes around the anchorage, complete with commentary.

"In the vast pantheon of the animal kingdom, there is nothing quite as snaky as the sea sneak." The fourth engineer accurately intoned the mellifluous tones of that great environmentalist and broadcaster. Then the fourth engineer decided he wanted a close-up photograph of the two ships moored together.

The fourth engineer was a Scotsman. I had got to know him when I was working in the engine room for a week, as part of my training. It was very hot, very noisy, and very greasy. Everyone wore greasy earmuffs, greasy boiler suits, greasy socks, and greasy boots. I didn't inspect the underwear. Donald – that was his name – would appear out of nowhere dragging a hammer on a length of twine.

"Hello." I would shout.

"Hoo are ye?" he would shout back.

"Fine."

"Bit warem."

"How's your hammer?"

"Jings crivens help ma boab. 'S tha' a hama?" In Scottish, this roughly translates as "Goodness gracious me. Is that a hammer?" Donald would peer at the workshop tool intently, then shrug his shoulders and walk on with the hammer bouncing happily across the steel-grated deck behind him.

At the end of my week learning the finer, practical principles of marine engineering at first hand, I was deemed proficient by the chief engineer. My understanding of marine motive power was advanced beyond measure. I had manufactured a new barbecue from an empty oil drum and some old angle iron.

Back in the lifeboat, I was now beginning to wish I was still in the engine room. The second mate had steered us close to the bows of the rafted-up ships, looking for the best camera angle. This was not a sensible thing to do. The current was running at three knots and more between the hulls. We bounced off a hanging anchor and were swept between the two vessels. The lifeboat's engine coughed and died. As the two ships flexed apart and back again with the shifting current, the lifeboat was sucked further between the very high, extremely hard, steel hulls. Each ship was around eight thousand tonnes. This was not a good place to be. Think of being stuck in a giant garlic press. Screws and rivets started to pop out of the squeezed lifeboat.

"Help!" There was no response. This was turning into one of those terrifying moments. I wondered what squashed bones looked like.

"Help!" We shouted louder. Again there was no response. The crews of both vessels had retired to the bar for an afternoon of jovial companionship and the construction of ancient Egyptian burial mounds.

You will be pleased to know we were finally saved by the junior engineer. His name was Keith. He was so junior he didn't even have a number. He, too, was a Scot.

"I were oon ma wee bunk, astral travellin'. I thought I heard a great spirit in the sky. He were calling me to paradise he were. It were magnificent. I asked him if this were heaven? 'Hell,' the great spirit replied. This confused me it did. I didna' think I'd bin tha' bad. Then he said it again. 'Hell,' but this time with a 'p' on the end. So I astral travelled outta me bunk and here I am."

Keith tut-tutted as he helped us winch the warped and cracked lifeboat back into its davits.

"We, and the rest of the planet's living organisms, owe you a significant debt of gratitude." Donald was still channelling a wildlife programme.

In later life Keith became a teacher of children with behavioural problems. This had been good training for him. Donald, on the other hand, joined Extinction Rebellion. In the meantime we all retired to my cabin for some oatmeal biscuits.

"They're good for your bowels." Our sweet mother would've been proud of me.

Donald and Keith worked with a greaser named Scantlebury. Scantlebury was a salt-of-the-earth sailor, but one who hadn't been at sea long.

One morning Keith took Scantlebury aside. "Did ye know Donald's brother's a pianist? He's giving a recital at the Albert Hall next week."

Later that day, Scantlebury raised this achievement with Donald. "Hey mon, ya bruddah he famous piano player."

Donald, his face a mixture of sadness and pain, looked Scantlebury firmly in the eye. "Me brother's got na' arms."

The next week Donald happened to mention to Scantlebury that Keith's brother had won a trial with Celtic, the famous Scottish football team.

Scantlebury raised this achievement with Keith. "Hey mon, ya bruddah he trial wid Celtic."

Keith, his face a mixture of sadness and pain, looked Scantlebury firmly in the eye. "Me brother's got na' legs."

The engineers used to leave their greasy work boots lined up outside the engine room. One night, Scantlebury filled Keith and Donald's boots with Swarfega, a green gel used by the engineers to clean their greasy hands. He was a quick learner.

Eventually we went alongside the wharf. Weeks earlier, while still at sea, the mate had offered me an opportunity for career advancement.

"When we ge' up the Gulf, 'ow about you take me watch?"

I had not really believed him then, but now, as the mate had suggested, I took over his four to eight watch, supervising the discharge of cargo between those hours. This upset the second and third mates. The four to eight is the plum watch, which is why the first mates take it. It is plum because it fits in well with normal sleep patterns and mealtimes. In the evening, at dinner time, the third mate also has to relieve the first mate at six o'clock, so the first mate can dine in a relaxed fashion in the saloon. The third mate, who takes the eight to twelve, therefore ends up doing an extra half to one hour of watch-keeping. That's what you get for coming third. The third and second mates therefore mutinied. This was resolved by me being allocated the eight to twelve, and them being rocked around the clock to the twelve to four and four to eight respectively. It was purely a numbers game.

While alongside, in our downtime, Donald and I would visit other ships on the wharf, taking movies to smooth the way. Let me tell you about shipboard movies. In some ports we could access a library of movies. These were not digital, downloadable, plug-and-play movies. These were the real thing. That is a pun. They came on reels of film which had to be fitted onto a projector and then projected onto a white sheet hung in the saloon.

Our sweet mother, for some unfathomable reason, took it upon herself to teach us what a pun was when we were young. Like Crunch, she too was a teacher. I realised early on that teachers liked to hunt in pairs. Maybe she thought she needed to test her skills. I don't know, but it is not easy to teach children why they should laugh at some things and not others. In fact, why would you even bother? Children will laugh at whatever they want to, whether that is a grubby joke about bodily functions or their sibling falling under the wheels of a bus. Some things are just funny.

To illustrate her point, our sweet mother explained that if someone took offence, they may also take a gate. She was obviously relying on the fact that 'offence' and 'a fence' sound similar. We found this insulting. We had been brought up to speak clearly. We knew the difference between a fence and making someone annoyed. Fences were for jumping over as you ran away from the offended neighbour whose letterbox you had just filled with worms. That is amusing, but only because of the worms, not the words. Secondly, as we pointed out to our sweet mother, offence is one word beginning with an 'o', and a gate is two words beginning with an 'a'. There is not even the hint of a giggle in that distinction. And even if you make a gate one word, you get 'agate', which is a coloured rock used to make cheap, second-rate jewellery. I wasn't laughing then and I'm sure you're not now.

Our sweet mother should have just cut her losses and run at this stage. Instead she felt the need to explain the exact relationship between a fence and a gate, as if her offspring were incredibly stupid and didn't know that a gate opens and a fence doesn't. She eventually realised that treating those same offspring as if they really were total idiots didn't reflect well on her own level of intelligence, and changed the subject.

"Have you all done your homework?" That wasn't funny either.

Unlike at a regular cinema on shore, the audience at shipboard movies could drink alcohol, shout, jeer, snore, fart, and pass interminable commentary on the action, just like in the pit of the Globe Theatre four hundred years previously. I was in charge of showing the movies. I had never worked a projector in my life. It took a while to get in the groove.

One night I showed a movie about a Canadian ice hockey player. It had three reels. I mixed up the reels and played the last one second and the second one last. At least the beginning was where it should be. No one noticed the movie had ended at half time. The second reel, which had become the last, left the plot hanging nicely.

"Must be one of them festival films." The inebriated audience were in total agreement as they wobbled off to their bunks.

One day Donald and I visited an Indian ship. We took a movie, the nautically themed *Gone with the Wind*, to swap for one of theirs. The Indians only wanted Bollywood, so we couldn't rid ourselves of our unwanted classic, but they did ask us to stay for lunch.

Donald's face lit up. "Oooh, I could murda a curry. National dish o' Scootland."

The Indians very proudly served us steak and chips with lashings of dead ross. After lunch they took us to a store room. It was full of unused clothing.

"Take whatever you want." Perhaps they felt bad for rejecting one of the great achievements of Western cinematography.

"Is this legal?" My veneer of responsibility and law-abidingness was easily peeled away, and Donald saw no reason to object. We walked back to the *Madrigal Star* with our spurned movie reels and four pairs of newly-pilfered jeans.

Another day we visited a ship from Czechoslovakia. Do you find this strange? I hope so, because Czechoslovakia was landlocked. Remember this is before Czechoslovakia dissolved into Slovakia and the Czech Republic, but even that excuse can't save you, because both those countries are landlocked too. Why then did Czechoslovakia have a merchant navy? The short answer is that it was advantageous for trade and the ships were based in Poland, which is not landlocked. The long answer goes on for about twenty pages of very small, eyesight-numbing print in an academic journal, but because this is a 'once-over-lightly' kind of book, we won't bother with the long answer. As an aside though, Czechoslovakia also had a real navy, one with guns and admirals and lots of beer. Okay, lots of beer isn't a particularly distinguishing feature, but you get my drift. It is the only navy in the world which has never lost a battle. It only fought one, on Lake Baikal in Siberia, in 1918, against the newly-erupted Russian communists, but that is a long story and we don't do long stories either, unless you are prepared to listen to Rodney for a couple of hours.

Boarding the Czech ship was like walking into a maritime version of *Mary Poppins*. Children ran about kicking footballs and each other, young mothers nursed babies on their hips, the air smelt of milk, coffee, beer and sauerkraut, and everyone was happy. This was not at all like the *Madrigal Star* where, most of the time, no one, apart from Keith and Donald, was happy. This was strange. We were always told it was the Commies who should be miserable.

"Hello," we said.

"Ahoj," they said.

You may find it irrelevant, but 'ahoj' is the Czech version of 'ahoy'. In this regard you may have noticed that while we don't do the long, hard, factually precise yards as mentioned above, we do do irrelevance, with a passion. In fact, as you've probably already realised, this whole book is irrelevant. But having come this far, you may as well keep going.

The Czechs made us very welcome, fed us food we couldn't identify and gave us beer. They didn't want *Gone with the Wind* either. We could understand this. For starters, they didn't speak English, and secondly, it probably wasn't suitable for under-fives. I got into a conversation with the second cook. I used up all the Czech I knew in five seconds.

"Dvorak."

The second cook sparked into life. "Tom Petty."

"Smetana."

"Led Zeppelin."

"Tchaikovsky." I showed my linguistic virtuosity and branched into Russian.

"Sex Pistols!" The second cook shouted so enthusiastically he spilt his beer.

For the next ten years, Petr and I exchanged music through the post. Western music was not readily available in Prague until the Berlin Wall came down. I now have an extensive LP collection of Czech and Russian classical music. This is slightly unfortunate because Dvorak and Smetana, the names of two great Czech composers, were the only Czech words I knew at the time. I was more of a Tom Petty guy myself, like Petr. I would have liked to keep the LPs I sent him.

I sadly lost touch with Petr in later years, so Petr, if you're reading this, do please get in touch – I have an LP of the Partridge Family's Greatest Hits waiting for you.

Walking back to the *Madrigal Star* we were approached by a group of Kurdish stevedores. Their clothes had all seen better days, their teeth, where they had them, were yellow and stained. They were wiry, fierce-eyed men. They mimicked a drinking motion at us.

"Av?" I thought this was the local word for water. I had hit the nail on the head. They seemed to understand me.

"Av. Av." They crowded around us, shouting. I was secretly proud of my ability with languages, although they did seem a little threatening. "No av. No av." They pressed closer. This was getting confusing. It was soon clarified. "Whiskey. Whiskey." I had insulted them by offering water.

We had no wish to cause another international incident and wind up in an Iranian slammer, counting the minutes before our hands, or our heads, were severed from the rest of us. It was one thing to give whiskey to the officials and the revolutionary guards. As long as no one said anything, no dhows were rocked. But to give whiskey to an oppressed and poverty-stricken people, that would have been well beyond the pale. The officials and revolutionary guards would not allow that to happen. We also had a sense that an Iranian slammer may not be the same cushy number as experienced by the second cook of the *Rangitoto* in Saudi Arabia.

"Sorry." We meekly raised our hands in submission and backed towards the *Madrigal Star*, confronted by this crowd of angry men. The hypocrisy, on so many levels, was sobering. I accept that was a poor choice of word, but it was true. These men, who lived and slaved in the heat and the dust for a pittance, were denied even a small comfort by an unjust world. It's surprising when you discover you may have a social conscience. I liken it to finding a useful gift inside a Christmas cracker.

"I wanted to say we coulda given 'em *Gone with the Wind*." Donald, unusually for him, was downbeat. "But I canna even joke aboot tha'."

We sailed from Bandhar Khomeini on a bright and sunny day. This was not unusual. Roughly two-thirds of the days in the Persian Gulf are bright and sunny. Captain Stretton and I were on the bridge. It was the eight to twelve watch.

"You ready to do this on yer tod?" Stretton's lifeless blue eyes pierced my skull.

"Beg your pardon?"

"Captain!"

"Beg your pardon, Captain!"

"On yer tod?"

I wasn't aware I had a tod. I decided to humour him. "Yes."

"Captain!"

"Yes, Captain!"

"Good." He disappeared into his cabin, which adjoined the bridge. He emerged two minutes later with a cold can of Coca-Cola in his hand. He thrust it at me. "You can't say I never do anything for you." I took the can. "You can't say I never do anything for you." Stretton repeated himself to no one in particular while looking off into the distance. He disappeared into his cabin again.

I drank the Coke. I was the officer of the watch. I was now responsible for thirty lives and millions of dollars' worth of vessel and cargo. I was barely out of short pants. What sort of intellectually challenged person was running this show?

The fifth engineer decided we needed a swimming pool. He was almost two metres tall and had to duck going through doorways, into the shower, and even lying in his bunk. He often sported band aids on his head and body to cover injuries caused by manoeuvring his large frame around the confined quarters of the ship. We called him Bob Geldof. If you don't understand why, go and ask your parents. Bob Geldof was always hungry. Off watch, at any time of the day or night, he would raid the galley.

"It's because I'm tall. It's a long way from my mouth to my feet and takes the nutrients forever to hit my toes. I have to keep topping up so I don't get gangrene."

At dinner one night, the stewards removed his plate and cutlery and replaced them with the equivalent of a small horse trough and a shovel. "Now you're on song." Bob sat down for his fifth meal of the day. When he eventually left the sea he leveraged his height and ran a scaffolding business.

Bob Geldof commandeered Donald and Keith to assist with building the pool. They worked like bunnies with a blowtorch up their backsides. In no time at all they had assembled a wooden framework from scraps of dunnage and secured a greasy tarpaulin between the frames. The pool was the size of a large puddle and deep enough to drown in. Four of us could swim at the same time if we all held our stomachs in. They filled the tarpaulin with seawater from one of the deck hydrants. It wouldn't have done for the Olympics but it cooled us down. Unfortunately, there was a slick of oil on the surface of the water. The oil was leaching out of the tarpaulin, or the engineers, I'm not sure which.

"Excellent." The appearance of a toxic pollutant in the water didn't worry Bob. "Less friction, we'll swim faster."

On the subject of oil, fires occurred in the engine room of the *Madrigal Star* on a regular basis. We'd be pottering across the tropical ocean on a magnificent, sunny day when *Boom!,* there would be an explosion followed by the emission of a spume of black carbon and other debris from the funnel. The engine would stop.

"Scavenge fire," the engineer on duty would report to the bridge. As everyone knows, the scavenge is a space where unburnt fuel, carbon and oil can collect beneath the engine cylinders. If this space gets hot enough, the fuel, carbon and oil can combust. Scavenge fires have caused several major accidents on ships. They are dangerous. On the *Madrigal Star* we'd average one a day. You'd think this state of affairs may have caused the ginger beers some angst.

"Ooch, another scavenge fire." Keith the junior engineer would skip eagerly down to the engine room. He would be closely followed by Donald and his bouncing hammer. Bob Geldof would hit his head on a steel frame in his rush to remedy the situation. After an hour or two there would be a heave from the engine and we would be on our way again. Scavenge fires weren't all bad. At nighttime, the explosion from the funnel was like a fireworks display. Stan and my brother would have loved it.

The rocky bit on the opposite side of Australia to Wilsons Promontory is called Cape Leeuwin. It, too, is marked by a lighthouse. We rounded Cape Leeuwin in the mid-afternoon, heading east. It was a clear day with a stiff breeze blowing and a long swell running up from Antarctica.

Boom! There was an explosion followed by the emission of a spume of black carbon and other debris from the funnel. The engine stopped.

"Scavenge fire," the engineer on duty reported to the bridge. We were three miles from shore. The currents and wind had us drifting towards that shore. This was not a good thing.

"Ooch, another scavenge fire," Keith the junior engineer lilted gaily and skipped eagerly down the companionway. For further detail return to the paragraph on scavenge fires above.

Six of us hung over the port bridge wing, binoculars clamped to our eyeballs, calculating the distance to the first reef. If you're thinking words are beginning to repeat themselves, they are. This was better than déjà vu, déjà vu. How many ships get the opportunity to bounce off both sides of southern Australia, on the same voyage? You wouldn't read about it.

We drifted closer and closer to the shore. I was wondering whether or not I should take the remaining oatmeal biscuits with me if we had to abandon ship. There was little conversation. This was becoming serious. Maybe we were approaching a terrifying moment. The complacency of our boredom had been buried in the bilges. We had one radar working now, but since we could see the shore, the radar just added to our anxiety by telling us how far we had to go before the hull was ripped open on the rocks and we were dashed to death in the chaotic surf. The phone from the engine room rang on the bridge. It was the chief ginger beer.

"How close are we?"

"'Arf a mile." The mate was showing little sign of stress. He had been taking his malaria medication.

"All right, we'll wind up the rubber band and give it a whirl."

A couple of minutes later the engine coughed, another plume of sparks flew out of the funnel, and we were on our way.

"That's a shame." Keith also showed little sign of stress. "I were aboot t'ask the lighthouse keeper's daughter oot on a date."

Three days later we entered the western end of Bass Strait. It was a bewitching balmy evening. The stars were crammed together like sequins on a glam rocker's jacket and I was on watch. The tangy eucalyptus scent of the Tasmanian bush mingled with the salt air and all was well with the world. A myriad of lights appeared just above the horizon, dead ahead. The closer we steamed, the more lights there were. Red ones, green ones, white ones, all pirouetting about on the ocean. Our course was taking us through a fleet of fishing boats.

I checked our one working radar. Going by the screen on the radar, there was very little room to manoeuvre. Bother, I thought. No I didn't, and my sweet mother certainly wouldn't have wanted me to repeat what I actually thought. "It wouldn't be seemly, William," she would have said. I could see the headlines now – "8,000 tonne freighter obliterates Hobart fishing fleet. Only the fish survive." I adjusted the range on the radar to get a closer impression of the fishing boats. Nothing changed. I tried again. Nothing changed. I gave the radar a kick. It made a satisfying deep echo. The radar was the size of a pinball machine, unlike modern radars you can almost put in your pocket. Nothing changed.

Then it dawned on me. There was a lot more actual distance between the boats than the dodgy radar, now stuck on a wide range, was showing. It had deceitfully condensed them into one homogeneous yellow blob.

"Oh, a life on the ocean wave, a life on the rolling deep." I croaked out an old nautical song as we proceeded to pass with ease between the fishing boats. I kicked the radar again.

"What's that bloody racket?!" I'm not sure if Stretton was referring to my kicks or my singing. He remained in his cabin.

"Just fixing the radar!" I pointedly stressed the words 'fixing' and 'radar'.

"Captain!"

"Captain!"

The *Madrigal Star*, with us still aboard, eventually arrived in Singapore. She was going to Gadani Beach in Pakistan to be scrapped. A skeleton crew would sail her there and the rest of us would pay off. Her days sailing the world's oceans were done and a less romantic future beckoned. She would be made into razor blades – the ship that shaved a million faces. This was sad. She was a gallant old vessel with teak decks and rails, truly a reminder of a fast-vanishing age.

Gadani Beach was the site of the world's third largest ship-breaking yard. It was also the subject of a Pakistan government initiative to attract tourists. As well as picnicking, camel riding, swimming and sunbathing, another of the attractions, according to a Pakistani travel guide was "the fact the coast is fascinatingly lined with rusting wreckage of ship hulls and mighty vessels which once ruled the sea." I didn't go, so I am not in a position to either confirm or deny that the presence of disintegrating steel plates and heavy metals on an industrial scale significantly improves a paddle at the beach.

One of the prized items to be taken off a ship before it is scrapped is the builder's plate. This plate, usually bronze, records the builder, the year of launch, the tonnage, and other information identifying the vessel. The plate on the *Madrigal Star* was screwed to the superstructure just beneath the bridge. One of Captain Stretton's final duties was to ensure the plate was returned to head office. A few days before we arrived in Singapore, Captain Stretton looked up to where the plate should be. There was just a faded rectangular shadow in the paintwork.

To his credit, Captain Stretton tried to be reasonable about the missing builder's plate. This went against every instinct he possessed. A message was sent around the ship that the plate should be returned to the bridge, no questions asked, no fingernails extracted, no shocks to the genitals. It wasn't returned. Another message was sent around the ship. The plate should be returned to the bridge, and if not, the perpetrators of this stunt would be reported to head office, tarred and feathered, and then keel-hauled until their innards spewed out. The plate was not returned. Another message was sent around the ship. The plate should be returned to the bridge, and if not, the local constabulary in Singapore would be invited aboard to search the baggage of every man before he could pay off, and the person or persons found in possession of the plate would be charged under local law, incarcerated in a rat-infested cell with fifty convicted members of the Chinese mafia, then, if they were still breathing, have their innards ripped out by a host of hungry vultures. The plate was not returned.

"I'll bloody get 'em." Stretton was giving instructions to the mate the evening before we docked. "I'll end their bloody careers, I'll bloody see to that." He angrily threw the suitcase he was about to pack onto his bunk to emphasise his point. It snapped open. From inside the case, out spilled the builder's plate.

The mate nodded in its direction. "It's a bit o' Donald Duck the Bill didn't find that then, ain't it?"

The next day I paid off.

"They say it's tough at the top, but it's a lot tougher at the bottom." The mate shook my hand before I headed down the gangway. I never saw Mike again. He was a decent man. He taught me a lot. Mike, if you're reading this, please get in touch. I know who took, then put, the builder's plate in Stretton's – sorry, Captain Stretton's – suitcase.

Did you know that whales have belly buttons?

The Good Oil on the Bad Oil of Big Oil

I'm back at the park on the waterfront helping the scrimmage sisters set up another installation. They seem committed to combating global heating using their whole arsenal of educational and artistic skills. The weather, perhaps appropriately, is unseasonably warm. A hint of cream-coloured cloud lacquers the sky and sunlight seeps into every crevice of the city. It smells like spring with a light garnish of exhaust fumes that are wafting in from the nearby road. All is well, at least on the surface of our small world.

"Where's the gore, the bones, the filth, the relentless decay and destruction, the threat of impending doom, the sculptures designed to keep psychologists in business?" I look around for the usual cardboard installations.

"We don't know what you're talking about." The scrimmage sisters are fastening the guy ropes of a tent-like puppet theatre. It is modelled on an old-fashioned Punch and Judy show but, instead of red and white stripes, is coloured like a fluorescent rainbow with a multitude of environmental motifs entangled in the colours. "What we do is very child-friendly."

Trixie and Sarah disappear behind the theatre. I stand next to a tree and wait. A few curious passers-by gather.

"Ooh, I haven't seen one of these for years." A grandmother points out the theatre to her two young grandchildren. "It's a bit bright, isn't it?"

"When do the puppets start, Mummy?" A five-year-old girl, holding her mother in one hand and a carton of chips in the other, has stopped to see the show. She is dressed like a fairy, with silver wings tied to her back.

We all wait, enjoying the relaxed balminess of the afternoon. I think I am about to fall asleep.

Suddenly, the air is rent by a screech.

"Screw Big Oil!" The high-pitched voice cuts the air like a squealing bandsaw.

"Fuck me." A startled young woman, who is holding a large Alsatian dog on a leash, can't help herself. "Sorry, sorry," she apologises to Fairy Girl, her mother, Grandma and her grandchildren.

"Big Oil is Bad Oil!" The voice screams louder.

"This isn't what I was expecting." Grandma frowns.

"BP, Chevron, ExxonMobil, Shell, TotalEnergies, Eni and ConocoPhillips." The voice is unrelenting.

The Alsatian barks at the theatre and strains at its leash.

A puppet dressed as a female ninja bounces up into the theatre. She is dressed in a black and bright orange hooded cloak and carries a miniature samurai sword.

"Petrostates and Big Oil have made an estimated $52 trillion of pure profit over the last fifty years." The ninja sounds suspiciously like Sarah with a peg on her nose. "That's $2.8 billion per day. How much of that have you seen, people?"

"Not a brass razoo." Rodney has turned up with his wife, Jeanette. They lean their bikes against the tree next to me.

"Not a brass razoo." The ninja flounces across the stage.

A model oil well, gushing dollars, pivots around the theatre. The ninja slashes at it with her sword and the oil well falls over.

"Yay!" cheer the children.

"Oil pollutes the atmosphere, heats up the planet, funds wars which kill millions of people, and causes worldwide environmental destruction." The ninja bounces around and slashes at thin air with her sword.

"Yay!" The children have no idea what the words mean but appreciate the violence.

A model ship appears in the theatre.

"Ships run on oil. That oil produces sulphur oxide and nitrogen oxide fumes when burnt. It also produces carbon dioxide and methane. If the shipping industry was a country it would be the sixth biggest polluter in the world." The ninja slashes at the ship with her sword and it sinks.

"Yay. Yay!"

A model plane joggles about the ninja's head. "Planes run on oil. The aviation industry contributes up to eight percent of global heating. Save the world by remaining at home, sitting in an uncomfortable chair, watching rubbish movies on television, eating last week's cold leftovers, and breathing in air from the hospital for infectious diseases next door. Fly like a ninja or don't fly at all." The ninja slashes at the plane's wobbly flight path with her sword and off comes the plane's tail.

"Yay!" The plane corkscrews downwards and disappears from sight.

A model car races around the ninja. "Cars run on oil. They.Just.Drive.Me.Insane," she yells in a highly punctuated fashion, then slices the car in half.

"Yay. Yay!"

The ninja pauses and looks warily around her. Another puppet dressed in a grey business suit appears, wearing dark sunglasses, and carrying a briefcase in the shape of a petrol pump. He points the briefcase at the ninja and squirts her with what looks suspiciously like black coffee. The ninja gags melodramatically and slowly sinks to an apparent prolonged and slippery death.

"Oh." The children quietly turn their faces to their elders, seeking emotional guidance and support.

"Oh," Grandma echoes sadly.

The Alsatian lies down, whimpers, and puts his head between his front paws.

"I rule the world!" The oil man puppet holds up his briefcase like a trophy and marches up and down. "Nothing can defeat me, I rule the world." He sounds suspiciously like Trixie with a bad case of bronchitis.

"Look, look." The children whisper excitedly to each other and point at the theatre. The ninja has returned to life and, now holding a solar panel instead of her sword, is slowly stalking the oil man who continues his triumphal procession across the stage. Suddenly, the ninja flies through the air and slices off the oilman's head with the solar panel. "Yay. Yay!" A small fountain of what looks suspiciously like raspberry cordial spouts from the oil man's neck.

"Subtle." Rodney takes a drink from his water bottle.

Shortly after, a human head appears in the puppet theatre. The ninja withdraws to one side. The head is wearing a fluorescent green academic mortar board and an obviously false bright yellow beard.

"No show without Punch." I recognise Bryan immediately.

"Hello, I'm Professor Pineapple." The head bows to the audience, almost losing its mortar board. "How many of you think that oil is a fossil fuel?"

A number of the audience, which has grown substantially, put their hands up.

"Well, I'm here to tell you that you are wrong. Oil is not made from fossils, or dinosaurs, oil is made from plankton, bacteria and decayed marine organisms, mixed with mud. The plankton, bacteria and other marine organisms settled on the ocean floor aeons ago. They were also joined by organic matter, such as dead plants and animals, which washed down rivers into the oceans and found its way into the sediment along with the plankton and their friends. Over time this biomass was buried deeper and deeper in the earth as sediment settled on top of it. Going deeper into the earth means hotter. The combination of pressure and heat resulted in the biomass becoming oil. So put simply, oil wasn't made from fossils. Calling oil 'fossil fuel' is a barefaced lie. Another lie by Big Oil!"

"This is boring." Fairy Girl pulls at her mother's hand.

"Can we go?" The grandchildren whine and look anguished.

"Did you say oil contains *dead animals*?" The ninja looks directly at the audience.

"That's right, and our ancestors were animals. For example, our ancestral primates first appeared on earth about one hundred million years ago. So the next time you fill up your car, you could be pouring great great great great grandma – add a few more greats – into your tank. Granny probably wouldn't thank you for that."

"I would not indeed." Grandma's face has taken a severe turn.

"Can we go?" The grandchildren whine again.

"No, we cannot." Grandma's face looks even more severe.

"Turning it around, how would you feel if your decomposed remains were sucked out of their final resting place, sent off to the other side of the equator, and burnt in a fiery internal combustion machine, just so some dude could drive down to the dairy for a packet of smokes and a creaming soda milkshake?"

The Alsatian lets out a plaintive yelp.

"Well, this is the fate which awaits us if we don't stop using oil." Professor Pineapple is getting worked up. "Your bag of bones won't be turned into oil for another one hundred million years or so, but that is not the point. It's a human rights issue and it's happening now. Bring on the revolution. No to oil!"

"No to oil. No to oil!" The ninja brandishes her solar panel and hits Professor Bryan on the nose by mistake.

"Yay. Yay!"

"No to oil!" I hear a youthful voice shout in my ear. I turn around to see Skater Kid.

"'Sup. Thought you'd be here, boomer." He recognises Rodney. "Hello, Mr Child Molester."

"What did you call my husband?" Jeanette looks at Skater Kid in a mildly threatening way. She is a strong athletic blonde woman.

Any reply is drowned out by the ninja knocking the mortar board off Professor Pineapple's head and leading the chant of "No to oil. No to oil!"

"Yay. Yay!" The children cheer as the Alsatian breaks loose and runs off with Professor Pineapple's headpiece.

"Are you stalking us?" I turn back to Skater Kid, raising my voice above the noise. "What's your name anyway?"

"Are you trying to groom me?" Skater Kid wipes his nose with the back of his hand.

Grandma looks sideways at us and shuffles her grandchildren another metre away.

"I don't believe a word of Professor Fruitface." The mother of Fairy Girl also sidles her daughter sideways. "But isn't this fun?"

"No to oil. No to oil!" The ninja and the audience are in sync.

"No to economic imperialism!" Professor Pineapple makes a new offering. His face is beginning to turn red in the heat. There is a stunned pause. "No to economoilism," someone's vocal chords stumble. "No to imperioil," tries another. Finding the phrase indigestible, they quickly rediscover their mojo. "No to oil. No to oil!"

"Rruff, rruff." The Alsatian, having been apprehended, has abandoned the now-shredded mortar board and is straining at its leash in an attempt to attack the ninja.

"This boy with a skateboard said you're a child molester." Jeanette confronts Rodney above the surrounding din. There is a hint of accusation in her voice, whether directed at Rodney or Skater Kid it is hard to tell.

I step in to help Rodney in this potentially embarrassing situation. "And an oldster."

Skater Kid points at Rodney. "He offered me an ice cream."

Jeanette mimes a punch at Skater Kid. "I think you're a little troublemaker."

"Want to be my gran?" Skater Kid grins and disappears into the crowd.

"No to oil!" The ninja gets tangled in Professor Pineapple's beard.

"Bring on the revolution!" Professor Pineapple shakes his head to dislodge the ninja and his beard detaches from one side of his face.

"Excuse me sir, but do you have a permit for this activity?" A uniformed police officer, who has wandered into the chaos, peers into the theatre at Professor Pineapple.

"It's not my show." Professor Pineapple is indignant.

"It's not his show." So is the ninja.

Fairy Girl starts bawling. The Alsatian has eaten her chips.

Elephants can identify themselves in a mirror – a big mirror.

Opus No 9

M y leave after disembarking from an extended tour on the
Madrigal Star coincided with Rodney's holidays again. This
was fortunate, or not, depending on how you looked at it. Rodney
had two holiday jobs. He was surveying archaeological sites and
killing gorse on the side. The gorse was being slaughtered in a nature
reserve. Rodney would cut away the heads of the gorse as best he
could, with saws, hedge clippers and secateurs, and then slap DDT
on the stumps. DDT was not a prohibited chemical in those days,
even though it was probably carcinogenic in humans and could
adversely affect reproductive capabilities.

"Fortunately, I hate children and I can't spell carcinogenic."
Rodney was not concerned. He carried the DDT in an open can and
painted it onto the stumps with a brush. Gloves? Respirators? They
hadn't been invented yet. Not on that nature reserve anyway.

Being a trifle worried about Rodney's future health, not that I
told him, I did some research on DDT by going to the local library
and reading those encyclopaedia things. I discovered that DDT was
also toxic to a wide range of animals and marine life. It was readily
absorbed into soils and waterways and could take decades to decay
away. What better chemical could you have chosen to use in
Rodney's environmentally-aware environment? Agent Orange
perhaps?

DDT was also a three-letter acronym. Mr Bojangles would
probably have attributed it to CNN. It stands for
dichlorodiphenyltrichloroethane. Try spitting that out in a heated

discussion with your main squeeze over who is responsible for weeding the front garden. I decided it was an act of linguistic mercy to acronym it.

I also learnt that DDT was first made in a laboratory in Austria in 1874. In 1939, a Swiss chemist, Paul Hermann Muller, discovered it killed bugs, such as mosquitoes and lice. He won a Nobel Prize for that. Wouldn't you think that if you knew it killed bugs, you might think that it wasn't so good for other animals, like us? Apparently Paul wasn't concerned. Nor was the Nobel Prize Committee.

The American military, not particularly well known for its people-first approach, also sprayed DDT directly on its troops to control typhus-spreading lice. Not content with that, the same military also sprayed it directly on civilians in places its armies had conquered, I mean liberated. It was a bit like fly spray, but a lot stronger. Imagine jumping out of the shower and spraying yourself down with a can of Mortein. Well it was worse than that. The Americans banned DDT in 1972 when they found out how bad it was. A few years later, and despite my warnings, Rodney was still using the stuff.

"On the upside," he said, "I haven't caught malaria."

When Rodney was not busy poisoning himself and all other surrounding organic life forms, he was hiking the hills, surveying Māori archaeological sites. He worked in partnership with a student acquaintance called Nigel. Rodney was bunking down with Nigel, at Nigel's mother's motel by the beach. Every morning, Nigel's mother would see them off by handing them a paper bag of sandwiches and two pieces of fruit. Around midday they would find a shady spot for lunch, often by a stream in the bush, and catch some meditative moments. Without fail, as he finished his last mouthful, Nigel, a man of few words, would say, slowly and deliberately, as if he was sculpting a verbal statue from granite, "Well, as they say in the Public Service, if that was lunch, I've had it."

Rodney couldn't believe his luck. "I knew as soon as I heard it, dude, that sentence was my epitaph."

When Rodney's work was finished, he decided that he, me and Bryan would go on a windsurfing safari.

"We haven't made a lot of progress." I was worried our book was stagnating. "Shouldn't we get stuck into a bit of writing?"

"We'll write on the road."

That sounded like a good plan, so we strapped the boards and masts to the top of Rodney's car and set off. We travelled along scenic country roads, winding around a seascape framed by soon-to-bloom pōhutukawa trees. Rodney's car was new to him. Bryan sat in the front seat.

"What's this?" Bryan pulled the cigarette lighter from its socket.

"Cigarette lighter." Rodney looked sideways.

"You don't smoke."

"I'm future-proofing."

"Does it work?"

"Future-proofing? I don't know. It hasn't happened yet."

"I meant the cigarette lighter." Bryan held the lighter up to his face and looked at the inside of it closely. He couldn't see any glowing redness. He put his thumb on the inside rings of the lighter to test for heat. For a clever man, Bryan had his lapses. "Sugar!" No, he didn't say that, you can substitute your expletive of choice. Bryan inspected the circle of seared flesh on the end of his thumb. The car's interior smelt like a rare-done steak.

"Seems it does." Rodney wound down his window to let in some fresh air.

Our first night on the road, we camped at a friend's family bach. This friend had usurped Grubby the redhead and been my sister's second boyfriend, before he too was usurped. It was trial and error in those days. We had no dating apps to provide wisdom and guidance.

There were three of us and five of them, including my brother. We combined our food and cooked sludge for dinner.

"Just like home." My brother poked at his portion with a fork. This was unfair. Our family meals were a compromise between Crunch's meat and three veg, and our sweet mother's desire to be avant garde. So our sausages would be curried and our rice pudding jasmine-scented. Stewed mince with anything was 'con carne'.

"It was still sludge, like her pavlova." I'm afraid my brother was right about the dessert. Every Christmas, our sweet mother would proudly present the table with her version of pavlova. It had concrete for a base and the upper level was the consistency of chewing tobacco. For years we thought this was normal. Only when we left home did we discover pavlova was meant to be a uniformly elegant crisp meringue with a light and fluffy texture on the inside. We thought it was something to scale your teeth with at the end of a meal, like a baby's rusk.

It was a bit rich for my brother to criticise food. He was an entrepreneur from an early age. At ten years old, he and a friend were manufacturing lemon and grapefruit cordial and selling it to the neighbours. This was based on a good business plan. There were no overheads. They collected the empty bottles from the roadside, they stole the fruit from their customers' gardens, and they mixed the beverage in our laundry tub, right next to the toilet. When I say right next to the toilet, I mean exactly that. The toilet was about a metre from the tub. There was no door, no wall between them. Not a drop of that cordial ever passed my lips. As with the cockroaches on the *Madrigal Star*, I did have my limits when it came to bacteria.

Later, my brother and his friend branched into ginger beer, the liquid version. This went well until one evening when a batch, already bottled and stored in the laundry, exploded. Crunch, who happened to be using the toilet at the time, rushed outside, corks flying in pursuit. Ginger beer was dripping down his face and he held his pants up with both hands.

"Where is he?" Crunch grimaced, his half-closed eyes stinging from the spicy liquid. But our brother was long gone, out the same bedroom window Mother had thrown his fireworks, over the offence and away up the road. He saw fit to lecture me later.

"In business, always have an exit strategy."

My brother had inherited his business acumen from Crunch's father. It may not surprise you to learn that Crunch's father was an eccentric. He didn't allow us to call him Grandad, or Grandfather, or Pops, or any other term of endearment usually reserved for those males close to extinction. Instead we called him Jim. Everyone called him Jim, even though his name was Theodore.

Theodore, I mean Jim, was a publican, an unregistered moneylender, and a freelance insurance salesman. This was a good combination of trades for working without attracting too much attention from the Inland Revenue Department. Jim gave me my first watch. He had been to the Returned Servicemen's Association bar that afternoon and was drunk.

"It tells the time." He looked at me intently.

"I hoped it might."

Jim looked around suspiciously to make sure no excise men were listening. "Off the wharves." He tapped the side of his nose with his index finger.

A lot of Jim's, and therefore our, possessions came 'off the wharves'. 'The wharves' was a big department store at the bottom of town where everything was cheap as chips and the shop assistants were burly men with tattoos of anchors and Marilyn Monroe on their arms. Jim shopped there often.

As part of his grand plan to remain undetected, Jim drove an incognito grey Morris Minor. Going down hills he would turn off the engine so no one could hear him coming. He also did it to save petrol. His business dress consisted of stained grey flannel trousers, a previously white, now grey, stained singlet, and a half-smoked, roll-your-own cigarette super-glued to his lower lip. If it was cold, he would wear a stained grey suit jacket over the singlet. He looked like he was homeless, but actually owned a good part of the town's real estate.

Jim's cigarette was always going out. When this happened he would fussily search for a match to relight it. He kept stashes of matchboxes in his pockets, his car and around the house, so he would never be caught without a light. He was an early positive influence on my brother's love of incendiary devices.

Jim was also an early (although some may not say positive) influence on my brother's education. At school, my brother, who like Crunch was a good cricketer, would throw books, pencils, protractors, and anything else contaminated by academic learning, out the windows, just to test his throwing arm. This was not popular with the teachers. With Jim, however, he was the model of decorum. Learning how a cash-only, tax-free business operated, he was too busy to misbehave.

An important part of this education occurred on the weekends when Jim would take my brother and me to collect the rents. We would tour the town, stopping at addresses in various states of disrepair to chat with the occupiers and watch as they surreptitiously handed a wad of cash to Jim.

Once all the banknotes were in Jim's pockets, the Morris Minor would coast silently down to the butcher's, where my brother and I would each be given a saveloy, which we would wash down with bottles of ginger ale. Saveloys were a staple gift from butchers to children back then. Butchers peddled them like drugs, to hook children into pestering their parents to be taken back to that particular purveyor of dead meat.

"Here, son, have a sav," they would say, looking over their shoulder in case Mum or Dad was watching. "It's our secret, orright?" Jim always knew when a saveloy had changed hands. In fact he encouraged it. He owned the butcher's shop as well.

Back in the car, Jim would exclaim, "Cor lubbaducks," after looking at the fuel gauge, and off we would go to the bowser to top up with that week's pint of petrol.

"They don't make weekends like that any more." My brother, often nostalgic, is now CEO of his own business which, in case you are doubting, does pay its tax bill.

Jim, unfortunately, died early. Taken to view his body, we noticed the funeral directors had dressed him in a smart new black suit. At first we thought we had the wrong dead person, but then saw that the funeral directors, affectionately, in a manner not uncommon in small towns, had also chosen to highlight one of Jim's most defining characteristics – they had placed an extinguished roll-your-own cigarette between his lips. My brother regarded our recently departed grandfather fondly. "Don't worry, Jim, you won't need matches – you're being cremated."

After our wind-surfing meal of sludge, we drank instant coffee. In those days this was acceptable. Then Bryan brought out his cardboard box. You thought I was going to write 'cards' or 'Monopoly', or some other item worthy of twentieth century after-dinner bonding, didn't you? Bryan possessed close to fifty wind-up plastic toys. There were alligators, Smurfs, cars, trains, the Easter Bunny, radios, a coconut, a shark, a television set, a pair of running shoes, a pram, and many others. He kept them all in the cardboard box. Why he had brought them on a windsurfing trip, I had no idea. Why he possessed them in the first place, I had no idea. He collected them, like his fridge magnets.

Bryan's version of a challenge was to place every toy on a table and attempt to have them all wound up and wobbling about at the same time. He took advantage of the fact that there were eight of us to help compensate for his burnt thumb. We tried hard to please Bryan, honestly, but the potato fell off the table, taking with it the telephone box, the angel fish, the Volkswagen Kombi, and a number of others. They wriggled about, like newly-caught sprats in the bottom of a dinghy, until their little motors wound down and they died.

"So sad." I sort of meant it.

"We were so close." Rodney exaggerated our levels of skill and commitment.

"What a fun night." Bryan described the evening with absolutely no hint of irony whatsoever.

We retired to our tent. On the way we paused underneath the bach's upper-storey deck. In a deeply felt gesture of thanks, we serenaded our hosts.

"Crazy 'bout you baby, yeah, yeah, crazy 'bout you baby, yeah, yeah. And her name was?..." We were interrupted by a pot of water being emptied over our heads.

Back in the tent Rodney dried his hair with a tea towel. "Why does no one else like that song?"

The next day was warm enough to go windsurfing. The deserted white dunes were ruffled with marram grass, oystercatchers poked their red beaks into the littoral fringe, the sun bleached our hair, the teal ocean lolled languidly upon itself, and the sea air teased our nostrils with the salty prospect of adventure and mysterious foreign lands. We sailed a steady breeze in and out of perfectly curved waves, nuclear war was not declared, and all was well with the world.

Wetsuits hanging around our waists, we prepared lunch on the beach. In an improvement on last night's meal, our menu listed luncheon sausage sandwiches made with the purest refined white bread, followed by vanilla wine biscuits, chosen for their high sugar content, an apple to clean our teeth and please our mothers, and all washed down with sweet orange cordial, drunk straight from a shared bottle. Exquisite.

Bryan made the sandwiches. He was cutting slices off a cylinder of luncheon sausage. In more modern times, such cylinders have been rebranded 'dog roll'. Bryan was cutting the sausage with his hunting knife. The blade alone was twenty centimetres long.

"Sugar!" No he didn't say that. Substitute your expletive of choice. Bryan had cut a slice off his thumb. The same thumb he had barbecued in the car.

"How did you do that, bro?" Rodney looked up from waxing his board.

"I was just cutting the luncheon sausage, like this." Bryan, demonstrated with his other hand. "Sugar!" No he didn't say that. Substitute your expletive of choice. Bryan had cut a slice off his other thumb. As we discussed earlier, Bryan had his lapses.

"Well, you can't go back in the water." I cleaned and dressed Bryan's damaged hands. "The sharks will come. So I guess you're on dishes."

After lunch, while Bryan struggled to wash and dry dishes with two bandaged thumbs, Rodney and I sat on the beach. I opened my exercise book and passed it to Rodney with a pen.

"Take this down." I thought hard for a minute. "Chapter Two." I paused, then paused some more.

"Is that it?"

"Well, you come up with something."

Rodney handed the book and pen back to me. He thought hard for a couple of minutes. "We windsurfed. Bryan cut his thumbs making lunch. There was blood on the sandwiches." He paused. "Did I ever tell you about Onion Man?"

I raised my hand.

"But I didn't tell you about Pong."

"Yes, you did."

Rodney looked out across the ocean. I waited for him to say something more, but he didn't.

"Is that it?"

"Big picture man, that's me, bro. You fill in the details." Rodney picked up his board and sail and strode into the waves.

I warned you Rodney had a short attention span. I went to see Bryan.

"All the dishes are covered in sand."

Bryan gave me the fingers. Fingers were his only functioning digits.

We windsurfed our way around the peninsula for another three days. On our last day we packed up the car, slightly depressed at the thought of having to return to the city. We were also slightly depressed at the fact we hadn't put pen to paper much.

"Do you think we lack talent?" I removed the cigarette lighter from its socket and hid it in the glovebox.

"Nah, we're just too busy." Rodney shoved his wetsuit into the boot.

Bryan didn't do much packing. His thumbs were still healing beneath their bandages. I lashed the windsurfers and masts to the roof rack.

"They'll never shift." I gave them a hearty shake. My maritime training was standing me in good stead.

We drove through the lush countryside. Sheep were bleating as they were mustered, cattle gazed dolefully across tree-speckled pastures, the traffic was light, and hawks circled on updrafts, searching for roadkill. All was still well with the world. Rodney spied an upcoming stretch of straight road.

"Let's see what she can do." He accelerated his new pre-loved car into the straight. Whoosh. An alien apparition flashed past the rear windscreen.

"What was that?" Bryan twisted his head so quickly his nose hit the door frame. "Ouch."

I put my left hand out the window and felt for the windsurfers. They weren't there. "Ah, better back up."

In the distance behind us there was a screech of brakes. Rodney reversed and we climbed out of the car. A station wagon had come to a halt, following an evasive manoeuvre, in the middle of the road. A young woman gripped the steering wheel with frozen hands. She stared far ahead into the distance, as if she had seen the numbing darkness of death. There was a toddler in the back seat.

"Who are these funny men, Mummy?" He started howling.

"You haven't seen our windsurfers, have you?" I asked this question as politely as I could given the circumstances. Mummy didn't, or couldn't yet, reply.

"It's all right, here they are." Rodney pointed to a ditch beside the road. There they were indeed, masts and all, still firmly attached to the roof rack. The whole rack had detached itself from the roof of the car, taken off like a glider, narrowly missed Mummy and her boy, and landed in the ditch.

"We're really sorry." I tried to penetrate Mummy's glazed visage. She managed a clipped half-smile, then retreated back into the gloom. This was serious. Mummy and her infant were suffering from shock. In a moment of inspiration all my first aid skills came to the fore. I grabbed Bryan's hands and manipulated his two bandaged thumbs, like puppets, in the direction of the toddler.

"It was an accident." Thumb One had a high-pitched squeaky voice.

"That was no accident." Thumb Two had a very low gravelly voice. "That was a woof whack."

"Woof what?"

"Woof whack." Thumb Two beat Thumb One over the head. The howler giggled.

"Ouch." Bryan wasn't giggling.

When Mummy also started laughing and we had reattached the woof whack to the car, we escorted Mummy and the toddler to their destination. I noticed Mummy didn't get too close behind us but she did give us a very friendly wave when she turned off the road.

"I told you the windsurfers would never shift off that woof whack." I was proud of the expertise I had gained in my whipping, lashing and splicing sessions with Mike the mate.

Soon after arriving home, Rodney and Bryan were due to run in a relay race, from one rural town to another. I went along as manager. There were six in a team. Bryan was down to run the first leg.

"How you feeling champ?" I took Bryan's tracksuit top from him before the start. It was made of lurex. I was taking my job as manager seriously.

"J'ai la pêche." Bryan flexed his biceps and posed for the crowd. That phrase is French for "I have the peach". It meant Bryan was bursting with energy. Bryan's hair was a lemon colour and he had a new silver stud in his left ear.

The crowd was admittedly small – the competitors, their support crews, a dementia-impaired pensioner who had lost his way going to the supermarket the night before, and a couple of mangy dogs. From a managerial perspective though, Bryan's positive frame of mind was promising.

It was a perfect day for running, if there ever can be such a thing. It was not too hot, not too cold, a few clouds and a gentle cooling breeze. The gun went and they were off. Bryan soon lagged behind.

"Come on, champ, you can do this." I was quite comfortable in the support vehicle. I also believed in positive encouragement, for others anyway. Sometimes I just liked to have a good moan. It was more satisfying than telling myself, as encouraged by self-help criminals, that I was a strong, motivated man who could achieve anything I had ever dreamed of. Well, I wanted fame, wealth and unbridled power, and so far not one of those three things had materialised.

"Move yer fucking arse, Bryan!" One of our teammates was not a fan of positive encouragement. Bryan fell further behind the leaders.

"Play him some music." I also believed in rock and roll as an agent of change. Rodney pushed play on the ghetto blaster.

"Running on Empty" erupted into the air. In the circumstances, Jackson Browne was not a good choice.

"Try something else." It made no difference. Bryan lagged even further behind. By the end of his leg, he was a spent man.

"My peaches just turned to jelly."

"Orange juice?" He collapsed at my feet. "How about a beer?"

The next morning Bryan was rushed to hospital. His appendix had burst. We went to see him in his convalescence.

"Don't make him laugh." The nurse who showed us to Bryan's bed was obviously new to the job. There was nothing in her contract which required her to give us an invitation. After five minutes the other patients started complaining about the noise. So the nurse moved us, Bryan and his bed into an empty ward.

"Sorry." I opened the door for the nurse.

"It's all right. We don't usually get children in this part of the hospital."

"Don't make me laugh." Bryan struggled to breathe while surreptitiously checking inside his hospital pyjama pants to see whether his stitches were still intact.

"Sorry." The nurse gave us a sheepish look before leaving.

"We should've put you out of your misery." Rodney referred to the race, a little cruelly, I thought.

I softened the message. "You could've dug a little deeper." I employed a kind and caring tone of voice, much like our sweet mother. Then I passed Rodney some of the grapes we had brought for Bryan. "You do know it was your fault we came last?"

"My appendix was oozing bacteria and yellow pus into my abdominal cavity. I've been under the knife. I could've died." Bryan theatrically pressed the back of his hand against his forehead.

Being largely ignorant of medical science, it was not until years later we realised this was true. Instead, between grapes, Rodney said, "Call that an excuse?"

We left Bryan with a vineyard's worth of produce, a year's supply of war comics, and a promise to return the next day.

"I hope they leave me in here." Bryan looked around his empty ward. "Those other buggers make far too much noise."

Rodney and I walked out of the hospital.

"What will you do when you finish law school?" Next year, Rodney would enter his last year of legal study.

"No idea, dude. Travel the world perhaps?"

I was pleased that Rodney knew the value of a solid state-funded education.

"Without education there will be no democracy. Without democracy there will be no education." You can quote me on that when the human species shrivels into an intellectually and emotionally desiccated hairball. You may argue it has done so already.

Glossary

Before I left on my next voyage in the new year, Rodney and I attended another grouping. This was to be a reading session where, instead of Ralph lecturing us about his renowned achievements, we would get the chance to show the world what real writing was about. Like a host of other words, we didn't know what 'hubris' meant. I like to think it wasn't that we were overtly arrogant, but more that we were temporarily afflicted by the overconfidence of youth.

We sat around the lounge at Maggie's place drinking tea and eating bran muffins. The budgerigars had all brought a plate.

"We didn't ask you to contribute." Rat Lady laid her cigarillo in an ashtray.

"I can conjure up a gingernut as well as the next man."

"Exactly."

There was some preliminary chat about Ralph's mother's health – apparently she now had only severe indigestion – and then the budgerigars took it in turns to read their literary pearls. Romance was a common theme. Maggie, who was wearing an orange kaftan and a carmine tie-dyed head band, read five pages of her novella about a suicide bomber who couldn't decide whether to flick the switch and wreak destruction on the infidel west, or marry his poverty-stricken, deaf and dumb cousin, who worked as a laundress. The way Maggie put it, death was preferable to marriage of any sort.

Rat Lady whispered in my ear. "She's been through a lot."

"Where's Mr Maggie?"

"Plural."

"Mr Maggies?"

"Exactly."

When Maggie got to the end of the fifth page, we applauded politely. She sat down, bashfully wiping tearful runs of mascara from her eyes. We all had the opportunity to comment on Maggie's work. Ralph said he thought it could probably do with a bit more psychological friction and structure, Rat Lady said she thought it was wonderful, the other budgerigars said it was challenging, totally believable, and that it "drew them in".

"It moved me." Rodney was sincere. "Either that or I've eaten too many muffins."

Rodney decided that I should read our one chapter.

"You wrote it. You take the consequences."

"You wrote the title."

"Big picture man, that's me, bro. You fill in the details – remember?"

I read our first chapter. I couldn't help noticing that the bran muffins were getting a hammering while I spoke. One of the budgerigars filled the teacups during the second page. Ralph looked at his nails with what I interpreted as a smug expression on his face. He made me nervous. I sat down to even politer applause than Maggie garnered.

"Who wants to go first?" Ralph was too cheerful, like an executioner during the French Revolution.

Rodney raised his hand. "It drew me in, although it could probably do with a bit more psychological friction and structure."

Ralph raised an eyebrow at him.

Rat Lady exhaled a plume of smoke. "A good first effort, well done." I don't think she meant to be patronising. Maggie and the budgerigars couldn't decide who should comment next, so Ralph stepped in.

"Please don't take this the wrong way. I don't mean to be harsh, but in my humble opinion, you and your... friend," he waved a hand in Rodney's direction, "have made a brave attempt at literature, but really, have you considered advertising?"

The budgerigars drew in their collective breath then spoke over each other.

"Oooh, that's a bit strong."

"It wasn't that bad."

"You've got to start somewhere."

Maggie gave Ralph a stare. "Don't you listen to him, boys, it's just his artistic nature."

I noticed we had been down-graded from 'men'.

"On the contrary they are here to learn." Ralph looked at us condescendingly. "There are no themes, no hint of deep and intricately linked plots, there is no suggestion of character development. I'm afraid to say it contains very little literary merit." Then came the clincher. "Unfortunately, it is, how do I put this gently, it is... boring." He finished with what I perceived as a concocted grimace of sympathy.

Rat Lady, bless her, broke what was threatening to become an embarrassing silence. "I've got an idea. Why don't you start again, after the first paragraph, I think that one's okay, and don't try to invent things, just write about what you know?"

"We don't know a lot, obviously." I was feeling more than a little chastened.

"You mean write about the beach, and sport?" Rodney didn't seem fazed at all by Ralph's criticism.

"And all that ship shit?"

"And nurses?" Rodney's face lit up.

"Exactly."

"Too easy." Rodney had enough confidence for both of us.

"And don't forget the mice." Rat Lady patted her hair as if to make sure there were no rodents hiding in it.

We reported back to Bryan.

"It's depressing being a writer." I dropped my exercise book on the table. "Look what happened to Ernest Hemingway."

"Understandable – he had four wives." Bryan smoothed back his peroxided mullet.

"Made squillions though." Rodney was still seeing the positives.

"He liked cats as well as weddings." I waited for Scrabble, who was on the back porch, to bark. He obliged.

"Look on the bright side." Bryan was about to do just that. "You've only wasted your time on one chapter."

"And the title." Rodney was beginning to deflate.

"And my note." I was not to be outdone.

"And we haven't made squillions." Rodney deflated some more.

"Scrimmage!" Sarah and Trixie bounded through the door and leapt on Bryan. "It's not about the money."

Bryan hit the linoleum in a flurry of limbs.

"Yes, it is." Rodney and I took up the challenge. Bryan tried to join in but couldn't find the breath.

Scrabble raced around the porch barking until Bryan managed to fill his lungs. "Tranquillity." The black and tan linguist lay down on the doorstep and regarded us all silently with his morose brown eyes.

Kim was also on the floor. She was sitting in the lotus position by the fridge. "Why don't you do what that vermin person says?"

Rodney let out a sigh. "Because we have no themes."

"No deep and intricate plots, no character development." I impersonated Ralph.

"It would be as boring as hell," Rodney mimicked.

"Not one iota of literary merit." Bryan got into the swing of things after finally casting off the scrimmage sisters.

"Breathe in, breathe out." Kim invited Trixie and Sarah to join her on the lino. Rodney blew his nose. There was a brief silence while Bryan adjusted his hair in the mirror.

"I suppose we might." I could think of no other options.

"This could be another turning point." Bryan twisted his torso to get a back view.

As Rodney suffered through his final year of law school, my next voyage took me through the Pacific Islands and up the western seaboard of the United States on a venerable vessel called the *Edinburgh Angel*. I had seen some of the Pacific years before when our family sailed to the United Kingdom. Can I make a plea here for nations to be more original in their choice of name? And not to lie? United is more than a glib throwaway word. I have yet to meet a truly united nation or state. Not to mention the fact it makes them sound like dyslexic football teams, although Kingdom United and States United are usually on the same side, except when they played against each other in the American War of Independence and then the 1812 War. Both these games featured a brawl, much like most modern football matches. The 1812 contest was a draw, but States United won the Independence encounter in a penalty shootout, after which both sides shook hands and had a cup of coffee and a biscuit. It should have been tea, but that had all been thrown into the ocean.

On my first visit to the Pacific Islands, our sweet mother woke me at five one morning. She took me to the wet market in Papeete.

"Why can't I stay and sleep like the others?" Our sweet mother was dragging me out of our cabin in the dark.

"You'll enjoy it." This was an order, not a vision of the future.

The wet market was bursting with colourful fish of all shapes and sizes, and various hanging cuts of meat of indeterminate origin. There was blood, gore and scales in the air, on the floor, and all over the exposed body parts of the vendors. Flies, rats and cockroaches were strongly encouraged to attend. It smelt like a rubbish dump.

I understood the primal earthy attraction of it, but where were the saveloys? I knew I wouldn't be going back there in a hurry.

"That's an experience you won't forget." Mother was now dragging me back to the ship. And I obviously didn't forget, because you've just read about it. I was being dragged back to the ship because it was about to sail. We climbed onto the gangway as it was being raised.

"Happy Birthday, William."

Not another experiential gift, I thought. Where are my new toys?

Our parents were keen on giving experiences and not material gifts. As a child, this was not pleasing. Once our sweet mother made me walk for five hours in the searing sun, just to see a flock of yellow-headed seabirds and some poisonous spiders in a jam jar. An elderly ranger, he must have been about forty, let the spiders run over his hands.

"I've been bitten before, so I'm immune."

Let's see how much older you get, I thought.

"Happy birthday, William." When we finally arrived home I sank into a heat-stroke-induced coma on the couch. Mother accepted a cup of tea from Crunch. "I think he really enjoyed himself."

On my present voyage we called in at Fiji. I had the afternoon free so went to see a local rugby match. As I walked towards the ground, the sky lowered and turned a foreboding shade of dark. Torrential rain began cleaving itself into individual molecules of hydrogen and oxygen on the surrounding earth. Then I was slipping and sliding in liquid heat. It was hard to tell what was rain and what was sweat. Coconut palms wilted under the weight of water.

Through the gloom and cascading flood, I found the rugby pitch. It was so dark I almost walked right into a scrum. I must have missed the pay booth, if there was one. The atmosphere was dark, the mud underfoot was dark, the ball was dark, and so were the players. I think they wore uniforms. It was impossible to tell. For all I knew they could have been naked. Everything was a very dark shade of dark. I think there were other people watching the game. Every so often I heard what could have been a cheer, but it was quickly washed away in the deluge. It was more likely the combined death rattles of drowning players, spectators and referee. Shadows of various shapes and sizes flitted across my vision. I heard grunts, shouts, and occasionally the bloated gurgling note of a whistle blown underwater. I smelt mud, blood, and kava. I was living out one of the more tormented circles of Dante's Inferno.

At some point the ground went silent. Nothing moved. Apparently the game was over and everyone had shape-shifted away into the blackness. Either that or they were dead. I walked back to the ship, a saturated mariner and none the wiser man.

"Saw you at the rugby." One of the big, bare-footed stevedores grinned at me the next day. "You can always pick a white face in a crowd."

Hawaii was our next port of call. We docked in Honolulu as the sun rose. Like most ports, the wharves were outside town in a place so bad no one wanted to live there. That night we taxied to the nearest bar. That was something sailors often did in port. The nearest bar was a strip club. Bars often became strip clubs when sailors were in port.

"What a coincidence." The bosun looked up at the pink neon lights as we climbed out of the taxi.

Inside, the women chewed gum and wriggled. The men drank beer and ogled. Describing such a scene in light of the #MeToo movement is dangerous ground. Was it degrading or empowering? The apogee of feminism, or its nadir? I feel physically unqualified to answer. Instead, by way of allegory, I think back to a good friend who once wrote lesbian poetry, under a pseudonym, for a student newspaper. The poems were so successful the editor kept demanding my friend post her more.

"They truly reflect the trauma and joy of lesbian love, the internal and external contradictions of a sexually marginalised existence," wrote the editor in one editorial. She was a lesbian herself. "I should know."

My friend continued writing until the pressure became too much. The editor wanted to meet in person, and he couldn't see how he could pull that one off.

At the strip club, members of the Hells Angels Motorcycle gang were acting as if they owned the place. Now I have nothing against clubs, teams, lodges, associations, fraternities, political parties, families, tribes, covens, or any other form of social grouping. They reflect all that is good in humanity, excluding perhaps the National Rifle Association of America, and do a good job of uniting people around a common interest. This includes the Hells Angels. They were united in wanting to bash our brains out.

Outside on the street, at two o'clock in the morning, we found ourselves facing off against three monsters with outsized whiskers, bulging waistlines, and tight black leather pants seemingly held together with silver chains. I am not sure how this happened, but I think one of their girlfriends, who was a stripper, took a fancy to one of our lads. He was a youngster from the Outer Hebrides and didn't know better. The Outer Hebrides exist in a time warp and out there strippers were what you used before painting the front door. He had drunk too much beer. Luckily for us, the Hells Angels were also drunk, or stoned, and probably both. They swayed like elephants.

The girlfriend appeared and pleaded with them not to hurt us. Plead is an exaggeration. Rather she drawled, "They talk funny, they're from England."

"I'm not, I'm Scootish." The words slopped from our young friend's lips.

"Oooh, that sounds sooo sexy." The girlfriend wasn't doing us many favours.

"No it doesn't." We sidled across the street, holding our young friend between us. One of the Hells Angels sat down in the gutter. He rolled sideways and vomited.

"Run?" This was the smartest thing the girlfriend had said. We accepted it as good advice and, without a qualm of conscience, turned tail and fled. The two Hells Angels still standing tried to follow us. Fortunately, their choice of pants held them back.

"I wanna goo back." Our young friend tried to turn around.

"No you don't." The bosun seized him by the arm and threw him into a taxi.

This incident illustrates one of the trials of sailors' lives. We existed on the littoral fringe of society. We were easy targets, without local networks and the security those networks bring. Our primary support was each other. While we could argue and fight like sewer rats on board ship, once ashore we all had each other's backs. It was just like living in a regular family.

We also had the Seamen's Mission. The Seamen's Mission was a building in a port where we could go for rest, reflection and spiritual comfort. The missions were a Christian charity. I went to a mission once. It was a Sunday, winter, raining, and the pubs were closed. The rest of the world was hibernating and the mission had its doors open. This was admirable. There were three of us. One was a Muslim, one a lukewarm Catholic, and one an agnostic Sunday school graduate. We were a water-soaked shivering joke.

As children, my siblings and I were sent to Sunday school, ostensibly to broaden our theological and philosophical understanding of the human condition. The truth is that our sweet mother and Crunch just wanted some quiet time on Sunday mornings. I won a prize at Sunday school. It was a book token to be redeemed at a Christian bookshop in town. I spent an hour trying to find a book that didn't mention God or Jesus. Please don't be offended by this. Some of my best friends are Christians. At the age of eight I was just more interested in comics and pirates. How many candidates for the clergy, aged eight, do you know? Not finding any comics, or anything on the subject of piracy, which is not surprising given the nature of that profession, I settled for a souvenir tea towel with the ten commandments on it. It became my Christmas present to our sweet mother and Crunch. That'll learn them, I told myself.

That wet, cold afternoon in the Seamen's Mission, we didn't require spiritual comfort, rest or reflection. We were simply looking for somewhere dry which was warmer than outside. In our time of need, the mission stood up. Sometimes, it is the simple things that make the world a better place. We had no need of PlayStation, X box, iPads, Tik Tok or Spotify. Our lives were complete with a cup of cocoa and a gingernut. Some may say this reflected a lack of ambition on our part, and that we should have been designing schemes to live on Mars. In reply, I would point out I have no desire whatsoever to live in a dry, barren desert with no oxygen. Such an environment is bad for your complexion.

We sailed up the west coast of the USA. In San Francisco we docked at the port of Oakland. I wandered through the adjoining residential area on the way back from a trip to San Francisco just across the bay. Many of the houses were boarded up. All were shedding paint. When the wind gusted, it was like walking through a ticker tape parade of lead flakes. Occasionally, I would see someone sitting on the steps outside their house. Sometimes, they would raise a hand in a desultory wave. Usually they would just stare at me. Weeds were the preferred form of flowerbed. The air breathed forlornness and unease.

The only other place I had experienced an atmosphere like this was Umm Qasr, in Iraq. There I had been intently followed by Muslim eyes from behind black burkas, and conversely ignored almost completely by robed men. I was the only foreigner in the place. I was wearing shorts and a T-shirt. I felt severely underdressed. In retrospect, I had probably insulted the entire local population.

Now on the streets of Oakland I was feeling a similar discomfort.

"How d'ya like our beautiful city?" One of the stevedores confronted me when I was back on cargo watch. He emphasised the word 'beautiful', like he was challenging me to disagree. He had outsized whiskers and a bulging waistline. I didn't want to take any chances.

"Great. Oakland was a bit quiet though."

"What the fuck were you doing in Oakland?"

"Walking. How else do you get back from the train?"

"Take a fuckin' cab, or an armoured personnel carrier." The Hells Angel who was masquerading as a stevedore continued to inform me that Oakland was a centre for heroin and cocaine distribution and had one of the highest crime rates in America. You see, I may have been lacking in intelligence, but I wasn't lacking in courage or ambition. I didn't have to go to another planet to live an adventurous life. I had walked the streets of Oakland, California, and not been shot, maimed, castrated, kneecapped, sent to rehab, or arrested. I eat your Mars project for breakfast.

Leaving San Francisco, we sailed under the Golden Gate Bridge. The sun shone, seagulls swooped and shrieked, wavelets contoured the water like a newly-ploughed field of blue earth. Until they didn't. One minute you could see the cars buzzing over the bridge, the next, they were stolen from our sight, along with the bridge itself, the city, and the sky. It was like they had all gone up in a puff of Haight-Ashbury cannabis smoke. This was magic. This was hallucinogenic. This was American exceptionalism. This was a thick sea fog. We were passing right under the bridge at the time. In a narrow waterway like the harbour, a ship our size had right of way. This was good for us, but not so good for the fleet of yachts which had been racing across our bows just before the fog descended. We could see them on the radar, dodging about like a colony of very upset ants. We knew they couldn't see us. We sounded the fog horn. We looked over the side for mangled body parts and wreckage. We imagined the newspaper headlines. "Pearl Harbour II. British ship attacks San Francisco." We cleared the two headlands at the harbour entrance and the fog lifted as suddenly as it had arrived.

"Bosun, go forward and check we don't have any stowaways on board." No way was the captain letting anyone get a free ride on our ship, even if we had run them down.

We ended up in dry dock on Vancouver Island. Sailors love dry dock because shore crews come aboard and do a lot of the major maintenance work. The sailors get to play football with the stevedores then go to the pub. Unfortunately my time in dry dock was cut short. I was whisked away to Liverpool for a shore course. 'Whisked' is a euphemism for spending thirty hours' travel time getting there, including changing flights four times.

The first flight was short, from Vancouver Island to Vancouver on mainland Canada. The plane had been built late on a Friday afternoon, just before everyone knocked off for a beer. Since then, it had been raided on numerous occasions by aircraft engineers looking for spare parts. It rattled like a can full of nails and we hadn't even taken off. We, the human sacrifices, were still walking down the aisle looking for our seats. When we sat down, the seats creaked and groaned around us. There were corrugations in the fuselage and wrinkles in the foreheads of the flight attendants. They had obviously been on this aviation throwback before.

After finding your seat on a plane, you usually fasten your seatbelt and settle back to enjoy the flight. My seatbelt wouldn't adjust. Its previous occupant had been a sumo wrestler.

"Is this normal?" I exhibited the gulf between my stomach and the webbing to one of the attendants.

"It's a short flight." She handed me two pillows. I stuffed them between me and the seatbelt.

We rattled out onto the tarmac for take-off. The pilot revved the engines. Then he revved them some more, just to see if they would fall off. They didn't, so we accelerated down the runway. Have you ever been to a children's birthday party inside a rock crusher in a quarry? Neither have I, but this was what I imagined it would sound like. We shuddered and fishtailed down the runway to a cacophony of metallic shrieking and grating noises. And that was that. Instead of rising gracefully into the air we ground to a halt.

Once the noise had subsided, the pilot's voice came over the intercom. "Well, that didn't go like they said in the training manual. Let's try again while we still can." I wasn't sure I liked his tone.

We turned around and taxied back towards the start line. The pilot just followed the trail of nuts and bolts to find it. Once satisfied the engines were still where they should be, the pilot accelerated down the runway for the second time. Again, we remained firmly attached to terra firma.

"Hmm," announced the pilot, "we're in last chance saloon now." He certainly had a way with words.

I looked at my fellow sacrificial offerings. They seemed resigned to their fate. No one said anything, until a lone voice started to sing. "Heart of oak are our ships, jolly tars are our men, we always are ready, steady boys, steady." Others joined in until a full choir expressed itself, exuberantly, loudly. They were Canadian Army Reservists. I don't know why they chose a British Navy sea shanty to sing. I was hoping to remain above the water. It was like whistling Colonel Bogey in the movie *The Bridge on the River Kwai*. We could make as much noise as we liked but we were still bathed in doom.

We careered back down the runway. We shook like a thousand tambourines at a Hare Krishna convention, the engines remained glued to the wings, the Canadian Army roared its lungs out, and soon we were shaking and grinding our way through the clouds. The army clapped and cheered.

"Well, how about that? I didn't think we'd make it." The pilot sounded as relieved as we were. He needed to go on a course in public relations.

I eventually arrived, still breathing, in Liverpool. We – that's me and the other course participants – were put up in a hotel called the Belgravia. That's a fine, traditional name, I thought. I was told it had sea views and a lively social scene at the in-house bar. All meals would be provided in the establishment's dining room. It sounded grand. The façade was a little jaded but in keeping with the old neighbourhood.

"Lav's down 'all, luv." The receptionist showed me to a shoebox with a single bed in it. I showered in a linoleum canister decorated with green mould and slept for fourteen hours.

The next day I went into town to open a bank account. I went to Barclays Bank. That's a sturdy English name I thought, and it's got a nice blue, nautical colour. My money will be safe there. When I finally got to the front of the queue, I politely asked the young teller if I could become a customer of her steadfast institution.

"Ye wha?" She looked at me as if I had just stepped out of a black hole.

"I'd like to open an account."

She laughed. I was beginning to regret my choice of bank.

"It's yer accent. Ye talk foony."

I remembered hearing this line before. I also remembered it wasn't as embarrassing as the time I had to obtain a visa to enter France from the French Embassy in London. When I arrived at the front of that queue, the young French passport officer checked to see if I was the person my passport alleged I was. She looked at the photo, taken a few years previously, then looked at me. She laughed too long and a little too enthusiastically for my liking. "You do not

look like zees now." She tried to stifle her mirth but it was quite clear
she thought I had aged without the benefits of Botox and an eyebrow
lift.

The Barclays' teller's voice brought me back to earth. "Wher' ye
frum?"

"New Zealand."

"Oer, I dort ye were a Cuckney frum Lundun."

It turned out that my money was safe in Barclays Bank, too safe
in fact. A few years later, when I tried to withdraw my remaining
pennies and close the account, the bank wouldn't let me. I had to
provide multiple forms in triplicate, references and referees,
mugshots and fingerprints, all so I could access my remaining twenty
quid.

"Keep it," I said. It is probably still washing around in some
sludge fund used by Russian oligarchs to launder their ill-gotten
roubles.

Accents proved problematic in Liverpool. On our course we had
various shades of English – Cockney, West Country, Scots, Welsh,
Irish, a Canadian, and me. Not one of us was from Liverpool. One
night I went to the bar in the Belgravia, along with everyone else on
the course. This was something we did regularly. The bar was busy.
Four of us sat at a table, drinking our bevvies as they call them up
there. Someone suggested playing cards. I went to the bar.

"Can I have a pack of cards please?" I made sure to say this in my
clearest, most accurately enunciated, non-Antipodean English.

"Der ye go." The barmaid handed me a pint of Carling lager.

"No, a pack of cards." This time I spoke very, very slowly.

"Ye wha?"

"Never mind." I took a sip of the beer and walked back to our
table.

"'E talks foony," I heard the barmaid say to her mate behind the
bar.

Another evening we went to a Chinese restaurant. We sat at a big, circular table. We were an Englishman, an Irishman, a Welshman, a Scotsman, me, and the Canadian. The waitress, who wasn't Chinese, not even a hint of Asian, took our orders. Half way through, she too started laughing.

"Ye all talk foony." She held her notebook in front of her mouth to try and hide her sniggers.

Enough was enough. I could not let this go. "Have you ever thought, unlikely as it may be, improbable as it may seem, that it's you lot up here, in the greyest of grey dregs of merry England, who may actually be the ones who talk – " I paused for effect " – foony?" I finished by stressing the last word with an exaggerated Scouse flourish. It made no difference. She giggled all over our rice and chicken chow mein.

I liked Liverpool, even though it was cold, bleak, shabby and grey. It had rough edges, rougher humour, and the ability to surprise. By way of example, one morning the sun shone. By way of further example, I once found a solitary kiwifruit in the marketplace. At the Belgravia we had song nights, quiz nights, and grab-a-granny nights. Grandmothers were apparently hard to catch, or in short supply. It was actually an opportunity to dance waltzes, foxtrots and other forms of movement to music which were the subject of historical research.

The dining room at the Belgravia... let me start again. What purported to be a dining room at the Belgravia was a cupboard with a table and some crockery hidden inside it. We would squeeze in there for baked beans on toast, or baked beans and sausages, or baked beans and eggs, and a cup of tea. That was the menu, whatever the meal. To its credit, the kitchen... let me start again. To its credit, what purported to be a kitchen at the Belgravia, also gave us a packed lunch to take to the training institute. The packed lunch consisted of baked bean sandwiches, made with white bread from the local mill, from which the local ladies emerged every afternoon decorated in veils of flour. If they went to the chippie on the way home they came out battered.

I wouldn't want you to get the impression it was all fun and granny-grabbing in Liverpool. We were, strange as it may seem, being paid to be there. We jumped off high diving boards into freezing water, in our clothes, while holding our noses to prevent our brains shooting out the tops of our heads, we hauled ourselves into liferafts in soupy, chlorinated swimming pools, we put out fires in a soot-laden steel mock-up of a ship, we sashayed about with ropes and sextants, we sent each other crude messages with dots and dashes, we moved model ships around model harbours, we attended lectures on spherical trigonometry given by salt-corroded old men, we purchased parrots, eye patches, crutches and spare legs, and, most importantly, we were taught when and how to say "Arrrrr".

'Arrrrr' as you may be aware, is an ancient nautical term which can mean anything you want it to mean. For example, if someone standing next to you on the deck at sunset says, "Did you see the green flash?", you might reply, "Arrrrr". If the steward in the saloon asks if you liked the Yorkshire pudding, you might reply, "Arrrrr". If you are standing alone on watch, in the middle of the night, observing the wonders of the firmament, you might say, "Arrrrr". If you want to greet some fellow sailors in a bar, you might say, "Arrrrr". If the ship is sinking beneath your feet, you might say, albeit in a slightly subdued tone, "Arrrrr".

'Arrrrr' is not to be confused with 'aye aye'. 'Aye aye' is another ancient nautical term which simply means yes. Aye is repeated twice in case the first aye is lost to the noise of waves crashing over the deck, or the thud of the chief gunner's bloody noggin hitting the bulkhead beside you in battle. It is a well-known fact that, to speed up onboard communications, Lord Nelson, who was a stickler for grammar, only required his men to answer with one aye in the affirmative.

Unfortunately, once he lost an eye, he became overly sensitive to the use of a single aye, and ordered a return to the duplicate version. Hence, aye aye remains the norm to this day.

'Arrrrr' is also not to be confused with 'ahoy', or 'ahoj' in Czech. Ahoy is another ancient nautical term which means 'hello matey'. It was Australian in origin. Ahoy can be used as a greeting in any situation. For example, you might shout "Ahoy" when hailing another vessel through a megaphone at sea when your VHF radio, UHF radio, satellite phone, Morse key, and semaphore flags are all out of action. You may also use ahoy when on the sets of such classics as *Mutiny on the Bounty*, *Master and Commander*, *The Love Boat*, and *Gone with the Wind*. When the director asks "Who the hell are you?" just answer "Ahoy skipper!" and salute. You'll be fine.

Arrrrrr!

The Short Chapter

I am visiting Crunch and my sweet mother again. They are still living in the apartment at the rest home complex.

"How's Mum?" Crunch and I are sitting at the dining room table. Crunch has been listening to a radio programme about the future of electric planes.

"Pigs will fly." Crunch turns off the radio. "It's fake news. The batteries are too heavy."

"Fake news is a fact."

Crunch gives me his quizzical we-are-only-slightly-amused look. "They'd fall out of the sky. Ask Isaac Newton."

"Is he in the rest home?"

Crunch gives me his you're-no-child-of-mine look. "I think we'll have to cancel the South Island. Your mother just can't travel."

Mother has recently been diagnosed with dementia and Crunch is looking after her. For a number of years he has managed to cover up her memory and reasoning deficiencies by taking on more of the running of the household. He is also expert at bailing her out of awkward social situations, but now her brain misfires are so noticeable no amount of camouflage can conceal them.

"Last night we watched a TV programme about Paris. Afterwards she wouldn't go to bed, said we had to make the most of our visit to this beautiful city and go up the Eiffel Tower at midnight. I told her it was being painted and was closed to tourists. She wanted to know if I was painting it."

"What did you say?"

"I wasn't tall enough."

Our sweet mother comes into the dining room. It is late afternoon. She is still in her dressing gown. "Hello, William." She gives me a hug. "I didn't know you were coming over." She sits down at the table and starts doing a crossword puzzle. She squints at the magazine. "I need my specs." She gets up and leaves again.

"I found the iron in the fridge yesterday, and the butter in the pot plant by the front door. When I took her to the movies last week, halfway through she got up and started looking for the remote to turn off the television."

"I'll come and stay for a bit, give you a break. You could still go to Te Wai Pounamu."

"Te Wai who?"

"The South Island."

"Not by myself. We only travel together."

Outside, the Major is leading his reluctant regiment down the driveway. He is wearing a red beret, a dark suit and his leather slippers. "Eyes right!" he orders as he passes the apartment. He salutes as he marches past, looking directly at us. Crunch and I stand to attention and salute him in return.

Mother comes back into the dining room without her reading glasses. She sees me. "Hello, William." She gives me a hug, "I didn't know you were coming over."

There is a knock at the door, but before anyone can answer it, in walks Rat Lady. Her grey hair is still coiffed in a bun.

"Hello, dear." Mother gets up and gives Rat Lady a hug. "I didn't know you were coming over."

Rat Lady holds her lit cigarillo out the window so as not to kill anyone but herself. "I was just passing. Thought I'd look in."

"Don't you have to be on the telly?" Crunch points at their new flat screen television across the room. Rat Lady has become a well-known actress who still appears as an ageing matriarch in a popular evening murder mystery series.

"Even I know it's pre-recorded." Mother has a moment of lucidity. She is fussing around with a teapot in the kitchen.

"Written anything lately, Rat Boy?"

"Only a shopping list. How's Maggie?"

"I'm going to her fourth wedding this weekend."

"The budgerigars?"

"Flown to the four corners long ago."

"And Ralph – who would've believed it?"

"You've got to hand it to him." Rat Lady tapped her ash into the flower bed below the window sill.

"I think we can take credit for propelling him on his way."

Rat Lady laughs in her throaty, exuberant fashion.

Our sweet mother comes to the table with the teapot. It is empty. She holds it up in front of us.

"Does anyone know how to make this work?"

There are 20 quadrillion ants in the world. That's 2.5 million for each person.

Chapter -11

After four years at university, Rodney graduated with a law degree. That is not a joke. "Now I really can earn squillions, bro." He was almost twenty-three years old.

We were celebrating Rodney's graduation in Bryan's kitchen. Bryan handed out the beer. Kim handed out the low calorie fat-free sugar-free food-free dip, and carrot sticks. Scrabble chewed on a bone.

The scrimmage sisters were with us. For once they didn't say "It's not about the money". We waited for it, but they didn't. Instead, Sarah, the shorter dark one, looked uncomfortable. "You couldn't give us a small loan could you? We're behind in our rent."

"Capitalism screws everyone in the end." Bryan served this up with a heavy dose of joie de vivre and went off to find fifty dollars. We cranked up the stereo and danced outside in the street.

"Scrimmage!" The sisters leapt on Rodney.

"I have truly arrived." Rodney looked up at the stars as Scrabble licked his face. It was a rite of passage thing.

Rodney couldn't find a job in town – "Lawyers aren't free thinkers. They wanted me to wear shoes in the office" – so he moved to a smaller centre in the provinces. He wore shorts and jandals to work. His boss was blind – "That's why I picked him."

Rodney justified his dress code in these terms. "You have to put yourself on the same level as the clients. It puts them at ease." Some of Rodney's firm's clients were violent drug dealers, but Rodney was no pushover. "These are the guys who used to chase me with cracker guns. I never inhale their excuses or their stock."

Rodney began playing hockey again and one day I received a letter from him. This was the only creative writing he had managed for months, although not having seen any of Rodney's legal submissions, I couldn't swear to it. I, on the other hand, had been productive. I had rewritten the first chapter as Rat Lady had advised, taking into account all her suggestions. I had also typed it up and sent it off to the publishers, as a replacement for our first first chapter. This is what I had written.

Chapter 42

Rodney and I sat on a beach and decided to write a book. We were unemployed and had nothing else to do. Unfortunately, neither of us had passed English, but being short of cash we had nothing to lose. We believed that writing a book was like receiving an inheritance from an ancient aunt.

"How hard can it be?" said Rodney.

"Piece of piss."

"Pass me a pen."

"I don't have one, but hey, isn't that alliteration?"

Just then, from out of nowhere, four beautiful girls, wearing nothing but bikinis, came and sat down beside us.

"Hi, we're nurses. What are you two hunks doing?"

"Writing a book."

"Wow, that's amazing. You must be really smart. Mind if we hang out with you guys?"

"Do any of you like mice?" I asked.

"Or tramping?" added Rodney.

"What do your mothers do?"

"That's a lot of questions. What we're really into is ships."

"*That could work,*" I said.

"*None of you are called Helen, are you?*" Rodney asked.

"*What's your book about?*" The nurses were rubbing suntan oil into our backs.

"*It's a book about what we know, which some people may say isn't much,*" I replied, humbly, "*but some people we know, who know about writing books, told us to write about what we do know, not what we don't know, so we are, but really, what would we know?*"

"*That's so humble,*" said the nurses, admiringly.

"*There are truckloads of themes, tonnes of deep and intricately-linked plots, and heaps of character development,*" added Rodney. "*The people who know told us to include those things.*"

"*So it's not boring?*"

"*Better than reading an advertisement for breakfast cereal.*" We laughed dismissively.

"*Can we read it?*"

I handed the nurses the exercise book I had been busy writing in. They looked at the first page.

"*Why is the first chapter called Chapter 42 and not Chapter 1? Where are the other forty-one chapters?*"

"*We don't really know why the first chapter is Chapter 42 either,*" I said, "*but what we do know is that we don't have an answer to everything.*"

"*That's so humble,*" said the nurses, admiringly, again.

"*What does the title mean, 'The Protestant Work Ethic: How to Live with It and How to Live without It'? Is it a religious novel, like the Bible?*"

"*We're not really sure what it means but it sounded good,*" I replied, "*and while we're on the subject of titles, I can tell you, and this is a secret, that the title of our next book is 'Winner of the Nobel Prize for Literature.'*"

"*Wow. That's amazing.*"

"Our friend Bryan says it's a great marketing strategy and he doesn't know why someone hasn't thought of it before," Rodney said, humbly.

"You guys are so cool."

Back to Rodney's contribution to creative writing – his letter. It read, "Yo bro, I was playing hockey at the weekend, right wing, and going like a train. A horse escaped from the knackers yard across the road. It tackled me as I was about to score a goal. I have a leg in plaster. It's broken. Send whatever you have."

I took Rodney's letter and wrote on the back of the same piece of paper. "I gave a lecture to the Anthropological Society yesterday. To illustrate evolution, I stripped naked and leapt about the room with a bone in one hand and a beer bottle in the other. I'm insolvent." I put the letter back inside Rodney's envelope, sellotaped the flap closed, and wrote "Return to sender" on the front.

A week later I received the same envelope in the mail with "Not known at this address" written next to Rodney's return address and my "Return to sender" crossed out. I unsealed the new Sellotape on the flap. Rodney had also written on the back of his original letter. "How does that illustrate evolution? My leg is still broken. Send whatever you have."

I found the last available space to write on. I wrote, "It doesn't. I just knew you were lying about the horse." I sellotaped the envelope closed again, crossed out "Not known at this address", and wrote a new "Return to sender" with an arrow in red ink pointing to Rodney's original return address, which I also underlined in red ink.

When it came to recycling we were in our element. It's amazing how much postage you could get for five cents in those days. The only limitation was the size of the envelope.

Halfway through his first year practising as a lawyer, Rodney was admitted to the bar. This doesn't just mean, as you would be quite entitled to think, that Rodney was allowed to have a drink after work. No, this is a legal term which means he was allowed to walk through the courtroom door *and* sit in the seats right at the front of the classroom, just a matter of metres from the judge.

"What a privilege this is, but I don't let it go to my head. Sometimes I take a deckchair and sit off to the side." Rodney told me this when I went to visit him. What he said is not quite true, but one day, keeping to the beach theme, Rodney did wear his jandals to court. They were bright yellow. He had forgotten to take his shoes to work. He was running late. He shuffled in and hid his feet under the desk at the front of the classroom. Luckily, he had remembered his jacket and tie. Even luckier, he was not wearing his budgie smugglers.

I was keen to observe Rodney fighting for right and justice, so one day I accompanied him to court. Rodney did remember his shoes this time, but he was running late again and was physically running to court. As we pounded along the pavement we heard a loud rip and a breath of fresh country air caressed Rodney's buttocks. The pants of the suit he had bought at the op shop for ten dollars had split down the seat.

"Lucky I'm not wearing my orange man-overboard undies." Rodney rushed into a nearby stationery shop with the paper shopping bag he used as a briefcase held strategically behind him. He bought some Sellotape. He had a lot of trouble getting the money out of his wallet with one hand while the other held the shopping bag in position.

"Would you like a hand?" The shopkeeper wanted to be helpful, but Rodney wasn't having a bar of it.

"I'm not falling for that old chestnut."

Rodney hid behind the cooking and hobbies section while I kept watch for stray housewives and children. He dropped his trousers and taped up the split from the inside. He crackled as he walked out of the shop and into court.

"What's that noise?" The judge looked suspiciously around the classroom when Rodney stood to address her.

"Old war wound, Ma'am. Fox hole in 'Nam." The judge gave him a severe look over the top of her bifocals.

"You wouldn't believe the rash," Rodney complained afterwards.

Rodney and the law were not highly compatible, but there was money to be made in other people's misery and misfortune. By the end of his first year in practice he had even managed to save enough to buy a ticket, on a plane, to the other side of the world. Before he left we went to a grouping.

"Back again?" Ralph seemed slightly put out that we had returned. He was wearing the same faded jeans, white polo shirt and creased blue suit jacket he always wore. He still needed a shave.

"We've got a lot more to contribute, bro." Rodney smiled without really smiling.

Today's subject was 'Do You Need an Agent?'. We settled ourselves among the budgerigars, drank our cups of tea and ate bird seed. Maggie called it Mother Nature's healthy trail mix.

"I dried the pumpkin seeds myself. Can you taste the linseed?"

I looked around for a little mirror with a bell on it so I could peck at my reflection.

"I preferred the bran muffins." Rodney pushed his handful of bird seed down the back of the couch.

"An experienced literary agent can make the difference between being published, or wallowing in self-pity, insecurity and doubt about your abilities for decades to come." The budgerigars wrote down Ralph's wisdom in their notebooks. "An experienced agent knows which publisher will be most attracted to your MS. He, or sometimes she – " Ralph acknowledged he was outnumbered on the gender front "– knows how to comb through all the contractual pitfalls awaiting new writers. And remember, a publisher won't write back to you if they don't like your work. They will only reply if they do. But they will reply to an agent no matter what..."

"Excuse me, Ralph." I raised my hand. "What do you mean by 'your MS'?"

"Manuscript." Rat Lady replied on Ralph's behalf.

I looked concernedly around Maggie's lounge. "I didn't think it was multiple sclerosis. No one here's got multiple sclerosis, have they?" Everyone, except Ralph, shook their heads. "That's good then. Carry on Ralph."

Ralph's face had slowly evolved from 'put out' to 'sour'. He looked at his notes and continued.

"A good literary agent is well worth their fee. While you may think that completely warranted cost is a little on the steep side at first, the joy and intense personal satisfaction one gets from being published makes the expense more than worthwhile."

Rodney put up his hand to ask a question. Ralph ignored him and carried on. "When I was first published, I was lucky enough to be taken under the wing of a very talented agent who was worth every penny and..."

"Oi, over here, dude."

"What is it?" snapped Ralph.

"You wouldn't happen to be an agent, would you?"

"As a matter of fact I am." Ralph pursed stony lips.

"We would never have guessed." Rodney and I spoke as one, with just the lightest touch of irony.

"Do you really think this writing gig is for you?" Rat Lady walked down Maggie's driveway with us after the grouping had finished. She was smoking a cigarillo.

"How do you put up with that moron?" I still hadn't warmed to Ralph.

"He's actually a very good writer and, as well as being a freelance agent, he works as an editor – a junior editor, mind you – at one of the big publishers. He's written a very literary novel and a collection of short stories, even won a prize or two, but sometimes he can be a real... " Rat Lady hesitated and pondered a suitable adjective of sufficient literary gravitas to describe Ralph. She settled on "... tit".

"If he's such a great writer, why does he come to the grouping? We're not exactly giants of literature." Rodney's legal mind was incisive.

Rat Lady blew a plume of smoke into the air. "He makes almost nothing from his writing and agency work, and junior editors are paid a pittance."

"So?" I wasn't feeling particularly sympathetic.

"Maggie lends him money."

"What's with his sick mother?" Rodney, at least, showed a hint of compassion.

"I haven't met her. Maggie hasn't either. In fact none of us have." Rat Lady didn't seem overly concerned.

"Which publisher does he work for?" I had an uncomfortable feeling.

"Stables & Stately." Rat Lady looked inquiringly at me. "Why?"

"No reason." I exchanged a glance with Rodney. I had no desire to reveal our attempt at publication in case we suffered a humiliating rejection.

We stopped at the end of the driveway.

"We've followed your advice." Rodney gestured at me. "The bro here has rewritten the first chapter."

"I've kept the first paragraph though."

"And the title." Rodney made sure we didn't forget his contribution.

"Well done, Rat Boy. Want me to read it?"

I adopted Ralph's voice. "Perhaps when I've developed the themes and fleshed out the characterisation a bit more."

Rat Lady hit me on the head with her MS.

Before Christmas, Rodney flew out to watch Kingdom United play the game of 'whack the poor some more' in London (it was the years of Margaret Thatcher) and I readied myself to sail out to see the sea some more, with a few lumps of dirt and rock thrown in.

There was a growing problem with the seagoing life. Traditional ships with all their lines, wires, derricks, and blocks and tackle were being superseded by container ships. Containers are those big, corrugated, steel boxes you see sitting on wharves, truck depots, building sites, and outside the houses of people who don't want to mow their lawns. In some parts of the world, where they don't have lawns, containers are the houses. In the trade, containers are called boxes, and container ships, which like to alliterate, are called box boats.

Working on a box boat was like playing with giant Lego. You ... well, not you, but a little blue and white Lego driver, with an orange Lego hard hat, in a Lego crane sitting high in the Lego clouds, just stacked the boxes one on top of the other in the holds and on deck, and stevedores locked the corners of the boxes together. All we had to do was fasten some steel wire lashings and close a hatch or two. Then you sailed to the other side of the world and another little Lego crane driver, and some other stevedores, took the whole Lego edifice apart.

Where was the skill and seamanship in that? You didn't need many eye splices, back splices, long splices, short splices, common whippings, West Country whippings, palm and needle whippings, square lashings, diagonal lashings, round lashings, tripod lashings, shear lashings, bowlines, reef knots, figure of eight knots, sheet bends, double sheet bends, g.coli, carrick bends, clove hitches, half hitches, rolling hitches, monkey's fists, sheepshanks, and a host of other arcanely named twists and turns of rope, such as Turks Heads, to be able to handle a box. (If you spotted Giovanni Coli in that list I commend you. You really are paying attention. He will not appear again. I promise.)

It appeared I had wasted all that time on the *Madrigal Star* learning my lashings, splices and whippings. Mike the mate and I would have been better prepared for the future if we had discussed LGBTQ+ rights, or the formation of black holes, or how to cook bran muffins or save the beetles. Life had almost cruelly passed us by and I, at least, had not yet groan up. That is not a spelling mistake. For those such as my sheep station owner who saw himself slip-sliding towards his mortal demise from the day he was born, groan is quite appropriate. His punishment, ironically, was to live a long life. Years later, I read in the death notices of that unreliable publication that he died aged ninety-eight.

We also never saw what was inside the boxes. All we had was a cargo manifest. A cargo manifest is a document which summarises what cargo is inside the boxes. As will be immediately apparent, some would say manifest, a piece of paper was a poor substitute for actually imbibing the scent of a consignment of raw ginger from Sri Lanka. The romance of the sea was being imprisoned inside twenty- and forty-foot steel cuboids. This would be akin to selling food in identical plastic packaging in a very large, warehouse-like, artificially lit, muzak-deafening, sanitised shop, where everything is gaudy and smells like air freshener. Can you imagine how bad that would be?

Further, apart from requiring less skill, and not really knowing whether you were carrying ten thousand pairs of false teeth, as declared on the manifest, or a tonne of cocaine across the Pacific, the main drawback of containerisation was that it was far more cost-efficient than traditional shipping. This meant we had less time in port, which meant less time ashore, which meant we got into less trouble, which meant a lot less fun. It also meant more time at sea and more of the boring days which just floated, one into the other, until you had a whole raft of boredom and you wished for something terrifying to happen, just to see if some supernatural being was listening and would act on your opportunistic request for salvation. I could see the writing on the wall when I joined my next ship which happened to be a box boat, the *Aotearoa*.

I had earlier picked up my tin of oatmeal biscuits from our sweet mother.

"Don't eat them all at once, William, they'll give you indigestion." She was in a hurry. She and Crunch were going on holiday and Crunch was impatient. He had loaded the car and our sweet mother was, as she used to say quaintly, putting on her face. Crunch decided to back the car out of the garage and down the driveway. There was a loud screech of metal, followed by some intemperate language.

"Oh dear, I've told him not to use those words. Not at that volume anyway. There's a three-year-old at the top of the street." The top of the street was twenty houses away.

Crunch poked his face into the hallway. It was a face that wasn't taking any blame. "I'm off to the panelbeaters." He had forgotten to close the left back passenger door before reversing. The car door was hanging on the garage door frame.

I pointed at the old family sedan.

"Cool. Looks like you've been in a demolition derby."

Crunch reversed past me. He put his head out the driver's window.

"Don't sink."

I blew him a kiss.

Due to this diversion I didn't settle into my quarters on board as soon as I should have and didn't have time to familiarise myself well with all the buttons, switches, lights and dials on the bridge. This was all very new and fancy. There were even two radars and, surprisingly, at least to me, both worked.

A storm lashed us the night we sailed. A ship's bridge after sundown was a dim place, the only light coming from various instruments and a red light for reading charts, the chart table itself hidden behind a black curtain. This was to preserve our night vision. In the gloom I was flicking switches, pushing buttons, reading dials and watching lights, most of which I had never come across before but had received some hasty instructions about.

"What does this big red button do?" I had been looking at it out of the corner of my eye as we carefully and slowly threaded our twenty thousand tonne container ship down the very narrow channel, towards the very narrow harbour entrance, which, just for fun, had a rock breakwater on either side of it. No one bothered answering, so, believing it to be a part of my sequence of duties, I pushed it.

In retrospect I concede that was a mistake, but it was just so inviting, like a wooden lamp post to a dog with a full bladder. In this regard, I do confess to having had desires to jump off tall buildings and to open the emergency exit door on planes, just to see what happens. Such actions would be neither responsible nor sensible, but they have an instinctual pull on me which is hard to ignore. The French call this state of mind, 'l'appel du vide', which literally translates as the call of the void.

I knew any excuse wouldn't wear well with the captain when he bollocksed me, so I didn't even raise one. I understood I was on ground that was not just shaky, but was collapsing into a sinkhole. I have to give credit to the chief ginger beer though. Through the cacophony of alarms, ringing bells and flashing lights, he had the good sense to call the bridge. "You didn't really mean that, did you?" He must've known I was on duty.

"Too dark to see up here." I promised him a bottle of whiskey.

I had pressed the emergency stop button.

We sailed further into the storm. The wind was gusting over seventy knots, that's one hundred and thirty kilometres per hour, and the waves were over eight metres high, that's over twenty-six feet. They were breaking over the ship and no one was allowed on deck.

"I can think of a few I'd like to send outside though." The chief mate was a genial Welshman who said everything with a smile. The ship was crawling along. In nautical terms this was called dead slow ahead, just enough speed to maintain our position into the waves.

"Pop down below and check we're not leaking." As expected, the mate smiled at me.

I popped and we weren't.

"That's a good sign then." The mate smiled again as the ship lurched to starboard. "We'll be walking on the bulkheads next. Come down to my cabin and let's listen to a tape of Wales versus the All Blacks in 1963."

It was like this for three days. Hot meals were cancelled after the dinner setting launched itself into space.

"Yer can eat off the deck, if yer 'ungry." The first cook fancied a bit of downtime. My old pupil, Benjamin, who had joined the ship as a steward, looked at the mess in the saloon and said – absolutely nothing.

One night I was jolted from a fitful slumber by the ship falling into a deeper than usual trough. Twenty thousand tonnes of steel shook like a Salvation Army donation box and came to a halt. Where's my lifejacket? I thought. This was one of those terrifying moments. A life jacket, about half a square metre of orange fabric and foam, would've been as useful a life-saving device in those seas as bailing a sinking supertanker with a spoon. Alliteration wasn't going to help either. I lay awake, wedged into the crevice between the bunk and the bulkhead, and pondered my existence as the vessel shuddered, recovering its momentum. Perhaps knowledge of my personal mortality was pushing at the porthole of my perception. Didn't you hear me? I said to myself, Alliteration... oh shut up.

Eventually, we anchored off the western entrance to the Panama Canal, caught a lighter ashore and went to a restaurant for dinner. It was a large cavernous room with lots of pillars and decorative plaster and every table was full. The air smelt of sweat, spice and cigarettes. Everything was bustling and loud. We had rice con carne and beer. It cost us a dollar each, including the beer. The carne was not stewed mince as I expected, but steak. For a dollar, I wasn't about to complain.

The second mate had married a Colombian woman and spoke Spanish. He did all the talking on our behalf. The rest of us smiled and nodded and laughed when the Spanish speakers laughed, even though we had no idea what they were laughing at. They could've been laughing at the state of the local economy, the state of the economy of Kingdom United, transubstantiation and its role in Spanish Catholic theology, or it could've been they were simply telling jokes about us. We had no idea, but laughing together made us feel safe in a city renowned for not being safe. Panama at this time was a narco state, a transit point for oodles of cocaine. It had diversified from opium and cannabis and was run by a couple of socially-minded souls called Noriega and Escobar. Just who was the politician and who was the drug dealer was unclear.

After the restaurant we went for a drink. One of our group was little Jimmy from Liverpool. He was the junior engineer. He could just see over the bar when he stood up straight. As he waited to buy a round, two tall lithe-limbed beauties in sequinned mini skirts sidled up to him, one either side.

"You are soooo hansum." The first one brushed some hair from Jimmy's forehead.

"Soooo strung." The second one squeezed his left bicep.

Jimmy bought them both a drink and forgot about our round. Half an hour later we looked about for Jimmy. He wasn't to be seen. After another ten minutes I heard a tap on the window next to my elbow. I looked down. There was Jimmy. He gestured to me to come outside. He was hiding behind a rubbish bin, in his underpants.

"I dort I were on te someding, d'ye no warra mean? Me and dem two birds, dey tooke me roun' de corner, I dort dey were taking me somewhere special like, d'ye no warra mean? But some big nob wid a knoife, 'e was waiting for us, an' 'e took me wallet –"Jimmy held out his empty wrist "– an' me watch – " he looked like he was about to cry "– 'an' me jeans. 'E sed dey'd fit 'is twelve-year-old boy."

"What about the birds?"

"Dey jus' sed, 'Go backa to your sheep, Leetle Jeemee'." He exaggerated the Spanish accent. At least they hadn't stolen his sense of humour. I hailed a taxi and took Leetle Jeemee back to the sheep.

We transited the Panama Canal. It is a unique experience. If you want to know more about it, read a travel book. No, sorry, that was rude. What I really meant to say was, if you want to know more about it, take a cruise. Look, I can see you're getting a bit hung up about the Panama Canal here, I'm not sure what the big deal is. The Panama Canal is only an eighty-one-kilometre-long waterway linking the earth's two largest oceans, only one of the most difficult and dangerous engineering assignments ever undertaken by humans, only a sordid example of States United gunboat diplomacy and conquest, and only twenty-five thousand or so people died during its construction. Other than that there's some water, some jungle, some locks, and that's about it.

Cristóbal and Colón are at the other end of the canal. Leetle Jeemee had started the voyage with two pairs of jeans and after Panama City only had one pair left. If he lost his last pair in Cristóbal and Colón he would have had to fly home in his underpants when he paid off. We couldn't allow that to happen as he also only had two pairs of underpants. Imagine if they too were stolen. We would have had to fly him back to Liverpool in a dog crate. So we didn't stop. We scooted on past and into the Caribbean.

I had first transited the Panama Canal when travelling to Kingdom United with my family. That time, we did stop at Cristóbal and Colón. Unlike Leetle Jeemee we had plenty of underpants to play with. Why is this place called Cristóbal *and* Colón? Apparently, back then anyway, the port was Cristóbal and the town was Colón. A railway line was the boundary between them. We must've jumped across that railway line a thousand times chanting "Cristóbal, Colón, Cristóbal, Colón" as we did so. Okay, we did it once. Can you imagine Crunch waiting patiently for us to do it a thousand times? Even once was pushing it. Cristóbal Colón is Spanish for Christopher Columbus. I didn't realise the foremost invader of the Americas had a split personality until we stopped in this fork-tongued town.

We proceeded from the railway line into Colón. For some inexplicable reason, maybe not known even to themselves, Crunch and our sweet mother let our brother buy a toy handgun. It was black with a revolving chamber. It looked just like a real handgun. It fired what looked like percussion caps. It sounded just like a real handgun. Why would you let your child buy such an item in a narco state?

The first thing our brother did on exiting the toy shop was let off a few rounds in the town plaza. It's just what comes naturally when you buy a new bang stick. You'd think our parents would've thought about that. Locals leapt behind cars, doorways, rubbish bins, and any other conceivable shelter. Some small people leapt behind big people. Two police officers patrolling the square grabbed their handguns from their holsters and pointed them in our direction. As far as we could see their handguns had not come from the toyshop. They looked a lot bigger, a lot meaner, and more like harbingers of doom. Luckily, when they saw it was a small foreign boy holding the town plaza to ransom, the police officers had the sense to realise his weapon was a fake and smile and wave. Either that or they thought we were a drug dealer's family from abroad come to invest in the bounty of their beautiful country.

Not content with a handgun, our brother also wanted to buy a monkey. I supported him wholeheartedly. When we arrived in Kingston, Jamaica, our brother showed his business prowess and negotiated a deal, to a background of reggae music and the scent of pineapple-flavoured rum, with a vendor in the market. The vendor was an old fellow with knotted grey hair and skin like tree bark. He was selling yams, but also happened to have a small juvenile howler monkey. Howler monkeys, apparently, live up to their name. I'm not sure whether the yams were a sweetener to sell the monkey or vice versa. Not that it mattered, just about everything seemed to be for sale.

I wondered if we could open our own stall and sell our parents. That probably wouldn't have been a good look in Jamaica, but this was the dark ages and, besides, because Crunch and our sweet mother looked fairly much European, there was some nice revenge discrimination inherent in the idea. Our sweet mother did tan up well, but not enough to be mistaken for a forced immigrant from Africa. She was descended from Aborigines and, before you ask, there is no record of anyone called Bojangles in the family.

The market deal was all of our combined pocket money in exchange for the monkey. It was the cutest little thing. It jumped up and danced on our heads as soon as we showed an interest in adopting it. I think it had been smoking ganja. We could see we were all made for each other. Our sweet mother and Crunch, however, had learnt their lesson in Christopher Columbus town. They closed the transaction down before we could settle.

"It would keep us all awake." Our sweet mother showed no hesitation when justifying their decision.

Crunch was less diplomatic. "You're both idiots."

Instead of a primate, we settled for some Black Jack bubble gum. It burst all over our faces and wouldn't come off for weeks. In retrospect, I think we had discovered the existence of dark matter. Either that or we just didn't wash often enough.

At the end of that childhood voyage we docked at Tilbury, up the River Thames, outside London, in dismal grey drizzle. What had happened to the gaiety, the colour, the intense tropical scents, the violence, the reggae and the ganja of the Caribbean? It had all been shovelled into a North Sea concrete mixer, had the life churned out of it, and been poured out as grey, monochrome, sooty, sausage slurry. Sausage is what it smelt like in our B&B in Baker Street. Before you ask, Sherlock Holmes and Watson were nowhere to be seen. They must have been in another book. Our brother didn't go to Baker Street. He came down with measles a couple of days before docking and was whisked off to a quarantine facility at Gravesend in a lifeboat. Our sweet mother went with him to make sure he didn't buy or sell anything he wasn't entitled to.

Now, almost a couple of decades later, I was on the *Aotearoa*, ploughing through the Caribbean and headed up the east coast of States United. I was, however, inspired by the geographical proximity and memory of my childhood experiences to consider writing them down. I realised that this was exactly what Rat Lady was on about. The truth inherent in those experiences, I now understood, would bring them alive on the page. I considered this possibility long and hard. Then I went and helped the rest of the crew build beer can pyramids in the bar. My innate aversion to work had asserted itself again. I was beginning to doubt we would ever write, let alone get past, Chapter Two. There was still sand from our windsurfing trip, two years previously, trapped in the spine of my stolen, I mean excess stock, exercise book.

We docked at Fort Lauderdale, outside Miami, to discharge some boxes. Some crewmates and I managed a run ashore for a couple of hours before having to return to the vessel and prepare for sailing. This is what containerisation was doing to us. Apart from a handful of socially maladjusted curmudgeonly malcontents, those on the run from the law, Irving Berlin (he wrote a song about it), and depressive artistic types, who went to sea to see the sea? Definitely not me. I do remember that everything in Fort Lauderdale was expensive, racial discrimination was thriving in States United, and the inhabitants thought we talked foony. Apart from that, Fort Lauderdale may just as well have been a blancmange.

We had also stopped there in our childhood. Our parents had taken us to an early version of SeaWorld to see captive ocean mammals embarrass themselves for our enjoyment. That too was expensive, unless you were aged under ten and entry was free. Crunch led from the front as we went through the ticket turnstile.

"Anyone under ten?" The ticket vendor cast a kindly eye over me and my siblings. Crunch pointed at me.

"No I'm not, I turned ten in Tahiti."

Our sister kicked me. Crunch gave me the death stare.

"It's okay, he looks under ten."

I poked my tongue out at the ticket vendor as we passed through.

It's quite comforting when you discover your parents can be dishonest. In my experience, telling lies is a great leveller. It is confirmation you may not be quite as bad, relative to your parents, as they had encouraged you to think you were. It also gives you leverage for the future.

We paid off in Philadelphia. Leetle Jeemee still had two pairs of underpants and a pair of jeans, so the company, quite generously I thought, bought him a plane ticket to Liverpool with a seat in the main cabin. I decided to see a bit of Philly before flying home via Kingdom United to catch up with Rodney.

"I'm not a bloody travel agent." The captain was not impressed when I explained my plans.

I took a room in a seedy hotel in a seedy part of town. I had asked the cab driver to take me somewhere nice but not too expensive. I think he was in the mafia. People came and went from that doss house all night. I moved the furniture up against the door so I wouldn't be garrotted in my sleep, or be delivered a bloody horse head. The receptionist sat in a steel booth at the foot of the stairs behind steel bars. The only way he could get out was with a blowtorch. The bed sagged so far it rebounded off the floor when I turned. It didn't exactly feel like the land of the free.

The next day I walked out to see the sights. This should give me something to write about, I said to myself. I had my notebook in my pocket and an eye peeled for the wet sloppy indelicate entrails of life. I felt like Leopold Bloom setting out into the streets of Dublin. I had made a conscious decision to use this leave to finish Chapter Two when bounced awake on the floorboards the previous night.

I passed a phone booth on the street. The phone rang. That's unusual, I thought, Who rings a public telephone? I looked around. I was the only person in the near vicinity. Maybe someone's trying to get hold of me, I logically surmised, or it's a wrong number and I can set them straight. The only decent thing to do was to answer it.

"Gidday." My voice was redolent with helpfulness and naivety.

I'm afraid I cannot repeat the response to my well-meant greeting. All I can reveal is that there was a lot of shouting about mothers, and a paired noun starting with 'f', and some rhyming slang words we may have encountered previously on the *Madrigal Star*. In a state of shock, I replaced the receiver and walked away as quickly as was possible without attracting attention. That person needs to learn some manners, I said to myself in our sweet mother's voice. I had stumbled across a drug deal which I knew from the movies was not a good stumble to make. Where were Starsky and Hutch when you needed them? If you don't know who Starsky and Hutch were, then you are definitely too young to be exposed to what was said on that telephone call.

I found myself at the Liberty Bell. This is a large bell with a crack in it. How they could market such a faulty item as something tourists must see, I had no idea. It is also apparently based on a lie, in that it was not actually rung when States United declared independence from Kingdom United. What value can be placed on liberty founded on a lie, I ask? Very little, I reply. A guide in a lemon squeezer hat, who looked like a boy with bad acne, informed me that the bell represented all the freedoms that existed in States United and that, if I was lucky enough, my country might also one day attain such an exalted status of liberty and human rights. Hubris was definitely in his vocabulary and was one of his strongest points.

The next day I caught a Greyhound bus to New York. It wasn't grey and it wasn't quick. This was just another falsehood to add to my experience of States United. At what they called a gas station in those parts, the bus stopped for a hopper, pop and shoo fly pie break. That's a toilet and snack stop to you. I watched a man pay twenty cents to pump air into his car tyres.

"I wonder how much it costs to breathe?" I intended this as a rhetorical question, addressed to no one in particular.

"Where yew frum?" A high-pitched voice behind me made me jump. I turned around. A couple of young black male students had heard me. "Noo Zeeland? Yew tark funny."

At the bus station in New York I noticed the police were contracted to provide the sanitation services. They were cleaning up the facility of all vagrants. They handcuffed the mostly black male decaying souls together and led them around the bus parks, stopping periodically to add a new piece of human flotsam or jetsam to the chain gang. There must have been a dozen poor homeless people, locked together in this conga line of social oppression. Where the police were taking them I had no idea. The salt mines perhaps? I was having another of those Christmas cracker moments. I hoped it would stop. Otherwise I might have to do something about it and join the civil rights movement, or something else equally outlandish.

A couple of days later I caught my company-funded budget flight to London. I wore both jeans and underpants. The plane didn't rattle and shake as much as my flight from Vancouver Island, but you could still have danced to it.

Fava beans contain the souls of the dead.

The Next Chapter

The scrimmage sisters are waiting to paint heads. They have popped up an open-air studio in a square, just around the corner from Kim and Bryan's apartment. "Shave and Save the Planet" reads a banner above them. I watch on from what I think is a safe distance.

"Roll up, roll up. Become a work of art, make a statement for the ailing earth. It's free." Bryan has managed to gather a small crowd. His bald head is a multi-hued collage of penguins, albatrosses and an endangered bat.

Trixie and Sarah have shaved off their hair and decorated each other's scalp. Trixie's head is one half vibrantly coloured coral reef, and one half bleached coral reef. Sarah's head is encircled by the slogan, "I'm No Oil Ranting", spelt out in large jazzy black and white lettering.

No one, understandably, seems keen to lose their hair. Bryan pleads with the crowd and waves a pair of electric clippers in the air. "Come on. Your hair will grow back, but homo sapiens won't." There are still no volunteers.

"You, sir." Bryan points at me. "You fly too much for your work. Make an artistic statement to atone for your sins."

"I offset my emissions." I guiltily touch my hair and step backwards.

Bryan laughs at my embarrassment.

Sarah joins in. "There are heat waves and wildfires all over Europe, America, India, and China. Global heating is making it worse. Paint up and be a rebel. Show you care."

Bryan cranks up the volume on their portable sound system and dance music blares around the square. A bare-gummed homeless man in dirty op shop clothes shuffles artlessly off-beat. Schoolgirls in blue uniforms jiggle and giggle.

"I'm in." A young university student with very short, artificial-looking, glaringly white hair steps forward. She has an array of studs and rings in her ears, nose, eyebrows, lips, and tongue. "Hold my bag." She gives Bryan her roughly woven orange and green Tibetan satchel. Sarah sets to with the clippers.

"Who else has the courage?" Bryan is buoyed by their first customer.

A young office worker in a suit is pushed forward by his mates. "They'll give me twenty bucks each if I do it." Trixie grabs him before he can change his mind and sits him down. "I'm almost bald anyway." He turns to the student. "What's your excuse?"

"I can't find anyone willing to pierce my skull."

Trixie begins painting a blue whale entangled in a fishing net onto the head of the office worker. Sarah is creating a pointillist design of a koala bear fleeing burning gum trees on the head of the university student.

"We have to stop pumping greenhouse gases into the atmosphere. Hurricanes are more intense, storms and floods are more frequent, droughts are longer, even the Panama Canal is drying up." Bryan is on a mission to educate his audience.

"Load of bollocks." Everyone turns to look at a man eating a sandwich.

"You're a climate scientist?" Bryan relishes sandwich man's challenge.

"No."

"You've read the reports of the UN's Intergovernmental Panel on Climate Change then?"

"I've read enough."

"He's done his own research," shouts someone, mockingly, from the back of the crowd that has grown substantially in size.

"What's wrong with that?" A frumpy woman with glasses puts her hands on her hips and confronts Mocking Voice.

"It's a load of bollocks, that's what."

"What would you know?" Frumpy Woman takes a step towards Mocking Voice.

"Peace and love!" Bryan throws handfuls of climate cookies into the cacophony of argument and beats.

"Get air." A skateboarder shoots out of the crowd and bounces off a concrete ledge.

"Gnarly." Skater Kid, who is close behind the first skater, almost knocks over Homeless Man.

"Doom to ye all!" Bryan throws more climate cookies into the crowd and gets tangled up in the student's Tibetan satchel, which he tries to push back over his shoulder.

"Excuse me sir, but do you have a permit for this activity?" A uniformed police officer who has wandered into the chaos confronts Bryan.

"It's not my show."

"It's not his show." Skater Kid does kick turns on his board.

"Oh, it's you, sir. I didn't recognise you... without your puppet." The police officer notices the satchel. "Nice handbag."

Later that afternoon Bryan, Kim and I are waiting in the apartment for Rodney and the scrimmage sisters to return from the police station.

"I'm buggered." Bryan has collapsed on the couch. Next to the couch is a shelf which holds some newly framed photos of Scrabble.

"You should conserve your energy." Kim sits on the other side of the room.

"Carpe diem." Bryan waves a hand in the direction of the shelf. "Scrabble did."

"And look at him now." Kim points to an urn on the shelf which contains Scrabble's ashes.

The intercom announces the arrival of the others and Kim lets them in.

"We got a warning." Trixie looks tired and relieved. "Rodney fought tooth and nail to save us."

"But only two heads painted." Sarah, on the other hand, is tired and dejected. She looks at me. "Offsetting emissions isn't enough, Will."

"Neither is painting heads." I am feeling churlish.

"Can I have a gladiator's helmet befitting my warrior status?" Rodney rubs the blank canvas of his cranium.

"It's all too depressing." Kim takes up a lotus position on the floor.

'I'd settle for a baseball cap.' Rodney is not reading the room well.

"And no, I won't carpe diem." Kim looks angrily at Bryan.

The scrimmage sisters and I sit on the floor with Kim. Our stiffer bones won't fold into lotuses, so we just sit. Rodney belatedly joins us, with Bryan, who lies down.

"Don't smear the paint." The scrimmage sisters adjust Bryan's head position.

Outside, a ship's horn sounds its solemn lamenting farewell.

Kim breathes deeply. "Someone's always leaving."

Bryan lightly strokes her hand. "I'm not."

Whales were small, hoofed, land dwellers until they went swimming.

Requiem

It was grey, dismal and drizzling when I stepped off the plane I'd taken from New York to Heathrow. I could smell sausages and baked beans, sautéed in aviation fuel. I caught the train to London. I was to meet up with Rodney at a pub in Marble Arch.

Finally, I thought, as I walked out of the Marble Arch tube station. It had only taken me the best part of fourteen years to get there. I looked around. I can't say I regretted aborting my bus trip there as a schoolboy. It was all cars, cabs, buses, and carbon monoxide.

"Yo, bro." I found Rodney already seated at a table. "Catch the cosmo flow."

"You haven't been to San Francisco again have you, bro?"

"Other coast."

"Fing is, though, they don't say 'bro' here, or 'dude.'"

"How do you communicate then?"

"Just moan and make up rhymes."

Rodney handed me a letter he had received from Bryan. He pulled it out of an envelope which had numerous "Not at this address" and "Return to sender" directions on it.

"You're reading the wrong side." Rodney indicated that I should turn the letter over. I had been looking at some of Rodney's handwriting dated four months earlier.

I turned the page and scanned the back.

"Gidday bro," it read. "You guys have got a letter from the publisher. I haven't opened it. My cut is a very reasonable twenty percent. Yours in purgatory, Bryan. PS. I've dyed my hair carmine."

I high-fived Rodney. "They don't reply if they don't want you."

"Champagne!" Rodney looked hopefully at the fridge behind the bar.

"Dancing girls!" I didn't know where to look for them. People stared at us from behind their drinks. I went to the bar. "Two pints of your best lager, and make it warm."

"How much have you written?" Rodney sipped his beer as our euphoria evaporated.

"Funny you should mention that. How about you?"

"We'll have to get stuck in now, or you will. I'll look after the big-picture stuff, like the cover."

"That could work – I'm unemployed again. Did you hear that? I just said work and unemployed in the same sentence. How contradictorily subtle is that?"

I had indeed resigned from my nautical career. It had lasted a little over five years but felt like a lifetime. Box boats were not to my liking. I loved the romance of the sea, the sway of a ship's deck under my feet, the ever-changing destinations, the polar cold and the tropical heat, the skies crammed with stars so dense and bright you could almost touch them, the sunsets more vivid than anything Turner ever painted, our unspoken subservience to the Gods of wind and water, the grime and grit of wharves and ports, the thick scents of cordage, oil, kelp and brine, the anticipation and satisfaction of landfalls made good, the camaraderie and trust of shipmates – but box boats were just too industrial and lacking in poetry. Their emphasis on steel and efficiency had, for me at least, diminished commercial seafaring as a way of life.

The best thing about resigning was that I received a tax windfall. Luckily, these were the days before computerisation, at least in the public service, and coordination between governments was almost unheard of. Computers at that time were metal boxes decorated with red, blue and yellow wires. They were the size of houses and lived in cavernous warehouses at institutions of tertiary learning. They only flashed their lights when fed cardboard cards with holes punched in them. After a month's rumination, they would spit out reams of green paper with serrated edges. Somewhere on that green paper, written in indecipherable code, was an answer to the question you had asked.

Unconcerned about being spied on by AI, I therefore wrote to the Kingdom United tax department asking for all my tax to be returned, as I was not a resident player on the Kingdom United team. For some reason, the tax office I had to write to was in Wales. I received a letter in reply, amusingly contained in a new envelope and written on fresh paper, which told me to let the New Zealand tax authorities know. I wrote to the New Zealand tax office explaining that, because I had spent so much time at sea, I had not been in New Zealand long enough during my seagoing career to be considered a resident player on the New Zealand team, and therefore was not liable to pay tax in New Zealand. Can you please confirm, I said. I also mentioned, in small print at the bottom, it may have been in invisible ink, that I also had not been a resident player for Kingdom United.

The New Zealand tax people were very understanding and generous. I know these are not adjectives commonly associated with the lovely people at the Inland Revenue, but I'm just stating the facts of one particular case. I received a letter from the New Zealand tax officials. It too was written on fresh paper and contained in a new envelope. No wonder we have to pay so much tax, I said to myself, their stationery and postage bills must be horrendous. The kind New Zealand tax people advised they didn't want to know me, not to take it personally, and to deal directly with the Kingdom United team in respect of any matters concerning the Queen's coffers. I advised the Kingdom United tax people that their New Zealand counterparts had said they washed their hands of the matter and it was all up to Kingdom United. Kingdom United was obviously very flattered by this act of genuflection from the colonies, and a very kind Welsh person subsequently sent me a cheque for all the tax he and his friends had so cruelly and erroneously deducted from my salary while I had been sailing the ocean wave. Thank you, Margaret Thatcher. I didn't think I would ever say that.

In London, Rodney was working for a suburban law practice on contract. He had been there six months.

"Fing is, I need to be able to leave in a hurry."

"What have you done?"

"Nothing, it's really boring. I move files from one side of my desk to the other and charge the clients squillions for it. I've worked it out. It's about two quid an inch."

Is that ethical? thought my law-abiding and respectable self. "What percentage are they paying you?" I asked.

"Not enough, but sufficient to spend a few months travelling round Europe."

We were sitting in the kitchen at Rodney's digs in Brixton, drinking 'Blacker than Brown' English tea from mugs the size of flowerpots. The tea had been stewing for two weeks. My elbow hit the wall as I raised my mug. I shifted in my chair to get more comfortable. My opposite elbow hit the opposite wall. There wasn't room to twirl a newborn kitten in the palm of your hand.

"What are you going to do now you're a dole bludger?"

I searched Rodney's words for a hint of sympathy but found none. "I'm off to Vanuatu to help a rich American run an interisland shipping line."

"Where?"

"Vanuatu. It used to be the New Hebrides."

"Who's this rich Yank?"

"He was a passenger on one of our ships. He wore ugly checked golfing pants. He offered me a job if I ever left the company."

"Can he be trusted?"

"I doubt it. But I'll go and find out."

"Isn't that irresponsible, young man?" Rodney faked a schoolteacher's tone.

"I hope so." I took a gulp of tea. "Where am I sleeping?"

"There are six of us. You're on the floor."

"In the lounge?"

"Here." Rodney pointed to the harvest gold vinyl flooring beneath our feet. "The hot bedders are in the lounge."

Rodney and his current squeeze, a nurse called Nora, occupied the only bedroom in the flat. Another couple slept in the entrance alcove and two more nurses shared the sofa in the lounge. These two nurses worked different shifts, so one slept at night, the other during the day. One of these two nurses, Jeanette, was Nora's best friend.

"I have a problem," Rodney said.

"What's that?"

"We're taking the van to France and Spain. Me, Nora and Jeanette." Rodney meant his Volkswagen Kombi van. He had picked it up for two hundred quid in Earl's Court. It had already done twenty trips around Europe and had close to a billion kilometres on the clock. They would sleep in the back and stay in campsites.

"What could go wrong?"

"It's Nora." Rodney paused and tried to look wistfully into the distance. He couldn't because the view outside the window was a water-stained brick wall. He focused instead on the tablecloth. After an aeon, or about two minutes, Rodney eventually mumbled into his mug. "Fing is, bro, I think I like Jeanette better."

Well, this was stunning news. I thought of everything that could go wrong. I thought of the emotional disaster the trip could become.

I thought of the stress the three of them would be under, cooped up at close quarters in a Kombi van, for days on end, in foreign countries. I thought of the tension in the air, the funereal silences. I thought of the sleepless nights, the screaming matches, and the taut, apologetic aftermaths. I thought so hard I laughed, in a sympathetic and caring way of course. I almost fell off my chair I sympathised and cared so much, but luckily the walls held me up.

"Do they know?" I finally managed to squeeze out of my ululating larynx.

"Not yet." Rodney looked intensely miserable.

"A trip in the outdoors, camping, should sort it out. Remember Helen?"

Rodney brightened a little at the mention of Helen's name. I'm not sure why. Maybe he was grateful to have escaped a psychologist fixated on stains as a mother-in-law.

"Crazy 'bout you baby, yeah, yeah, crazy 'bout you baby, yeah, yeah." I could still remember how to croak the words, if not the tune.

"And her name was?" Rodney joined in, squawking while drumming with his hands on the table.

"And her name was?" I almost screamed in reply.

"Mary Jane!" we chorused at the top of our lungs.

Nora walked through the door. "What's going on?"

I stayed for a week with Rodney. It was awkward, especially when Jeanette, or the other hotbedder, wanted to cook baked beans on toast at two o'clock in the morning. This happened regularly, and I would get up each morning with a rash on my face. The first time it happened I was alarmed. I thought I had measles, or the pox (small or monkey, take your pick), or the black plague (this was London after all), or some rare tropical infection. It turned out to be splatters of dead ross from the baked beans. I got into the habit of just licking my face and pillow if I felt peckish during the night.

When I left to catch my plane home, I had some valuable advice for Rodney. "Good luck. You'll need it." I worried all the way to the airport. Not about Rodney and his slowly unfolding, soon to be a tsunami, trauma of the heart, but the fact I had just sounded like Crunch.

As I settled into the flight on our national airline I noticed one of the cabin crew looking at me. She served me a cup of tea.

"Hello, Will."

She seemed familiar. I studied her face.

"Helen?"

"You remember."

"How could I forget?"

We exchanged the usual pleasantries.

"That's a rock." I nodded at the large ring on her wedding finger.

"Craig is so gorgeous. He's a dentist. It's the most stressful job in the world."

"Did Craig tell you that?

She ignored my question. "Have you been tramping lately?"

"No. How's your mother?"

"She thinks Craig is wonderful."

Neither of us mentioned Rodney.

A few days later I would be sitting at Bryan's kitchen table with our letter in my hands.

The land, the forests, the mountains, the lakes, the sea and the sky, will all be here, long after we are gone, gently or not.

The Rug Tying the Room Together

A German man called Rudi Dornbusch once said that crises take a lot longer to arrive than you can possibly imagine, but when they do, they happen a lot faster than you can possibly imagine. This is known, quite appropriately you may think, as Dornbusch's Law. I had been pondering this law on my flight back over the seas I had so recently navigated. Rudi was an economist, and he wrote this law about currency crises. I had no idea what a currency crisis looked like, so I put that to one side. As long as I could buy a loaf of bread and a plate of caviar I was fine. Just joking about the bread. Rudi's law applies to other crises too. I could see that Rodney's romantic crisis had been a long time coming, but I could also see that once it arrived, the proverbial mucky stuff would hit the proverbial blowy thing with a speed and intensity not witnessed since Ghenghis Khan and his band decided they wanted to go on tour. In fact, as Rudi had warned me, and Rodney later related to me, I was in no way prepared for how quickly it did actually happen. This incident, like so many others, was added to Rodney's repertoire of stories. I have faithfully recorded his account here.

After I departed the flat in London, Rodney, Nora and Jeanette drove their van into the unknown. They ferried across the English Channel and spent the next night at a campsite in Normandy. The air was tensioned to the point of emotional implosion. Rudolf Nureyev couldn't have tightened his tights more tautly. Nora came out of the van where she had been plucking her eyebrows while Jeanette was in the shower.

"I need to talk to you, Rodney."

"Fire away, honeybunch."

"Don't you honeybunch me." The sterner than usual nature of this reply gave Rodney an inkling his life may be about to change. "I've seen you."

"Y...e...s." Rodney dragged out his reply while he tried to think of a strategy to weather the upcoming storm.

"Seen that look." Nora started to lean into her work.

"Y...e...s." Monosyllabic Rodney now understood it wasn't going to end well, whatever his strategy.

"You don't deny it then!" Nora exploded like a supernora, I mean nova.

"N...o....o, honeybunch." Rodney spoke as slowly and as gently as he could.

"I.said.don't.honeybunch.me." Nora spat out each word like a machine gun. She hit Rodney over the head with a map of France then dissolved into one huge viscous tear drop.

The neighbouring French campers glanced over, sucked on their Gauloises cigarettes, shrugged their shoulders and looked at each other. "C'est rien. C'est l'amour." Then they went back to their game of pétanque.

"What's going on?" Jeanette arrived back from the shower looking like a Sultana with her hair tied up in a towel.

It all worked out well in the end. Rodney and Jeanette crossed the romantic Rubicon and had an inspiring tour of Europe. The van only broke down a dozen times and cost them five times as much to fix as Rodney had paid for it. Nora took the next ferry back to London, cuddled up to a surgeon she'd noticed more than she should have some months earlier, plucked more hair from her face and became engaged. Sometimes a crisis, once over, makes the world a happier, more settled place.

Back in Bryan's kitchen we had no worries about any further crises. Like most people, except clairvoyants, mediums, fortune tellers, economists, and other charlatans, we were ignorant of the future and could only deal with what was in front of us. Bryan and I were almost twenty-five years old and so was Rodney, even though he was in another hemisphere. The world was our oyster, although if we'd known more about global heating at that time we would have more realistically described the world as our green-lipped mussel. 'Green-lipped mussel' doesn't convey quite the same promise of unlimited potential and endless opportunity as 'oyster', and would have been far more accurate. It was William Shakespeare who first drew this weird analogy about the world being a bivalve and, in hindsight, I think oyster was a misrepresentation and someone should have sued him for misleading us.

"Why don't you open it?" Bryan pointed at the letter in my hands. The envelope was previously unused.

"They must have money to burn." I held the envelope up to the light.

Kim was sitting in the lotus position by the fridge. "Ooom," hummed the rectangular white box which kept things cold. It was a Buddhist fridge.

I slid my finger under the flap at the back of the envelope and extracted the letter. "They've even used a new sheet of paper."

I read the letter aloud.

"*Dear Messrs Rockwell & Herringbones. We apologise for the rather extensive delay in our reply.*"

"So they bloody should." I looked indignantly at Bryan. "It's only been four and a half years."

"*The two letters comprising your initial submission were inadvertently placed with the Children's Book section, then somehow found their way to Engineering, before being lost among Women's*

Health & Beauty. The submission, in its entirety, has now, however, come to its rightful place."

Bryan was not impressed. "What sort of intellectually challenged persons are running this show?"

"Thank you for repeating the title. Being publishers we are not known for our skills in reading."

"That's sarcasm." I was proud of my ability to decipher nuance.

"We also do not think that TPWE:HTLWIAHTLWI is a helpful acronym."

Bryan shook his head. "Rodney won't like that."

"So now we turn to the submission itself. Firstly, we do not believe Messrs Rockwell and Herringbones are your real names. The use of pseudonyms has a lengthy literary tradition so we are prepared to accept these rather obvious attempts at concealment for present purposes."

"Talk about up themselves." I had always suspected Stables & Stately of arrogance.

"Secondly, however, we believe that your submission to this honourable firm contained many further untruths, or to put it more colloquially, porkies. Ridiculous as it sounds, we would not have been surprised if you had claimed to have given birth to kittens."

"Lucky I said to take that one out." Bryan patted himself on the back.

"Thirdly, we gained the distinct impression that you consider us to be incompetent at our profession and, to put it mildly, completely lacking in intelligence."

"You did say they were morons." Bryan, unfortunately sometimes, had a very good memory.

"Fourthly, we have been unable to find your names in any list of awards or residencies for which you claimed to have 'heaps.'"

"Your twenty percent isn't looking good."

"Sounds like we're in trouble."

"We are also in possession of your letter containing the first draft of your first chapter. We are fully aware of the timing of the Nobel Prize for Literature, thank you, and need no help from you in this regard."

"Oooh, hoity toity." My suspicions of arrogance were confirmed.

"Finally, we do not believe the second draft of your first chapter adds anything to your submission, and we are definitely not, to use your unfortunate term, losers."

I put the page down. "They don't leave much room for doubt."

"Their loss." Bryan shook his head in disappointment.

"Ooom." The fridge hummed in the background.

"Read the other page." Kim was placing an ankle behind her neck.

"What other page?"

"The one you dropped." There was indeed a second page, lying lonely on the lino.

"Page Two." I started reading.

"Given your obvious disdain for authority and your propensity for dissembling, we believe your approach to the world of literature has nothing more than off-piste merit."

Bryan squirmed. "I'm getting piste-off with all these words. Why can't they just get to the point, say what they mean?"

"Writers don't do that." I carried on.

"We have therefore decided that because your title and both drafts of the first chapter show little commercial promise, we cannot accept your submission."

"Bugger." Bryan showed that he, at least, could be succinct.

"There's more."

"While you are no doubt aware we don't usually reply to submissions we have chosen not to accept, we are making an exception in this case as it is possible you do have some nascent ability. You may therefore wish to engage one of our Writing Mentors to assist you in the writing and completion of your book. This can be arranged through Mr

R. Scraggs, one of our editors, whose contact details are below. We have made your submission available to Mr Scraggs. Yours faithfully etc. etc."

There was an indecipherable squiggle purporting to be a signature at the end of the page.

"Never heard of R Scraggs, perhaps he edits Women's Health & Beauty." Bryan, once more, was not impressed.

"Scrimmage!" Sarah and Trixie burst through the door.

"Scuppered." There was a touch of sadness in my voice.

"What's the matter?"

"Our book's not going to be published." I failed miserably to sound nonchalant.

"Sympathy scrimmage!" The scrimmage sisters leapt on top of me.

I eventually disentangled myself from Sarah, Trixie, and Scrabble who had taken the opportunity to sneak inside and join in.

"Bungalow." Scrabble cocked one eye at Bryan, hesitated, then meandered back to his kennel.

"Can I get anyone anything?" Kim had risen from the floor. I was about to request fame, wealth, and unbridled power, but, before I could open my mouth, she said, "Don't even bother."

"No squillions then?" Trixie put a hand on my shoulder.

"Not a brass razoo."

"You could try another publisher." Sarah put a hand on my other shoulder.

"We could." I wasn't enthusiastic.

"Did you make the mistake of already spending the money, like we do?"

"Need help with the rent again?" Bryan couldn't help smiling.

"I was going to give our squillions to charity." I said this with a straight face.

"Haha." Bryan didn't believe me for a second.

"There's a very good charity for helping models who've lost their looks and can't find work." Kim handed out tea and biscuits.

We all paused and looked at her. Finally, the scrimmage sisters broke the silence. "What's it called?"

"MOTH. Some people say it stands for models over the hill, but we just call it MOTH. They run dances and things to raise money."

"Moth balls?"

Kim nodded at me.

"Well, when we do make squillions, I'll definitely consider it." I said this as kindly as I could.

I wrote a suitably literary letter to Rodney to advise him of our bad fortune. "Bro. Opened the letter. We were right. Publishers are bastards. Give your feather stick back to its seagull."

The next week I went to a grouping. I didn't want to go, as I felt a bit let down by the literary community, but Rat Lady had called and said it was important to be there.

"Where's Rodney?" Maggie looked over my shoulder as she opened the door.

"Womanising in Kingdom United."

"Where?"

"The mother country."

Maggie was wearing a purple kaftan and a vermillion tie-dyed head band. "That's a pity." She glanced back up the hallway. I followed her into the lounge.

"Surprise!" The budgerigars screamed and hugged me. It was like being scrimmaged with incense.

"Hello, Rat Boy." Rat Lady was leaning against the wall and coolly drawing on her cigarillo.

There were plates of muffins, Mother Nature's healthy trail mix, cups of tea, and even some gingernuts, on a table in the centre of the room.

"What's all this about?"

"We have a party whenever anyone gets rejected by a publisher." Rat Lady tapped her cigarillo against an ashtray.

"We've had a lot of parties." The budgerigars seemed strangely happy about that state of affairs.

"How did you know we'd been rejected?" I asked this softly, not wanting to emphasise our failure too strongly.

Rat Lady waved her non-smoking hand at Ralph.

Ralph was wearing the same faded jeans, white polo shirt and creased blue suit jacket, but today he had made a big effort. There was a maroon silk cravat knotted at his neck, and he had even shaved. His hair was still plastic but something seemed different. I realised he was almost smiling.

"Mr Rockwell, or Mr Herringbones perhaps?" Ralph was acting a trifle haughtily, I thought.

"How did you know about Rockwell and Herringbones?" I suspected Stables & Stately.

"I knew it was you as soon as I saw the first paragraph. If you'd like a guiding hand, just ask." He saw my unenthused look. "I give a discount for members of the grouping."

Maggie thrust a bowl of yellow goo at me.

"Would you like some seameal custard? I gathered the seaweed myself."

I sat in a corner and munched on a muffin while the party carried on.

Rat Lady came and sat down next to me. "What's up Rat Boy?"

"No offence, but I smell a rodent. Is Ralph's surname Scraggs? Rat Lady nodded. I showed her our letter from Stables & Stately. "Recognise the signature?"

"That scrawl could be anyone's."

"Including Ralph's?"

Rat Lady seemed surprised, then nodded. "I see what you mean. It would be unusual for a publisher to write a letter like this."

We both stood up.

"Ralphie boy." I beckoned to Ralph across the room. He licked some seameal custard off his fingers then came over. He probably thought he was going to get some paid work.

"Breach of confidence telling everyone about our rejection, isn't it?" I didn't think I was ever going to warm to Ralph.

Rat Lady held up our letter in front of him. "Did you sign this?"

Ralph took the letter and looked closely at it. He glanced at the signature page then scoffed. "Of course not. That would be unethical."

Rat Lady stared hard at Ralph. He stared straight back. The room had gone quiet.

"We could take the letter back to Stables & Stately." Rat Lady's voice was gentle, but threatening. She addressed the others. "Who else over the years has received a rejection letter from Stables & Stately, signed with an indecipherable scribble and recommending you contact Ralph?"

The budgerigars timidly raised their hands.

"And you chose him as a mentor?

The budgerigars nodded.

"And you all paid him for this mentoring?" Rat Lady was on a roll.

The budgerigars nodded again.

There was an uneasy silence. Eventually Maggie broke the tension.

"Ralph, how could you? After all the help I've given you and your poor suffering mother. You didn't need to..." – she searched for the right word – "... steal from these dear ladies." She clenched her fists and stamped her foot. "How many other rejected manuscripts have you taken and then written to the ever hopeful authors, inveigling your way into their confidence, asking them for money?

And using your firm's letterhead. It's beyond the pale." Maggie sat down and dabbed at the mascara running down her cheeks.

Ralph looked around, like a cornered hyena. "What's the problem? They got first class tuition." He paused. "And I had to contribute to my mother's care."

"What's she got this week? Smallpox?" Emotional blackmail wasn't going to wash with Rat Lady.

For a few seconds Ralph stared at us condescendingly, then, throwing back his shoulders, retrieved his scruffy satchel from where it hung on a chair by the door. He turned to the room. "My mother died when I was five. None of you can write for shit." With that he stalked imperiously out of the house.

We all looked at each other. Rat Lady took a long drag on her cigarillo." Well, it's great material for a book. Has anyone got a bottle of wine?"

How do we prove we are not living in a simulation?

Bequest

Two months after the rejection party at the grouping, I picked up Rodney and his new wife from the airport. He and Jeanette had been married at a registry office in Brixton.

"Safety in numbers." Rodney put their baggage in the boot of the car. "I needed protection." He was alluding to Brixton's high crime rate. "It was either get married or get knifed." Jeanette hit him.

"Are you sure you know what you're doing?" I asked Jeanette.

"Getting married?"

"To him." I pointed at Rodney. She hit me too.

Rodney took a flyer from where it had been placed behind a windscreen wiper and looked at it. "Bloody oath, bro." He handed it to me.

There was a photo of Ralph on it, but not the Ralph we thought we knew. He was wearing tan chinos, an expensive-looking blazer, a crisp white open-necked formal shirt, and his hair was coiffed, almost beyond recognition. The text read – "Ralph Scraggs Media Ltd. For all your advertising needs. You can trust Ralph!"

It was midday. We stopped in for some fish and chips on the way back from the airport.

"Hey Rodney, heard you were coming home." Ajit wiped his hands on his apron. He and Stan were flipping burgers at the takeaway shop Stan had opened down on the seafront.

"What'll it be?" Stan waved a basket of sliced potatoes in our direction.

"Three fish, three chips, and a bucket of dead ross." Rodney shook their hands across the counter.

"And three creaming soda milk shakes." I picked out three plastic straws from a tall cup next to the till.

"Just flown in?" Stan plunged the basket of chips into the fryer.

"Two hours ago." Jeanette stifled a jet-lagged yawn.

"Come over tonight, we'll have fireworks." Stan rubbed his hands together in anticipation.

"Isn't deep-fried food bad for your liver, bro?" Rodney looked at Stan with concern. It was two years since Stan's second liver transplant.

"Only if you eat it." Stan put our fish and chips on the counter. "On the house."

Ajit handed over their milkshakes. "You don't fancy a game of world domination, do you? I'm off shift in an hour."

We walked across the road and sat in the sun on a rock wall.

"Shame about the book." Rodney buried his toes in the sand. "Are we going back to the grouping?"

"It folded soon after Ralph tossed his toys."

Rodney threw a chip to a gull which was standing on one leg to make us feel sorry for it. It worked. I threw it another chip.

"I feel like I've done my bit for literature, a title's nothing to be sneezed at is it, bro? Big picture, that's me."

"No offence, but I thought we might have had to change the title."

"I suppose Bryan did have a point about restricting the market."

We watched the three-inch high wavelets lapping on the sand. The sun was at its zenith, the heat teasing us gently through our clothes.

"You don't get this in Kingdom United." I gazed out upon the warm languid seascape.

"Not yet." Rodney was prescient.

We ate our fish and chips with tomato sauce. We stirred the remnants of our milkshakes with our plastic straws. All was peaceful, all was good in the world.

We've led a charmed life, so far, I thought. Perhaps we really will grow up. Perhaps we will publish our book one day and make squillions. Perhaps we'll even give some to charity. I thought a bit harder. Not MOTH though.

I looked out upon the island sitting like a green splash against the creamy sky-blue sky. Rodney and I had charged past that island in our racing catamaran.

"Do you think time is an emotionally constructed linear flow, or just a random collection of events?"

Jeanette looked at me like I was an idiot.

Rodney thought hard for two seconds, then offered me the last handful of chips. "It's what you want it to be, bro."

I ate more chips then threw the last one to the lying one-legged seagull.

Rodney squinted at the sun, shook the newspaper wrapping, then flicked the crumbs of our meal to the remaining members of the flock.

"Well," he said, "if that was lunch, we've had it."

Our breath endures after we are gone.

It All Comes Down To This

Bryan is addressing the Nutrition Society in an inner-city hotel which is next to the headquarters of the international media giant now known as RS Communications. On my way past the glass and steel facade of that global influencer, I hope to see its founder, Ralph, not that he would probably recognise me – it's been so long since the days of the grouping. I just want to congratulate him on taking his own advice and trying advertising.

Inside the hotel's theatrette the decor is a tribute to mediocrity. Bryan is positioned on a small stage at the front of the room and there are approximately twenty people in the audience, most of them well-presented and conservatively dressed women. Jeanette, Kim and I are sitting up the back. Bryan is nearing the end of his talk but Rodney still hasn't arrived. He wanted to cycle to the venue.

"You can't eat heat." Bryan glows under the spotlights like the ceiling of the Sistine Chapel and his eyes are on high beam. His re-painted head is now a tropical rainforest. "We're unlikely to all survive an unmitigated global heating crisis. Food will be in short supply. And according to Dornbusch's law, while the global heating crisis has been a long time in the making, well over a hundred and fifty years, it's now hovering above us like a giant vat of hot, slow-seeping, simmering molasses." As Bryan says this, a large, black, vat-like vessel swings out from the wings and positions itself over his head. Inside the vat, which inclines towards the audience, can be seen a dark brown substance.

"Oooh." The nutritionists look nervously at the vat.

"The molasses has been oozing out slowly for decades, but now we can see the whole dark mass of it, damming up behind the vat's gaping black mouth, storing up its kinetic energy, and preparing to launch in an overheated avalanche of sweet inky destruction." Bryan keeps his eyes on the audience. Small dark-brown drops begin falling out of the vat, bouncing off the rainforest and splattering at his feet.

"Who's going to clean that up?" An elegant woman in her forties who is wearing a fashionable designer dress has her mind on more mundane matters than the impending implosion of humanity. She sits tautly upright on the edge of her seat, as if attached by a wire to the ceiling.

"This great, flaming, sticky torrent will spill much faster than we can possibly imagine." Bryan's voice begins to rise dramatically. "For a while, we'll use our human ingenuity to keep it from enveloping us. We'll eat as much as we can, we'll put it in bottles and sell it, we'll feed it to cows, we'll make armies of gingerbread men, we'll fake our tans with it, we'll dye our hair with it, we'll make moonshine with it, but in the end, our ingenuity will run out of ingenuity, and the whole earth-sized vat will pour over our heads, drowning us in boiling viscous syrup, and sending us all to the big toffee shop in the sky."

The nutritionists exhale in collective dismay. "Toffee. That's not food."

"It's 'l'appel du vide', the call of the void." More drops splatter around Bryan. "We know causing global heating is bad, but we just can't resist pushing ourselves closer to the cliff-edge of... obliteration!" He brings his speech to a crescendo, the lights suddenly go out, and there is an explosive flash from the vat. Women scream and the theatrette is littered with a cloud of what, in the darkness, the nutritionists believe could be boiling molasses. Some try to hide under their seats, others protect their heads with their handbags.

"Thank you." Bryan bows calmly as the lights come back on.

The nutritionists are shocked. Ms. Elegant and Taut picks at the mess around her. "It's alright, they're only chocolate buttons." The rest of the audience breathes a sigh of relief.

As the nutritionists debate whether it is better to use chocolate or pomegranate molasses in a tagine, the scrimmage sisters, appearing from the wings, begin cleaning up the now-shredded vat and its scattered contents. Bryan comes towards us. His face seems to have filled out, his gait is a little quicker, and his whole being more vibrant than it has been.

"You're looking good." I haven't seen Bryan like this for months.

"I'm in remission."

"Champagne. Dancing girls!" I clap my hands together.

Kim has a big smile on her face. "Don't you dare." She puts up her hands to halt the momentum of Trixie and Sarah who have geriatrically bounded over to share in the good news.

"Crazy 'bout you baby, yeah, yeah." Our song attaches itself to my vocal chords.

Bryan looks around. "Where's Rodney?"

"That'll be him now." Jeanette takes her phone out of her handbag. But it is not Rodney, it is a police officer telling Jeanette that Rodney has been in an accident, a collision between his bike and a car, and is in hospital. "I'll be there right away." Jeanette suddenly looks crushed and pale.

I go with Jeanette to the hospital. We are hoping Rodney's accident is minor and that any injuries he may have will only require minimal treatment and an immediate discharge. Neither of us states the obvious; we haven't heard anything from Rodney himself.

At the hospital we are directed to a small room with orange plastic chairs and an old Formica-topped table. The sickly-sweet congealed smell of fear, hope, antiseptic and decay infuses us as we wait. The door has been closed behind us. Jeanette bites her lip and tugs at her hair. We don't speak. Conversation would be meaningless, either raising false hope or inducing worry. Instead I give Jeanette a hug and look out the window at the headlights of cars, trickling like drops of gold along the rain-polished road. We are two distinct worlds. Inside the building we are actors in an acute drama of existence where not every ending is a happy one. Those outside, heading home in their vehicles after a day's work, or going out for dinner or a movie, seem shut off from such a choiceless, brutal place, blissfully taking their pleasure and routine for granted, until their turn comes, and they too will be forced to inhabit this other unwanted realm. We are separated only by a cold pane of glass, but such is the depth of our disconnection, we could be on another planet.

Eventually, a young doctor with a stethoscope hanging over her shoulder hurries into the room. She seems distracted and uncertain. "We think Rodney may have had a stroke, while he was cycling. We think that is what caused the accident. We have put him in a medically-induced coma to protect his brain from damage."

Jeanette looks alarmed. "Nothing else you could do?"

The doctor shakes her head.

Jeanette wipes a tear from her cheek. "Can I see him?"

We follow the doctor down the bleached harshly-lit corridor to another room where Rodney lies on his back, under crumpled white linen, on a hospital bed. Beneath a web of tubes and sensors protruding from his face, chest and arms, and surrounded by computerised machines and screens, he seems almost beatific, the only living thing in a sea of electronic artifice. Jeanette takes his hand and whispers to him. I cannot hear what she says, and do not want to. I have never imagined seeing Rodney in this situation. I feel as if I am looking down on him from far above, a part of his life but, at the same time, divorced from it. I am simultaneously an observer and a player in this most serious of games.

We stay with him for a number of hours. Staff at the hospital continually monitor his brain activity and vital signs. They work around us, almost as if we aren't there, respectful of our grief and expectations.

In the early hours of the morning, another doctor says she thinks we should get some rest. She says the hospital will call Jeanette if there is any change in Rodney's condition, so we walk out of the hospital lobby into the night, like cave dwellers seeking the sanctuary of shadows. The darkness is a cool cloak to salve us, somewhere we can shelter and hide our apprehension, somewhere we can forget, for a few fragile, delicate minutes, that our world has changed irrevocably.

I see Jeanette home, then return to my boat. Unable to sleep, I retrieve our old manuscript from the depths of a storage locker, *The Protestant Work Ethic: How to Live with It and How to Live without It*. For some reason I could never discard it, nor the rejection letter that accompanies the manuscript like a satellite orbiting the moon. The manuscript was an extension of our lives that seemed just as real as we were ourselves, and to have thrown it away would have been denying a vital part of our history. The paper on which it was written has yellowed and is stained at the edges, the typewritten text looks positively archaeological. I cannot help but read the first chapter that was all we ever completed. I laugh a little. "It's rude to laugh at your own jokes, bro," I hear Rodney say.

Then I know what I must do. I take the manuscript and, opening my laptop, transcribe the text into a new file. Seized by an energy I cannot identify or explain, I then write, and write some more. At some stage I sleep, but on waking, return to my laptop and set down, almost in a frenzy, the burgeoning collage of images and events that are the sum of our lives together. Perhaps I am writing for distraction, perhaps for hope, perhaps for grief, or most likely a combination of all three, but I know that, this time, I will keep writing until our book is finished, no matter its quality, no matter its destination. I know that Rat Lady, Maggie and the budgerigars would understand if they were here to bear witness, although I'm not one hundred percent sure about Ralph. I write and write to save Rodney, his stories, and his memories, and soon Rodney is sitting up in his pristine, shiny, altar-like hospital bed, without any tubes protruding from his unblemished skin, and saying, "Hey, bro, what's up?", and I know this is the ending I want to write. This is the ending I want to be true.

Ingram Content Group UK Ltd.
Milton Keynes UK
UKHW042006200623
423745UK00004B/183

9 781738 600311